Simple Choices

Kimberly Collins

Blue Mingo Press

PUBLISHED BY BLUE MINGO PRESS

ISBN-10: 0990420809
ISBN-13: 978-0-9904208-0-4
First Edition

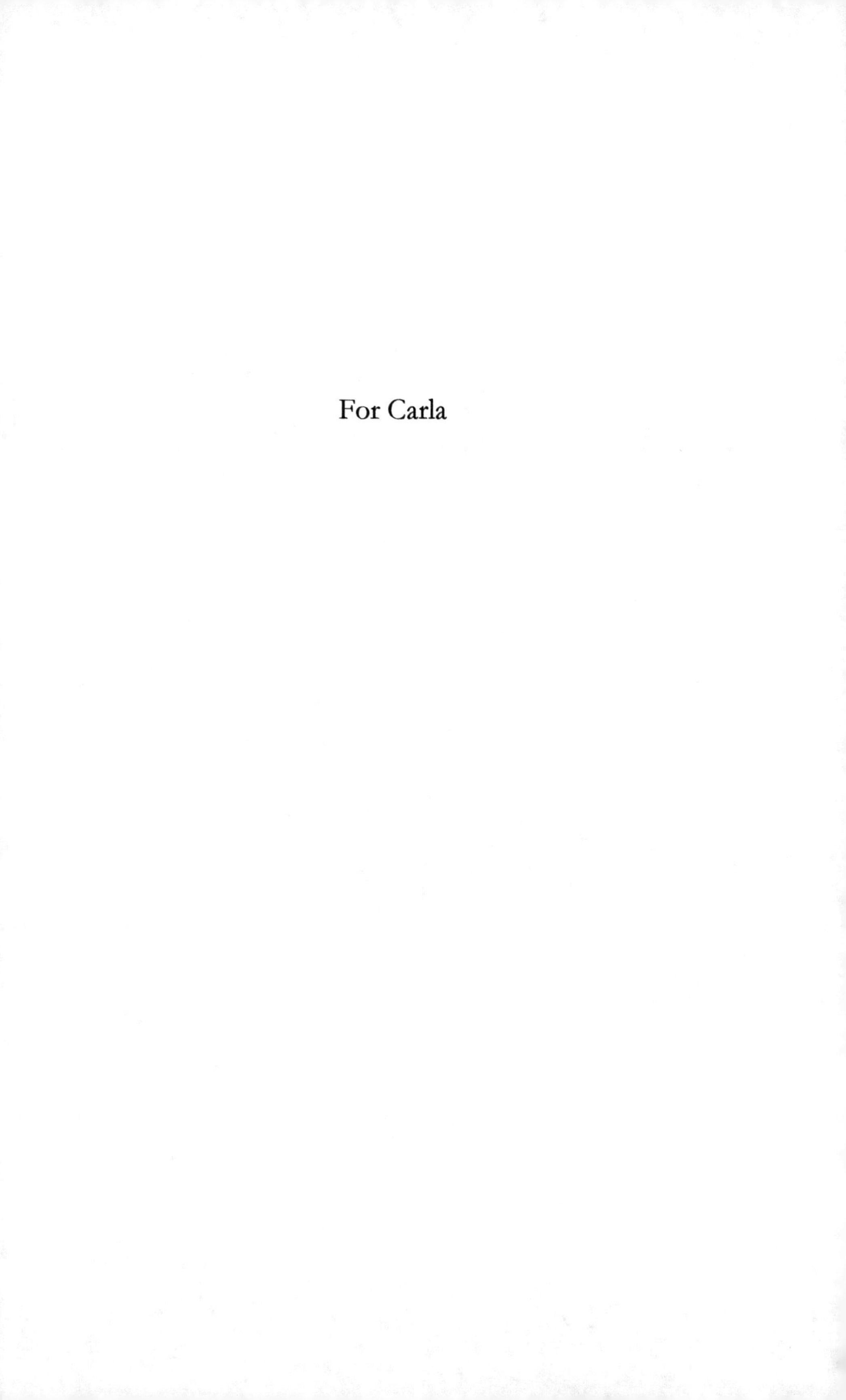

For Carla

MINGO

"All things work together for good…or bad…depending on
your choices." — Kimberly Collins

Southern West Virginia, Mingo County. The mountains are
close and steep and high. The sun's shadow doesn't arrive
until ten, and by five, it's sinking beyond the closest
mountain.

This is the heart of the billion-dollar coalfield. Where coal
is king. At least coal used to be king—a once-powerful ruler
brought to its knees, mostly by greed and politics. Over the
decades, coal has waxed and waned from king to pauper and
back again.

Living in the mountains requires a certain tenacity. Mostly
descendants of a prideful Scots-Irish heritage, the people of
Mingo hold on.

There are several roads into Mingo County. Route 119
runs through Pikeville from the south or Charleston from the
north, and into Williamson; Routes 49, from the east, and 52,
from the west, meander along the banks of the Tug Fork
River and dump you out in Matewan or Williamson. No
matter which road you choose, once you cross the county
line, the roads twist and turn, as you wind your way back into
the mountains and hollers.

The mighty Tug flows between Mingo County and
Kentucky. Along the banks of the Tug sits Matewan—a tiny
town that is no stranger to violence. It's home to the Hatfield

and McCoy feud and the legendary mine wars that sparked right in the middle of downtown in 1920.

The Tug has wielded its own power over the decades. Early spring rains pretty much guarantee she will rise up and demand respect as she overflows her banks. People have come to expect it. Prepare for it. Well, as much as one *can* prepare for such a thing. The flood of 1977 nearly wiped Matewan off the map, as it did every other small town situated on the banks of the river, including Kermit and Williamson.

After the '77 flood, the U.S. Corps of Engineers came in and decided to build floodwalls in Williamson and Matewan. The wall in Matewan was supposed to separate the town from the angry Tug; bad planning also routed traffic around town, isolating it from the flow that once made it a bustling little town. The floodwall was built to protect; instead, it alienated. This historic little mountain town was saved and decimated by the same act. There are still a few businesses left—a restaurant, the bank, a liquor store. But it's nothing like the busy coal town it used to be. Weekday and Saturday mornings Matewan used to be busy with people shopping, banking, eating. That was all before the floodwall. And the drugs.

The riders come from all over now with their four-wheelers to tear up the Hatfield & McCoy Trails. The mountains are beautiful with wild horses and rolling peaks. There's a lot of history in these mountains. A lot of love. A lot of living.

As the people and businesses drift away, there's even less to do. Less to occupy a person. The most convenient form of entertainment is getting high. The drugs crawl in and wrap around your heart, your neck and your ankles. This is a problem not unfamiliar across the country. But in a small community like Matewan—and the whole of Mingo County—it's more poignant, and the destruction is more obvious, even to the most casual observer.

Drugs are sweeping an entire generation away. Even the generation before them has gotten in on the action; this lover does not discriminate.

The mighty Tug keeps flowing and the mountains will always be almost heaven. Who knows, maybe with the ebbing of the coal industry, the mountains will flourish and the tourists will have a reason to keep coming, and Mingo can heal.

In the meantime, there are drugs to sell, drugs to do—or to do you—and murders to commit.

CHAPTER ONE
A Simple Start

"If bad companions tempt you, don't go along with them."
— Proverbs 1:10

Darlene slipped a bundle of carrots into the plastic bag and looped the top into a knot.

"Miz, I'm sorry, but you need to put those back and follow me," a voice said over her shoulder.

"Oh, my goodness, Mickey! What are you doing, crazy girl?" Darlene stood on her tiptoes and gave Mickey a hug and a kiss on the cheek.

"I saw your mommy buyin' bakin' stuff and decided to avoid that aisle," Mickey said in a conspiratorial tone. "Figured I'd let her shop in peace and avoid a bad scene here in the middle of the Piggly Wiggly."

"Oh, Mickey, you know Mommy loves you. You been part of our family forever," Darlene said, hoping Mickey couldn't see she doubted her own words as they came out of her mouth. Darlene's parents agreed with her husband, Dave, that Mickey was a bad influence. They had watched her change from a sweet little girl to a pothead in high school, and now her lifestyle left much to be desired.

Darlene's daddy had helped Mickey get out of a couple of DUIs, but he had washed his hands of her on the last one. He had done what he could, but she still lost her license for a year, spent twenty-one days in jail and had to pay a $1,000 fine. In addition to the DUI, she was charged with resisting arrest and assaulting an officer. She had slapped the cop and spit in his face. She didn't stop there. When they put her in the back of the squad car, she repeatedly kicked the back of the seat and caused enough damage that it had to be replaced. Darlene's dad had talked the cop into dropping the assault charges, which saved Mickey from a year or more in jail. After that, he refused to help her again. Millie, Darlene's mother had voiced her opinion of Mickey over the years and advised Darlene not spend too much time with her. Millie tolerated Mickey and was polite, but that was as far as she went.

Darlene wanted to shift the conversation. "What'cha doin' for Easter? Your sister gonna be here?"

"No, she's stayin' in North Carolina. I suppose it'll be just me and Mommy. She wants to drag me to church, but I don't think that's gonna happen. How 'bout you?"

"We're goin' to church, and then there's a big Easter egg hunt after service, so we'll let the girls do that. Then we'll go to Mommy and Daddy's for dinner," Darlene said, examining the green onions for the best bunch.

"Hey, I got some kick-ass weed if you want some. I can stop by this week," Mickey offered in a hushed tone.

"Oh, Mickey, I don't know. Dave would have a cow. Besides, I haven't smoked a joint in ages. Probably last time was with you. It'd sure be nice just to visit though. I miss you, Mick."

Mickey put her hand on Darlene's shoulder. "You okay, Darlene?"

"I just get real lonely, Mick. Livin' up the head of Rutherford Holler ain't my cup of tea, and with no car, no friends, it gets lonely. I'd just love to have company. Why don't you come by one day next week and we can have lunch and just talk and get caught up? It's been too long. Please?"

"Sure! Tell me what day…here comes Millie. I'll call you tomorrow."

Mickey said hello to Millie and darted off to the baking aisle.

Millie took a plastic bag from the dispenser and began filling it with carefully selected tomatoes. "What did she have to say? I suppose she's still up to no good."

"Oh, Mommy. I don't know why you're so hard on her. She's been my best friend forever. So she parties and smokes a little pot. There are a lot worse things."

"Maybe so, but she ain't no good for you, Darlene. Grab us some eggs and buttermilk, and I'll meet you at the checkout."

***

The next Thursday Mickey was on her way to Darlene's. She was looking forward to just hanging out. Even though they had been best friends for many years, they had seen each other only a handful of times since Darlene married Dave four years earlier. Dave had hated Mickey since high school and tried to convince Darlene what a bad influence she was. Mickey hadn't lost too much sleep over it. She smiled as she patted her jacket pocket holding the bag of pot she brought for Darlene.

Mickey and Darlene had met when they were in second grade at the home of a woman all the children called Aunt Penny. She didn't have any children of her own, but she was Millie's younger sister, so she was Darlene's real aunt. She sold Avon, and Mickey and her mother were there for a lipstick party. Aunt Penny had also invited Millie and a couple of other ladies. Mickey and Darlene were the only children in attendance that day.

Normally Mickey would have preferred to spend the day riding her bicycle and playing soldier with the neighborhood boys, but this was an afternoon at Aunt Penny's, and they were never missed.

Aunt Penny was Mickey's mother's age, but she seemed much younger and not so uptight. She laughed a lot, and during Mickey's teenage years, the older woman always explained things to Mickey that her mother wouldn't even discuss with her—things like her period, kissing boys and how to walk in high heels. Aunt Penny treated Mickey like an adult.

"Michele, this is Darlene, my niece." Aunt Penny made the introduction. "Darlene is seven, almost eight, and in second grade. She goes to school at Matewan. Darlene, Michele just turned eight and is in second grade at Red Jacket."

"Hi," Mickey said to Darlene. "Everybody calls me Mickey, 'cept Aunt Penny and my mommy when she's mad at me, then she calls me Michele. Other'n that, I'm just Mickey." Mickey looked Darlene over. "You really seven? You're awful little. My mommy says I'm tall for my age. You must be short for your'n."

Mickey was amazed at Darlene's tiny frame and big green eyes. With dimples and lots of red curly hair, she looked like a little doll. And she smelled good. Mickey rarely took time to brush her hair, and getting her to wear a dress was nearly impossible. She didn't understand how Darlene could play all day and not get dirty.

Mickey and Darlene were instant friends and remained friends all through elementary school, middle school and high school, with a momentary split in seventh grade. They had gone to separate elementary schools and had been so excited about starting seventh grade, so they could finally be together. Darlene was smarter—a lot smarter—and placed in mostly honors classes, so PE and West Virginia History were the only classes they had together. They managed to get the same homeroom and hung out at lunch every day and sat with each other for ballgames, student assemblies and other events.

One thing they hadn't counted on was Mickey's other friends from elementary school. She had spent a lot of time with the kids from Newtown and Red Jacket, and she wasn't ready to stop hanging out with them. Besides, they were fun.

They smoked pot, drank beer, cussed, and didn't give a shit about much of anything—least of all, school and their grades.

Mickey invited Darlene to join them in the parking lot at lunch a few times, but it was awkward. Darlene didn't smoke pot and was a bit of a goody two-shoes. Mickey was surprised at how uptight Darlene was compared to her other friends. Their friendship became strained, and Mickey tried to play both sides of the fence. She cherished her friendship with Darlene, but the Red Jacket and Newtown kids had a pull on Mickey she couldn't resist—didn't really want to resist. She enjoyed smoking pot at lunch; it helped her get through the afternoons.

As the school year wore on, Mickey started spending more time with her other friends than she did with Darlene. The bond between the two girls cracked. Darlene hung out with the brainy kids and cheerleaders and Mickey with the stoners. They still had lunch together when Mickey wasn't outside getting stoned. They still sat with each other in West Virginia History class, and Darlene was always happy to help Mickey with homework. From Mickey's perspective, Darlene was the one who had changed. She dressed in all the latest fashions and ran with the snooty kids. She was a straight-A student and had tried out for cheerleader.

They were still friends, just on different paths. At Aunt Penny's birthday party that year at the end of seventh grade, they reunited. There was no discussion of the split; they just started hanging out. Mickey convinced Darlene to try pot that summer. Darlene wasn't as fascinated with pot as Mickey was, but she would smoke occasionally, trying to look cool.

Eighth grade was a little better than seventh, but Mickey still ran with the stoners; Darlene was a cheerleader. They reached an unspoken agreement and remained best friends, but none of their other friends could figure out why or how. Everyone called them the odd couple, and they were—in looks and personality. They loved each other and promised to always be best friends. Looking back at how different they really were even then, Mickey was surprised they had managed to stay close all these years—especially after Dave entered the picture at the beginning of senior year.

Mickey pulled into the driveway, and Darlene came out on the porch to greet her. It was a warm spring day, with a thunderstorm grumbling on the other side of the mountain.

"Hey, crazy girl! It's so good to see you." Darlene held the door for Mickey. "Come on in. I made chicken and dumplin's and cornbread."

"Lord, girl, I ain't had chicken and dumplin's since Mommy got too sick to cook. I love your cornbread, and I'm starved." Mickey stepped inside and picked up Renee. "Look at you, little girl. You're gettin' so big. You look just like your mommy. Big green eyes and all those red curls. Darlene, she is the spittin' image of you. Where's Amy?"

"She's gettin' dressed for you. She wanted to wear her princess dress and tiara. Her highness should be out shortly. Bein' a princess is hard work."

A few minutes later Amy came out of her bedroom wearing a pink and purple taffeta and lace princess dress, a tiara and sequined shoes. She was carrying her scepter, which had pink, purple, and blue ribbons hanging from the end.

The storm moved closer as they ate lunch. Darlene served Mickey and then made a plate for the girls. "Mick, tell me who you're datin', what you're doin'?" Darlene put Amy in her booster seat and then lifted a squirming Renee and placed her in the highchair.

"Nobody in particular. Just datin' around—you know spendin' time with whoever's there. I ain't lookin' to get married or have babies, Darlene. I like to play it fast and loose." Mickey crumbled her cornbread in her dumplings. "What about you? You and Dave gonna have more babies?"

"Oh, goodness, I sure hope not. Two's plenty enough for me. Dave would like to have five more, probably. I ain't wantin' no more. Don't get me wrong. I love my girls more than anything, but I want a life, too. I really think I want to go back to school, Mickey. I just need to finish the last semester. I may need a few makeup classes, just 'cause it's been so long."

Renee held her mouth open like a baby bird waiting for the next spoonful of dumplings.

"Well, that whole nursin' thing didn't go over so well last time, so how you plan to swing it? Has Dave changed his mind about his wife havin' an education and a job?" Mickey asked.

"Well, I ain't quite sorted all that out just yet, but I'm workin' on it. If I have to go part time, I still have plenty of time to make it happen. I'm barely twenty-five."

A thunderclap banged directly over the trailer and caused both women and the two girls to stop and look up.

After lunch Darlene put the girls down for their afternoon nap.

Mickey cleared the dishes just as the storm came rolling over the mountain. The rain sounded like tiny rocks as it pounded against the trailer. "Mick, you might be stuck here longer than you planned." Darlene said, coming from the back bedroom.

Mickey peered out the window. The raging creek licked the bottom of the bridge that crossed into their driveway. "Yeah, looks like a flash flood out there."

***

The girls had been sleeping for about thirty minutes. The rain tapered off a bit, and the creek began to slowly recede. Mickey pulled a joint, a bag of pot and a pack of papers out of her pocket. "Here, this is for you. You need it. I've never seen you so uptight." She handed the bag of pot and papers to Darlene. "We'll smoke this one now," Mickey said, holding up the joint as she fished for her lighter.

"Mickey, we can't smoke in here, and I can't keep this in the house with the girls. They are too curious and into everything. I ain't got nowhere to hide it." Darlene handed the pot back to Mickey.

"Nope. You gotta keep it," Mickey said. "Where *can* we smoke this?"

"We can't. It's still rainin', and the porch doesn't have a cover." Darlene threw up every excuse she could think of.

"Well, we won't melt. You got an umbrella? We can keep the door open, and you can step back so you don't get soaked."

Darlene relented and got the umbrella from the hall closet. Mickey stepped out the back door, popped the umbrella up and lit the joint.

They stood on the back porch and smoked for a few minutes until they were rained out. Mickey watched as Darlene's face softened from the effects of the pot.

Back inside, they giggled as they dried off from the rain.

Darlene was looking for a place to hide the pot when she saw Dave's truck pulling across the bridge. "Oh, shoot, Mickey. Dave's home." She stuffed the evidence into her purse.

"Buzz kill!" Mickey said. "Guess I'll be leavin' now. Love ya, girl. Call me when things settle down."

She met Dave in the driveway. "If you'll back up, I'll be on my way!" She motioned for Dave to move his truck.

"What the hell you doin' here, Mickey?"

"Just visitin' my friend, Dave. That's all, nothin' else!" Mickey got into her car.

Dave backed off the bridge and let her out. As she pulled away, she could see him stomping onto the porch; she wondered how Darlene managed to deal with him every day.

***

Dave slammed the door behind him. "You gonna tell me what that drugged-out whore's doin' in my house?"

"She's not a drugged-out whore, Dave. And you need to keep your voice down before you wake the babies." Darlene went to the kitchen to put away the dishes Mickey had washed.

"Tell me why she was here!"

"She came to have lunch with me and visit. That's all. Why do you have to make somethin' bad out of it? She's my friend, always has been, and always will be, Dave. She just came for lunch, for cryin' out loud."

"You fed that fat whore my food? Food I worked hard in the mines to pay for? Is that the kinda wife you are, Darlene? Disrespectful's what it is."

Darlene had not seen him like this in years and thought he might hit her. "I'm sorry you feel that way. Dave, I get lonely sittin' here all day, day after day. I don't have any friends. You won't let me have any friends. I just needed someone to talk to and laugh with and talk about girl stuff." Darlene hung her head.

"Darlene, I've told you a hundred times, you don't need friends. You've got a husband and kids now. Besides, Mickey ain't nothin' but a drugged-up whore, and you know it." Dave sat in front of the door and took off his muddy work boots. "She tried to come between us before, and I'll be damned if I'll sit by and let it happen again."

Darlene didn't have the energy to fight with Dave. She knew he would never see her point of view. He would never accept Mickey. She just wanted to keep peace in her home. "I'm sorry, Dave. It won't happen again. I'll just tell her she can't come visit anymore, that my family's more important." She turned back to the sink and finished putting away the dishes.

"Why are you home early?" Darlene asked.

"The miner broke down and can't be fixed until late tonight, maybe even tomorrow mornin'. So they sent a few of us home. Sorry to spoil your little party."

Darlene prepared Dave's dinner and went to the bedroom to finish the laundry while he ate. She understood why Dave thought Mickey was a whore. In Dave's world, a woman lived only to serve her family, and Mickey was the complete opposite of all that. She lived a free life and came and went as she wanted. She had a job and a car. And drugs.

Keeping Darlene from women like Mickey was Dave's top priority. His form of love was control, and it seeped out and wrapped around Darlene like a vine. Dave's need to be the only thing important to Darlene was suffocating. She loved Mickey like a sister. She couldn't and wouldn't completely turn her back on her. She just needed to make Dave see how important Mickey was to her.

She was folding towels when Dave stomped into the bedroom. "What the hell's *this*?" Dave held the pot out in front of him like it was a bag of anthrax. He threw it at Darlene's feet. "Are you fuckin' kiddin' me? You were smokin' pot? Here? In my house with that whore? With my kids in the house? Darlene you've gone too far this time. This is just too much." In two steps, Dave was across the room.

He backhanded her across the face.

"You need to choose what you want, Darlene. Your husband and kids or that used up whore you call a friend. Choose! 'Cause this ain't gonna happen again. I can't stand to look at you." He pushed her back onto the bed and stormed out of the house, not waiting for an explanation. Darlene slid to the floor and cried.

***

She bathed the girls and put them to bed. Her head throbbed, and her stomach was still in knots. A bout of diarrhea had attacked minutes after Dave stormed out. She flushed the pot down the toilet and put the papers in the garbage. Perhaps a hot bath would ease the tension in her body. With the plug securely in, she turned on the hot water. She bent over and gathered her hair into a ponytail high on top of her head. A cascade of curls sprung out like a waterfall. She brushed her teeth and stood looking at her reflection. A slight bruise was coloring in on her cheekbone.

Nothin' a little make-up won't cover. Ain't like it's the first time.

The steam from the bathwater swirled around her, clinging to the mirror, and her image of herself gradually faded—much like her life had done. She had turned her life and her choices over to Dave years ago, without any protest. Her reflection was just a shadow now. She rinsed her mouth and stepped into the hot water.

***

Dave was disgusted with Darlene. He hadn't meant to hit her, but sometimes that seemed to be the only way he could make her understand. Seems like she would make the connection that the only time he hit her was when Mickey was involved. He couldn't believe she had Mickey in his house. *His* house. What was she thinking? She knew he hated Mickey. She knew she wasn't allowed to spend time with Mickey. Hadn't he made that perfectly clear to her? She had done pretty good at staying away from Mickey these past couple of years. She had known how he felt about Mickey since high school. She was a dope head then and was even worse now.

When he met Darlene, it was love at first sight. She was about the prettiest and sweetest girl he had ever come across. His parents moved from Phelps to Matewan the summer before his senior year. He didn't want to move and begged to stay with his grandma in Phelps so he could play football. His daddy knew the coaches at both schools and had arranged to have him play at Matewan. That first day of practice, he was glad his father had insisted he go there. The cheerleaders were practicing that day, as well, and that was when he saw her. He asked around to find out who she was and if she had a boyfriend. Not that it would have mattered. He was determined to have her.

He thought Darlene was joking when she told him her best friend was Mickey. He thought maybe he had Mickey confused with someone else. He had a couple of classes with Mickey, and she was about as opposite of Darlene as anyone could be. Mickey was big and rough looking and usually smelled like a cigarette; Darlene was tiny and sweet as a spring day. Darlene sure seemed to like Mickey and talked about her as if they were sisters or something.

When Darlene told him she wanted them to meet, he was determined to take the opportunity to push Mickey out of the picture completely. Mickey had a bad reputation, and he didn't want Darlene picking up any ideas or bad habits from her.

They decided to meet on a Friday night after a football game at Giovanni's pizza in Matewan. Mickey looked like she was no more excited to meet Dave than he was her. But it was important to Darlene, and Dave didn't want to look like the bad guy, especially over some stoner. After they ordered, Darlene left the table to go say hello to Mr. Steele, who taught English and drama and was Darlene's favorite teacher. Mickey and Dave were alone.

"So you and Darlene been friends a long time, I hear," Dave said.

"Yep. We go way back. All the way back. Darlene's my girl."

"You sure seem different. I can't see Darlene bein' friends with you."

"Really? Why's that, Dave?"

"Well, it's just that you're a stoner and you run with that bunch from Newtown."

"Well, Dave, it don't matter what you think of my other friends. Darlene's my *best* friend, and that's all you need to be concerned about."

Dave realized his attempts at maintaining the upper hand weren't going to work on Mickey. He decided not only was she a stoner, she was a belligerent bitch.

Just before Darlene slid back into the booth, Dave leaned over the table toward Mickey. "Just for the record, Darlene's *my* girl now."

The pizza arrived. "Damn, that's hot," Mickey said.

Dave shot her a disapproving look. "No need to cuss, Mickey." She was a stoner bitch with a foul mouth, and he realized then he needed to get her out of Darlene's life. He'd been trying to do that ever since.

By homecoming of their senior year, Dave and Darlene were well on their way to becoming a steady thing. Dave hated that Mickey always hung around at lunchtime. Didn't she have something else to do? Couldn't she eat with her other friends? As if that weren't bad enough, Mickey stayed with Darlene almost every Saturday night and apparently had since they met in second grade.

Dave made sure he changed that. On Saturday nights he began taking Darlene to movies or for pizza or just came to her house and watched TV—anything to keep Mickey away. He made it clear he didn't want to share Darlene with anyone. Especially Mickey.

Turns out, Mickey was the least of his problems. Darlene decided she wanted to be a nurse, which required four years of school at Marshall University. Dave's plan was to get married as soon as they graduated, so her going to school was out of the question. But Mickey was there whispering in Darlene's ear that she should do whatever she wanted. Dave supposed that's what women like Mickey did—whatever they wanted. He was determined Darlene wouldn't be one of those women.

Looking back, Dave thought he must not have been listening or just thought she was talking nonsense about going to college. When Darlene announced her plans, however, he listened.

"Well, I did it!" she said one day at lunch to him and Mickey. "I sent my applications for nursin' school."

"Cool. You should. You've talked about it since seventh grade. Where did you apply? Marshall? WVU?" Mickey asked.

"Both. Southern as a backup."

"Marshall? WVU? Whoa, hold up one minute. You've never said anything about this to me," Dave said.

"Well, yes I have. It ain't a secret I wanna be a nurse. Besides, we talked about it the other night. I asked you what *you* were plannin' to do after graduation, and I told you *I* planned to go to nursin' school."

"Yeah, but you never said anything about goin' to Marshall or WVU. Don't you think that's a bit selfish?"

"Selfish? Are you kiddin' me?" Mickey asked. "How is bein' a nurse selfish? You're such a moron, Dave."

"You ain't in this discussion, Mickey, so shut your face." Dave was sick of Mickey's interference. The last thing he needed was Mickey telling Darlene nursing school was a good thing.

"Hey, you two, stop it." Darlene held up a hand in both their directions. "I said I was just *thinkin'* about Marshall. I gotta be accepted first. So, keep your panties on, Dave."

"You are so rollin' over and playin' dead for him. Who are you? Do what you want, Darlene, and don't let him guilt you into doin' what he wants." Mickey got up, emptied her tray, and left the cafeteria.

Yeah, that's right. She's gonna do whatever I want. Dave had to find a way to convince Darlene this school thing was nonsense.

It took some time, but she finally gave it up. Not exactly the way he wanted or for the reasons he wanted, but she had quit school, and he had won. *So, fuck you, Mickey.*

Now, four years later, here he was dealing with the whole Mickey issue again. Dave drove around for the next few hours. He wanted to let Darlene wonder where he was. She needed to be taught a lesson about who was in charge. Again.

***

Darlene wondered where Dave had gone and then realized she was glad he was gone. It was nice to have the time to herself. She added more hot water to the tub. It eased the tension in her body and mind. She loved her family, and she loved being a mother, but she needed something more. If she hadn't dropped out of nursing school the last semester or had gone back and finished the next fall, how different things would be. Or would they? Darlene yearned for some of the freedom Mickey had. She soaked and cried and retraced the steps that had brought her here to this spot, this day. She wondered if there were a way to rewind or undo some choices.

The explosion that ensued when she had told Dave she had been accepted to Marshall University lasted for two weeks. Dave's relentless pleas not to abandon him held her emotions hostage. She told herself it was okay to compromise for love and decided to go to Southern, the community college.

Her decision to forego Marshall wasn't an easy one to make. She loved Dave and didn't want to lose him. She felt she needed to do the thing that would make *him* happy. She wanted to do what would make *everyone* happy. She now knew that was impossible. Dave would never be happy with anything she did or whoever she was. He wanted her to be something she found impossible to be. She struggled daily to meet his expectations and failed miserably at every turn.

Telling everyone her decision about nursing school was one of the most humiliating days of her life.

"So, Marshall or WVU?" Mickey had asked.

Darlene looked at Mickey, then Aunt Penny and then her mother and dropped her eyes to her bowl of soup. "Neither. Southern. I'm goin' to Southern," Darlene said.

"Oh, my," Aunt Penny said.

"Darlene?" her mother said, "What are you thinkin'? You have scholarship money and have been accepted."

"Southern? *Really*? You caved to him? What has happened to you, Darlene?" Mickey dropped her spoon and sat back in her seat. "You don't want to go there. You want to live on campus, get out of Matewan."

"I know, Mick. But…but, I love Dave, and I want to be with him. I don't want to just up and leave him here. He ain't goin' to college. His daddy got him a job in the mines at Massey, and he's goin' to work right after graduation. I can't just up and leave him." Darlene stopped eating and carried her bowl to the sink.

Aunt Penny shot Mickey and Millie a look of disbelief. "Well, I think you should really think this through, Darlene. Unless you intend to marry that boy right after school, you need to pursue your dreams, sweetheart. Even if you do marry him, you need to follow your dreams or you will regret it forever. Trust me, I'm old and have many regrets."

"Amen to that," Millie said. "Look at my life, Darlene. I love your father dearly, but if I had it to do over, I would go to school and get the hell out of here and see the world."

"Darlene," Mickey said, "I know you love him and all that, but he's just so controllin' of your every move. It's like you suddenly became his property, and you're always lookin' to him for his approval and permission or somethin'. Like you need to get his permission to do anything."

"That ain't it at all, Mick. I love him, and I respect him. I don't want to lose him. Sometimes you gotta compromise for those you love, and my compromise is to go to Southern." Darlene saw the disbelief and dismay in their eyes, but she needed to convince herself as much as them.

"Southern has a great nursin' program, and I can be an RN in two years instead of four. No, I don't get to have the whole campus experience, but my education will be just as good, and I can go for the bachelor's and master's later." Darlene sounded more defeated with every explanation she offered for choosing the community college over the university.

Darlene knew the other women were disappointed and frustrated with her. But she had made her decision, and right or wrong, at the end of the day, all that mattered was she was going to be a nurse, by hook or crook.

The first year of college flew by. She loved school and made straight As, even though Dave constantly berated her and hounded her to quit school and get married. He couldn't understand why she didn't have much spare time to spend with him, but he seemed delighted that she didn't have any spare time to spend with Mickey, either.

As the school year came to a close, Dave's demands to get married that summer were constant and took an angry turn. His mantra—no woman of his would need a college education and career; he would take care of his woman—was the complete opposite of what she wanted for her life. She knew she had to leave or Dave would make it impossible for her to finish school.

She wanted to get a jump on her bachelor's degree and decided to take a few of the core classes at Southern during the summer session.

Dave went ballistic.

"Darlene, we have plans to go to Myrtle Beach for two weeks durin' miners' vacation. How's that gonna happen if you are in school all summer? Let's go on to Myrtle Beach and get married. You can finish school on a regular schedule. You don't need to rush it. You don't even need to go to school. I'll take care of you. I've got a good job, and my uncle Bob said we could buy his trailer up Rutherford Holler. We're all set, girl. Come on, Darlene."

"Dave, I want to marry you, but not until I graduate."

"Darlene, I just don't understand why you can't be married *and* go to school." Dave said.

"I want to finish school first, Dave. I want to be able to focus on school and not have all the distractions of bein' a wife. When we get married, I want to be a wife and not studyin' all the time. Dave, the quicker I get out of school, the quicker we can get married." Darlene hoped this would placate him. "You can still go to Myrtle Beach without me. Take your cousins, Terry and Johnny, and go have a good time."

"Let me get this straight, I ask you to marry me and you tell me to go on to the beach without you? Why? What're you gonna be doin' while I'm gone?"

"What? I'll be in school, Dave. Studyin'. Homework."

"You plannin' to run around with Mickey while I'm gone? Is that why you're so eager to have me go without you?"

"No! What on earth are you talkin' about? Why do you bring Mick into every argument we have? This is just stupid. What are you accusin' me of? I've not even done anything, and you are accusin' me of somethin'."

After many more arguments, Dave went to Myrtle Beach with his cousins, and Darlene went to school that summer. Those two weeks without his hounding her every move had been wonderful.

She enjoyed every minute of school that summer. Dave was another matter. She dreaded seeing him. He called every morning before she left for school and showed up at her house every evening just to make sure she was there; then he would call before she went to bed.

Summer classes finally ended, and Darlene was at Aunt Penny's for lunch, when Mickey arrived.

"Hi, Mick! Man, have I missed you." Darlene stood on her tiptoes to hug her friend.

"Hey, little britches, how's school? I saw Millie the other day at the bank, and she said you were doin' really good. She sure is proud of you," Mickey said.

"School's great, Mick. I love it. I took a full load this summer—all core courses I'll need for Marshall next year, for the bachelor's program. I'm exhausted and have a little over a week before fall classes start."

"What'd you say? You're gonna do it? You're goin' on to Marshall next year?

"If I can get accepted again. That may not be possible, and it might make sense to just finish this program and be an RN and then make the jump. I need to talk to my advisor and figure out what makes the most sense."

"Soooo…what about Dave and the big weddin'?" Mickey said.

Darlene moved the food around on her plate. "Dave don't know. I ain't told him yet. He'll make my life miserable, and I don't need the distraction. I just want to get through the next four months of school."

Aunt Penny poured Darlene more sweet tea. "I understand why you don't want to tell Dave. He'll just obsess over it, but you can't lie to him, honey. Why does that boy want to rush into marriage?"

"I don't know, Aunt Penny. He acts like I'm gonna run off or somethin' if he doesn't make it legal right away."

"Well, is he right?" Aunt Penny asked. "Are you sure you want to marry him? Don't get me wrong. He's a nice enough boy, but I don't think he wants the best for you or even knows what is best for you."

"Well, he ain't a nice-enough-boy, Aunt Penny." Mickey said. "He's a jackass."

Darlene shook her head at Mickey. "I don't know, Aunt Penny. I love him, but I ain't all that excited about gettin' married. I just want to get through school. I don't think Dave's all that thrilled about me bein' a nurse, though. I think he would lock me in the basement if he could."

"So, why marry him?" Mickey asked. "I mean, if you don't want to, don't."

"But I do love him. I just don't know about gettin' married. I'm only nineteen. Why rush it?"

Darlene and Mickey left Aunt Penny's to go for a drive.

"Let's stop at the Gas 'n' Go and get a six-pack of Bud," Mickey said. "It's a beautiful day, and you've had your nose stuck in a book all summer. I think a drive and a few beers'll do you good."

"A cold beer would hit the spot. Heck, it might hit a couple of spots."

After they got their beer, they headed toward Williamson. "Darlene, get in my backpack in the back seat. In the inside pocket, there's a joint of the finest weed this summer has grown. Light that thing up."

"Oh, man. I've not had any since our high school graduation night, Mick, and we had to sneak away from Dave to do that." Darlene fished the joint out of Mickey's bag. "All

I do is study and go to class and deal with Dave's bullshit." She lit the joint.

"You don't have to put up with his shit, Darlene. You're smart—too smart for his dumb ass. And you're beautiful, and you can do anything you want. I'll say it again. If you don't want to marry him, don't." Mickey took the joint from Darlene.

"You're right, Mick. You are so right." Darlene drank her beer, and turned up the music.

Darlene and Mickey drove around for the rest of the afternoon to no place in particular. They made a stop at Walmart to buy shampoo and tampons. Then they stopped at Taco Bell. They sat in the Taco Bell parking lot talking and eating for about an hour before Mickey dropped Darlene back at Aunt Penny's to get her car.

"Mick, I had a great time. Let's get together again this weekend. I need more fun before I go back to school. I only have ten days of freedom."

"Sure thing. I'll call you."

Darlene got in her car and drove home. When she pulled into her driveway, her stomach churned. Dave stood next to his truck, scowling. "Where you been, Darlene?"

"I was at Aunt Penny's, and then me and Mickey went to Taco Bell and got somethin' to eat." Darlene felt the day's joy drain away.

"You smell like pot and beer. Where you been? Where'd that whore take you?"

"I told you. We drove around, drank a few beers, smoked a joint and ate a burrito. That was it, Dave. Why do you have to accuse me of somethin' every time I do stuff without you?"

"'Cause you been with that whore, and I know what she does."

"Really, Dave? What does she do exactly? She works, she lives her life and does what she wants. And that's what you can't stand. You can't control her, and you hate it." Darlene was fed up with his trying to control her every move.

"See there what she's done already? You're actin' just like her. You're drunk, Darlene. I don't know if I want to marry a girl that drinks and smokes pot. You're gettin' too independent and actin' all uppity 'cause you're goin' to school. And now you're runnin' 'round with Mickey. I just don't know, Darlene. I don't know who you are anymore."

Darlene laughed at him. "Really, Dave? Fine. Don't marry me. You're right, you don't know me. You don't know me at all."

Darlene handed her engagement ring to Dave and then turned and walked into the house.

Dave's tires squealed as he pulled out onto the road. Darlene went straight to bed and slept like a baby.

Dave called relentlessly over the next two days. Darlene left to spend the weekend at Mickey's after telling her parents to tell Dave she wasn't taking his calls. Darlene and Mickey spent Friday night at Mickey's place drinking beer, smoking pot, and watching movies. Saturday morning Darlene and Mickey decided to go to Tennessee to visit Darlene's cousin Rachel. Rachel and her family lived on Norris Lake; visiting them was always a good time. They called Rachel and made plans to leave that afternoon.

"Mick, I'll go home, shower, and get my stuff and be back here in about an hour. Be ready and we'll hit the road. I'm so excited." Darlene left to go home.

Darlene was packed and on her way back to Mickey's when she passed Dave in Red Jacket headed in the opposite direction. In her rear view mirror she saw him turn around and catch up to her. He was on her tail and not about to let up. He was blowing his horn and motioning for her to stop.

Mickey had moved into her grandmother's house after she passed away the previous year. It was a small house that sat about a quarter mile up a dirt road in Newtown. Darlene laid on the horn as soon as she pulled off the highway. She prayed Mickey could hear her. Dirt and rocks flew as she slid to a stop in front of the house. She got out of her car just as Dave pulled in behind her, blocking her.

Dave got out of his truck. "Darlene, what the hell's wrong with you? Now this nonsense has got…got to…to stop." He was drunk, and his words were slurred and running together. "You won't take my calls, and now you're all laid up with Mickey all…all the time. I ain't leavin' here without you. I don't care if I gotta fight Mickey, you, and the whole damned bunch. Now get in the damn truck, and we can forget this." He hit the hood with his fist.

Dave was red-faced and looked as though he hadn't had a bath in days. He smelled like three-day old whiskey and cigarettes. And he was angry. Darlene had never seen him like this, and it scared her. She ran for the front door. She was not quite fast enough and made it only as far as the front porch. Dave may have been drunk, but he was still taller, faster and stronger than Darlene.

"Where you think you're goin', Darlene? Why you runnin' from me?" Dave rushed behind her and grabbed her right arm.

"Dave, let go of me!" Darlene screamed and jerked on the door handle, but Mickey had locked it. "Mickey!"

"Look, Darlene, you just need to stop and listen to me. Stop squirmin', damn it."

Darlene pulled away from Dave and fell down the steps, banging her ribs and hip. Dave grabbed her by the waist and dragged her to his truck. "You're goin' home with me, and that's that. So stop fightin' me and just get in the damn truck."

Darlene struggled against him. She kicked his shin and scratched his face. "Dave, let me go. You're drunk and you smell disgustin'. I don't want to go with you. You can't do this." She struggled to get away from his grip.

Dave backhanded her across the face just as Mickey opened the door and stepped out onto the porch. Dave froze when he heard the pump of the shotgun Mickey had aimed at his head.

"Okay, tough guy, you let her go, and I won't knock your dick in the dirt. Let her go!"

Dave quickly let go of Darlene and threw both hands up in the air. "Okay, Mickey, okay. Don't shoot me. I just wanna talk to Darlene. That's all. She wouldn't stop squirmin' and screamin'."

"Didn't look to me like you was doin' much talkin'. I suppose you need to say whatever you came to say and then get the fuck out of my yard."

Darlene ran and stood behind Mickey.

Dave shuffled his feet in the dirt. "Darlene? Shit. This is crazy. Where you been, Darlene? Here?" Darlene stayed behind Mickey on the porch and just stared at him. She felt a wave of pity for him despite the blood trickling out of her nose.

Dave kept his eyes on Mickey and the shotgun. "Darlene, why you doin' this? Why you actin' so crazy?"

"Why am *I* actin' so crazy?" Darlene stepped out from behind Mickey. "You're drunk off your ass, you chase me down, and then you hit me. You're the crazy one here. You're nuts, Dave. You talk about how bad Mick is for smokin' a little pot, but you go on a four-day bender? Then come here and hit me? You just need to leave." She wiped the blood from her face.

"Is that all you got to say, Dave, cause this shotgun's gettin' real heavy, and you just never know when my finger'll slip." Mickey adjusted her aim.

"Darlene, I love you. I wanna marry you." Dave leaned against his truck for support. "I'm sorry I hit you. I didn't mean to hit you. You just wouldn't stop squirmin'. I won't ever hit you again, I swear. I wanna marry you." Dave pounded his fist on the side of his truck and wobbled as he tried to stand straight. "So, come on and let's get out of here. You had your fun this weekend, now just come on and get in the truck and we can fix this."

"Dave, I'm not goin' with you." Darlene was overwhelmed with pity for Dave. He looked so defeated. The situation was just too crazy. "You just need to leave, Dave. You're drunk. Go home and sober up, and we can talk later.

For cryin' out loud, I've got blood runnin' down my face, Mickey has a shotgun pointed at your head, and you're actin' like everything's normal. Go home, Dave."

"Dave, leave. I ain't tellin' ya again." Mickey readjusted the shotgun against her shoulder.

"Okay, okay, I'm leavin'. I ain't givin' up, Darlene. I'll…I'll go home and sober up. But I'll be back." Dave staggered back to his truck. The wheels threw dirt and rocks all over Darlene and Mickey as he turned around and headed down the drive.

"What the fuck was that?" Mickey asked as she lowered the shotgun.

"Oh, God, Mick. I don't even know what to say." Darlene dropped down on the steps, and Mickey sat down beside her.

"Well, all the more reason to pack up and get the hell outta here. I just need to grab my bag." Mickey got up and turned to go inside and get her things for the trip to Tennessee.

"What? What is it? Don't tell me you're thinkin' about not going?"

"No, it ain't that. I know it sounds crazy, but I feel so sorry for him. I ain't never seen him like that, Mick. He just looked so pitiful standin' there." Darlene looked at the ground so she didn't have to look at Mickey.

"You wanna see pitiful, go look at your face where that son of a bitch hit you. You gotta bloody nose, a swollen lip and I'm pretty sure you gonna have quite a shiner on that right eye." Mickey walked inside.

Despite the crazy start, Darlene and Mickey had a great time in Tennessee. Darlene had to explain her black eye and swollen lip to her cousins, but they were supportive and ready to kick Dave's ass.

The few days in Tennessee went by in a hurry, and after a couple of days back home, it was time for school again. Sunday night Darlene was getting her books together for school. Her first class was bright and early Monday morning.

"Darlene, Dave's here. He's waitin' outside. He said he ain't leavin' until you talk to him." Millie shrugged her shoulders as she made the announcement.

"Mommy, what should I do?"

"Well, just stand your ground. He hit you, Darlene, and that's not acceptable under no circumstances."

Darlene walked outside to find Dave sitting on the back porch holding a dozen red roses. She felt that familiar tug when she saw him. She did love him but couldn't take the controlling and stalking.

Dave stood up. "You're all tan. Where you been?"

"I went to Tennessee for a few days to visit Rachel." Darlene purposely left out that she went with Mickey.

"Oh, I see. I called you about a million times. Your mom said you's out of town." Dave shifted nervously from foot to foot. "Here, I brought these for you." She took the roses and thanked him. She buried her nose in the center of the flowers and took a long deep breath. That scent was something she would never tire of.

"You go back to school tomorrow?"

Darlene nodded.

"So, I guess you won't have any time for me? But you won't be seein' so much of Mickey either, so that's a plus."

Darlene dropped her head back and rolled her eyes. "We back to that already? You been here five seconds and you start in on Mick? Let it go, Dave. Just let it go."

"I'm sorry, Darlene. I just want to spend time with you, and you seem to always be with her or with your nose in a book." Dave sat back down.

"Dave, you got drunk and hit me. You stalked me, you cussed me, and then you hit me. I think Mick is the least of our problems." Darlene sat beside him, holding her roses.

"I'm sorry, Darlene. I didn't mean to hit you. I wouldn't hurt you for nothin'. You know that. You just...you just make me crazy sometimes when you won't listen to me and do what I want."

"Seriously? So, anytime I don't do what you want, you're gonna hit me? Why is that okay with you?" She pushed the roses back at him. "No. No. Take these and leave. You need to leave. I can't marry someone who thinks it's okay to hit me—under any circumstances or for any reason." Darlene turned and walked back into the house. She had turned the porch light off, leaving him sitting in the dark, holding the roses.

Looking back on those days before they got married, Darlene knew she should have stopped the relationship then. Why hadn't she run when she had the chance? She knew Dave was controlling and abusive. She was so absorbed with school, she didn't have time to think about what a relationship with Dave entailed. She didn't want to face the truth. She had hoped it would pass, that he would grow out of it. She should have just left it there on the steps of her parents' back porch, but she didn't.

School started that September, and Dave was doing everything he could to woo her back. He sent flowers every Friday. He called every night. He begged. He promised. He pleaded. Maybe she believed him or maybe it was just easier to stop fighting about it and go along to get along.

Now it was easy to see that what she had felt for Dave was more pity and misplaced obligation than love or passion. She failed to see the choice had been hers, and she let him choose what her future would be. By early November that year, they were back together. By Christmas, Darlene was feeling sick every morning, and her breasts were full and tender. She was pregnant.

Now here she was, four years later, with an abusive husband, two kids, and a wasted education. She felt trapped and helpless. Could she leave him? Could she take the girls and just go? Where? Where would she go? How would they survive? How would Dave survive? Wasn't she responsible for his happiness, too? For making him feel like the man of the house? Wasn't that her role as a wife? Dave had certainly convinced himself that was her role. She got out of the tub, dried herself, and patted the new bruise on her cheek. She had never been more confused and alone.

***

It took a few weeks after the blow up over Mickey and the pot, but things started to mend between Darlene and Dave. The bruise faded, and they resumed their lives with no mention of the fight. Dave wanted another baby and used the incident with Mickey as a bargaining chip. Darlene went off birth control pills and was pregnant by late June. She wasn't sure she could handle another baby, but she realized she didn't have much of a choice. She didn't enjoy being pregnant. The morning sickness, which was really all-day sickness, was overwhelming. Every smell sent her running to throw up. She was miserable.

They lived at the head of Rutherford Holler, nothing more than a tiny, twisty one-lane road. The pavement stopped about twenty-five yards shy of their driveway. From there, the road was packed down with wash-and-wear gravel—it kept washing away with every rain or wearing away with every car that passed.

Their home was a single-wide trailer Dave's uncle had sold them when they first got married. They were saving their money to build a house. The trailer sat on the side of the creek bank, and the yard was a giant mud puddle most of the time. No matter how much grass they planted, it seemed never to take root. One good rain and the creek would rise and flood the yard. What grass had started to show signs of life would be washed away and replaced with discarded bleach bottles, blue plastic grocery bags from the Piggly Wiggly, and pretty much anything that would float.

Late August, Dave was rushing Darlene to get out of the house. He wanted to get to church early. Darlene was fighting nausea and struggling to get two little girls dressed and out the door. It had rained all weekend and their yard had been replaced by a giant slush of mud. Dave was in the process of redoing their walkway and had rigged a temporary walk of wobbly cinderblocks and a few boards of plywood. He was in the truck blowing the horn, impatient as ever. The girls ran ahead. She slipped on the wet, muddy plywood and fell backwards. She hit the bottom step, hard. She woke up in the emergency room with a slight concussion. The baby had not been so fortunate.

After the miscarriage, Darlene was depressed and sad and lost. Dave was very caring and loving, and things were calm, almost normal…for a while. But as Darlene expected, he quickly slipped back into his demanding ways.

Not long after the miscarriage, she started having a recurring dream that she was drowning. She was out in the water, and it was dark. She didn't know how she got there; maybe she fell out of a boat or she swam too far out. Her arms and legs grew tired from trying to stay afloat. Knowing the bottom was there, she pointed her toes and strained to find the bottom. *There, there it was.* Relief flooded her brain, and she stood up. But it was a lie. The bottom was not solid; it was thick mud that sucked her down farther and farther. She couldn't get her feet free. The water inched higher and covered her mouth, then her nose, then her eyes. Then darkness. She would always wake up at this point, sometimes screaming, sometimes in a cold sweat.

Darlene couldn't find her way out of the sadness. The miscarriage had triggered a new level of anxiety that blinded her to any sense of normal most days. On really bad days, a full-blown panic attack would send her into a downward spiral, leaving her confused and scared. She slipped into a dark hole and was more alone and isolated than ever. No one but her mother ever came to visit. The only places she went were the grocery store and church. They had only one car, and she could never escape that damned holler. She felt more like a prisoner than a wife and mother. She had nothing to look forward to. Her daily choices were truly simple—*Oprah* or *General Hospital.*

***

In late September, Mickey stopped by to see how she was after the miscarriage. Darlene was thrilled to see her. Mickey had called first to see if it was okay to stop over. After the last visit, she didn't want to risk running into Dave. He was working that day, and Darlene thought it would be fine. She needed a friend. She reasoned that Mickey could come for a few hours and leave before he ever knew she had been there.

The trees were turning, and the leaves were bright yellow and red against a crystal blue sky. Darlene dreaded winter and just wanted to enjoy the beautiful day.

Mickey brought stuffed animals for the girls—a lamb for Amy and a giraffe for Renee. For Darlene, she brought a bag of pot, four Lortab and five Xanax. Darlene knew she should have said no. She should have known better. But some demons you just can't sweep under the rug for too long. And her demons of anxiety and depression had moved in and made themselves at home.

They smoked two joints on the back steps while the girls took their afternoon nap. Five feet from the bottom step was a straight-up mountain full of giant, craggily rocks Darlene feared one day would come tumbling down on them in their sleep. It was a peaceful afternoon, and it felt good to laugh and talk about silly stuff. The pot had been exactly what Darlene needed. The tension and anxiety melted away, as usual. The babies were still sleeping when Mickey left. Darlene ate half a bag of Snyder's potato chips and polished off half a bag of Chips Ahoy chocolate chip cookies and fell asleep with the girls.

Dave came home from work and had no clue Mickey had been to visit. No clue Darlene had a bag of pot, four Lortab and five Xanax stashed in her tampon box. As far as he knew, her worst choice that bright sunny day in late September was eating half a bag of cookies.

If it were only that simple.

CHAPTER TWO
Tricks and Treats

"We make up horrors to help us cope with the real ones."
— Stephen King

September flowed into October. Without much to look forward to, Darlene drifted into a ditch, and she couldn't crawl out. As each day smeared into the next, her mood grew grayer and dimmer. She rationed the pot Mickey had left her by smoking half a joint once a week. The pot calmed her anxiety and made life a little more tolerable. Her mid-afternoon weed breaks took place on the back porch while the girls napped. Because she never smoked in the house, her days of getting high were limited to nice days, when she could sit outside. She limited the Lortab and Xanax to her period, when the headaches and anxiety were unbearable. She continued to hide the pot and pills in her tampon box so Dave was none the wiser. After the initial shock of the miscarriage, Dave slowly returned to his controlling and demanding ways. He no longer asked if she needed anything from the kitchen while they watched TV at night. He just slipped back to his true self, which held tightly to the belief that the woman's only purpose was to serve her husband. Like the good little wife she had always been, Darlene did as instructed.

Halloween came on Friday that year, and Dave was working a double shift as he always did on the last Friday of every month. Darlene's parents had planned to take the girls for the night. Amy and Renee were excited about Halloween and hanging out with Nana and Poppy. Amy dressed as a Hershey Kiss and Renee was a tiger. Millie arrived at five to pick up Darlene and the girls in order to make the rounds to Aunt Penny's, a few family friends and Dave's parents. Millie had identified eight people as worthy treat-givers for the girls. After twenty minutes of picture taking, they loaded up the car and set out on their adventure.

"Darlene, how're you and Dave gettin' along?" Millie asked as they wound their way down the holler.

"Fine, I suppose. He's gone back to bein' Dave, and things are normal," Darlene said.

"What does that mean? Normal?" Millie asked.

"Just normal, Mommy. He's just Dave. He's a good man, a good father, he works hard, and I appreciate all he does. But..." Darlene's voice trailed off.

"But, what?" Millie asked.

"I'm lonely and bored, Mommy. I can't have friends. I don't have a car and I can't go anywhere unless you come get me. And I *hate* livin' up this holler. Most days I think I'm gonna lose my mind." Darlene struggled for the right words. "I don't know, I feel like I'm wastin' my life. I told Dave I wanted to go back and finish nursin' school, and he told me absolutely not. Said he wasn't gonna pay for me to go to school. Wanted to know what could I be thinkin'; I have two little girls to raise and take care of. I tried to explain to him that women with children go to school and work all the time. It's like he lives in the eighteenth century or somethin'." Darlene rested her head back and looked out the passenger window.

They were nearing the mouth of the holler and turning left to go down the back alley to Aunt Penny's.

"Darlene, I know you get lonely and bored livin' at the head of this holler, but you're a mother and wife, and you need to do what's best for all of you now. Not just what's best for you. You'ns need to sort out your troubles and make this marriage work."

"I know Mommy, but sometimes what's best for me *is* what's best for all of us. If I'm miserable, how am I gonna be any good for anyone else, especially my kids?"

They pulled into Aunt Penny's driveway and the discussion ended.

After thirty minutes at Aunt Penny's, they loaded the girls into the car again and set out for the next seven stops. The girls collected more candy than they normally had in a year. They each collected about $20 from Dave's parents, as well.

After trick-or-treating—with everyone oohing and ahhing and declaring the girls were adorable—Millie took Darlene home. Darlene ran in and got the girls' overnight bag and took it out to the car.

"Remember, Mommy, they need a bath and pajamas as soon as you get home or they'll never go to sleep." Darlene put the overnight bag in the passenger seat. She leaned into the back and kissed the girls goodbye and then kissed her mom.

"Honey, I love you. Things *will* work out. Just be patient," Millie said.

Darlene waved goodbye and walked back into the trailer.

She could hear the phone ringing as she stepped up on the porch. The caller ID said it was Mickey. "Hey, Mick. What's up?" Darlene hurled herself sideways into Dave's recliner.

"Hey, girl. What'cha doin' tonight?"

"Nothin'. Absolutely nothin'. The girls are gone with Mommy for the night, and Dave is workin' a double. I have a peaceful, quiet night all to myself."

"Well, maybe not. Wanna go to a party with me? The party's over at Belfry, and I can pick you up at eight."

"Oh, I don't know, Mick. Dave freaks if you come to visit. He would totally derail if I took off for a party with you." Darlene was torn. The thought of a party, with no kids and no husband sounded wonderful. She was bored out of her mind, but Dave's wrath would not be worth it. "Mickey, I can't. Dave would totally kill me. There just ain't no way."

"Oh, Darlene. Come on. The party doesn't really get started until late anyway. There'll be a ton of people you know there. We can drink and get stoned, just like old times. Please, please, please."

"Mickey, I don't know. It sounds like fun. Dave would never allow it." Even before she heard Mickey's exasperated sigh, it occurred to her that she had been asking Dave's permission before she did anything for far too long.

"Dave can I go to the grocery store?" "Dave, can I go to my mommy's with the girls?" "Dave, can I buy a new dress?" "Dave, can I have friends?"

"You ain't been out of that holler in months, except to go to the grocery store and church. Dave treats you like a prisoner. You're young, and you need to get out and have fun," Mickey said.

The more she thought about the situation and the more Mickey pleaded, Darlene began to convince herself she should go with Mickey. She needed to get out of the house without the kids before she lost her mind.

"Okay. Okay, I'll go. But I must be home by eleven because Dave gets home from work at midnight," Darlene said. "Oh, one more thing, Mick, do I have to wear a costume?"

"Great! No need for a costume. I'll pick you up at eight sharp."

As Darlene hung up the phone, she was excited and nervous about the party. Dave would have a cow if he found out. She frantically dug through her closet for something to wear. She hadn't been shopping in so long. Trying on several outfits, she realized she had completely lost her cool factor. Until she got married she had always worn the latest fashions. Dave rarely let her buy anything new for herself. She finally decided on a pair of jeans. Even if they weren't the latest fashion, she at least looked great in them. She paired the jeans with a blue sweater Aunt Penny had given her for her birthday.

Mickey arrived at five minutes after eight. Darlene grabbed her purse and jacket and headed out the door. Once in the car, Mickey passed her a joint. "Let me get the car door closed first," Darlene said. "Hold it down, I don't want my neighbors to see it."

"Man, you are really paranoid. You need to get out more. You'd think I had a gun to your head. Relax," Mickey said.

Darlene took several hits off the joint and immediately felt better. Mickey passed her a large travel mug.

"What's this?"

"Vodka and cranberry juice. Have a swig. It's good stuff."

Darlene took a small sample sip and liked it. Then she took a nice long drink. "This is really good. Do you have more?"

The party was at a huge, old three-story house. It seemed that every square inch of it was decorated. Skeletons hung from the trees, and at least thirty carved pumpkins lined the railing of the front porch. Each pumpkin was carved to represent an element of Halloween—witches, ghosts, goblins, black cats, and some things Darlene couldn't quite make out. Cars were parked everywhere: in the yard, in the driveway, on the street, at the neighbors'.

The music was loud. Frankenstein directed them to the living room where Dracula was tending bar. A very skinny neon skeleton approached and hugged Mickey. Darlene thought he said his name was Bob, but the noise was so loud she wasn't certain. She decided to just call him Neon. He took them to a smaller room off the kitchen. Neon offered Mickey a very large joint, which she immediately lit up and passed to Darlene.

Most people were in costume, but some were not. Darlene didn't recognize anyone but talked to almost everyone. One young man, whose costume Darlene couldn't figure out, came over and offered her cocaine, which she politely turned down. The man's costume was a red T-shirt with a black letter "P" sewn on, and he had his eye blacked out. "What's your costume supposed to be?" Darlene asked.

"I'm a black-eyed pea," he told her. "Get it?"

"That's really funny." Darlene giggled. She didn't know if it was really that funny or just the pot making it seem that funny. Either way, she couldn't stop laughing at his ridiculous costume.

"Excuse me, I've got to go pee," she said, and laughed that much harder. As she roamed around the first floor of the house looking for the bathroom, she happened to see the clock on the kitchen wall and nearly peed right there in the hallway. It was 10:30, and she had no idea where Mickey was. They had to leave right away. It would take at least twenty-five minutes to get home, and she had to be there, showered, and in bed before Dave got back from work.

Darlene used the bathroom on the second floor and then set out to find Mickey. She found her outside on the deck smoking pot with Neon, who was not so discretely passing a bottle of pills to her.

"I'm sorry to bust up the party, Mick, but it's 10:40 and we really gotta scat," Darlene said as she took the joint Neon offered her.

"No problem, little britches," Mickey said. "I'll see *you* tomorrow," she said as she turned to Neon and kissed him goodbye.

Mickey drove like a crazy woman to get Darlene home before Dave arrived. Before Darlene closed the car door, she leaned in. "Mick, thanks for tonight. I really needed it—all of it. I haven't laughed so much in a really long time. You're the best. I love ya, crazy girl!"

"No problem. We'll do it again."

Darlene took a shower, threw her clothes in the wash, and straightened up the house. She found the huge joint in her purse that Neon had given her as they were leaving. She hid this in her tampon box with the few remaining Lortab and Xanax. She dried her hair, put the clothes in the dryer and crawled into bed. She was exhausted and just wanted to sleep. She couldn't believe she had gotten away with sneaking out to a party.

Dave came home as scheduled a quarter after midnight, showered, and crawled into bed with her. He never knew she had gone to a party, and she fell asleep with a smile on her face.

CHAPTER THREE
Let Us Give Thanks

"O Lord that lends me life, lend me a heart replete with thankfulness." — William Shakespeare

The girls had finally settled down for a nap, and Darlene was at the kitchen table making out her grocery list for Thanksgiving dinner. She would make the desserts at her house and take them to her parents' and Dave's parents'. She would also make a few dishes with her mother. She was checking her pumpkin bread recipe when the phone rang.

She took a deep breath and picked up the phone. "Hi, Mick."

"Hey, Darlene, what'cha doing?" Mickey asked.

Darlene had kept her conversations with Mickey short since the Halloween party. The party had certainly picked up her spirits for a little while, but she had slowly drifted back into the gray ditch. And her nightmares of drowning were still frequent. She spent most of November feeling guilty about going to the party. She knew keeping secrets from Dave was wrong, but he would never understand and would probably beat her black and blue if he found out. So she kept the secret to herself, and as often as she could, still smoked half a joint in the afternoons when the girls were sleeping. Her stash was dwindling and would soon be gone. She promised herself she wouldn't get more. She couldn't.

She looked forward to the next time she and Mickey could get together and just enjoy an afternoon. No kids, no husband, no pressure. Just hanging out with her friend. She knew that would never happen unless she sneaked behind Dave's back. The Halloween party had been a fluke, and she knew this. A perfect storm—kids gone, Dave working, Mickey with a party.

"Just gettin' my grocery order together for Thanksgiving. I need to start bakin' tomorrow or I'll never get it all done. You know Mommy. She wants to have most of the desserts at her house Saturday. Her cousin Judy and her family will be here Saturday night, and Mommy has to have enough food for an army. What are you up to?"

"Well, I wanted to see if you were game for another party. The same place we went for the Halloween party. It'll be Saturday after Thanksgivin'. Think you can swing it?"

"Oh, Mick, there ain't no way. I just feel so guilty about the whole Halloween thing. I just can't. Besides, we have so much family comin' in for the holiday—Mommy's family and Dave's family. There's no way I could do it. It would create a war with Dave *and* Mommy."

"Well, you're sure gonna miss a good time. I have some great coke, girl. Have you ever tried it?"

"Oh, goodness, no. You know me, pot and an occasional pill is about as far as I go." She was a bit shocked that Mickey would have cocaine. "Where'd you get cocaine? Ain't that a little hardcore?"

"It's the dust of the fairies. I got it from a new friend of mine. His name's Ray. He owns The Place at Red Jacket. Have you been there? It's a pizza joint."

"No, I've seen it, but I don't go to Red Jacket or Newtown too often. Is it beside the old elementary school?"

"Yeah, that's the place. Man, it's crazy. He sells cocaine, pills, pot, whatever you want right out of the pickup window. But only to people he knows."

"What? Right there? Beside the school? That's crazy, Mickey." Darlene was thinking Mickey must be exaggerating just a bit.

"The school ain't used for nothin' but Girl Scout meetin's and little league basketball games. Most people don't know about Ray's side business. He sells mostly in the back of the restaurant. If you call ahead, he'll just slip it into your pizza box. Pretty cool, huh?" Mickey was laughing.

"Well, sounds kinda risky to me. Mickey, be careful with those people. Drugs like that are crazy."

"Okay, little mama. Don't worry. Ray's cool. You'd really like him. Maybe we can go for pizza one day."

Renee's crying broke through the conversation. Darlene stood up. "Oh, Mick, the girls are awake. Let me call you back. I'm sorry I can't go to the party. Maybe next time."

"No problem. There'll be more parties."

"Oh, Mick, one more thing. You gonna be able to stop by Thanksgivin' day? Mommy would love to see you. If not then, maybe Wednesday night? Aunt Penny and Judy will be there, and we'll be cookin' and singin' and actin' a fool. Just like old times," Darlene said.

"Sure, I'll probably stop by Wednesday night. Why not? Sounds like fun," Mickey said, and they hung up.

Darlene picked up Renee and held her close. She soothed her crying and thought about the party. Several scenarios rolled around her mind that would make going to this party possible. None of them made sense in the real world. She longed to go, to get dressed up again, and just be free for a night. It would never work. Dave had the weekend off, and she had too much family in town.

Renee stopped crying and was sitting on the couch playing with her favorite doll, Dot. Just as Darlene was about to return to her grocery list, Amy woke up and came waddling down the hall. Darlene picked up Amy and held her close. "Oh, my angels, why would I ever risk hurtin' you? I don't need a party. I just need my girls. With the two of you, the world is right." Darlene kissed each of the girls and returned to her grocery list.

***

The next week was filled with preparations for Thanksgiving. Darlene was busy with grocery shopping, helping her mother clean and getting ready for the holiday company. She dropped off some of her baked goods at her parents' house on Saturday afternoon. The place smelled wonderful. Her mother had made a pot of vegetable soup and a pot of chicken soup and had baked fresh bread.

"Lord, Mommy, you think you have enough soup here? Who's comin'?"

Millie was in the laundry room moving area rugs from the washer to the dryer. "Well, you and your bunch, Penny, Judy, her husband, her two grandkids and her daughter Beth. Who, by the way, is goin' through a nasty divorce. Judy says she's turned into a wild child." Millie emerged from the laundry room with a basket full of towels.

"Here, Mommy, I'll fold those. So, why's Beth gettin' a divorce?" Darlene asked, trying not to sound too interested in the ways a woman would go about splitting from her husband.

"Apparently, he was cheatin' on her with her best friend. Now, this is all Judy's tellin'. So, I assume that's what happened. But, they's always two sides to every story." Millie checked the last loaf of bread in the oven.

"They were married for quite a while, weren't they? Her oldest daughter must be six years old by now." Darlene continued folding towels.

"Yeah, six and five, I think. Little, still."

Judy was Millie's first cousin. Millie, Judy, and Aunty Penny had grown up together, and Judy was like a third sister. She lived in Piqua, Ohio, now and came home nearly every Thanksgiving. Millie and Penny had gone to visit Judy in Piqua every summer for as long as Darlene could remember until about five years earlier, when they decided they needed to just go away and visit some other places. One year they went to Asheville, North Carolina, to tour the Biltmore Estate; another year they went to Myrtle Beach; yet another, they drove to Savannah, Georgia, and fell in love with the place, deciding that would be the summer destination forever more. They giggled like little school girls every time they got together. Darlene hoped she and Mickey would be like that when they were older—if Mickey were around that long. Darlene worried about her friend's lifestyle and the drugs. Some days Darlene agreed with her mother that it would be a miracle if Mickey didn't OD or go to jail before she was thirty.

"By the way, Mommy, Mickey said she would stop by Wednesday night. She wants to see you and Daddy and Aunt Penny."

"Oh? Well, I sure hope she ain't drunk or high."

"Mommy, she won't be. She respects you too much for that. I don't know why you're so hard on her now." Darlene carried the folded towels to the linen closet in the hall.

"It's just that she ain't the same little girl no more, Darlene. She's changed. She's wild, and there's somethin' that just seems mean about her. She's got too many sharp edges. There's a hardness in her eyes. It's like she's just lookin' for trouble of the worst kind, and she don't care who gets hurt along the way. She changed when you girls started high school. There's just somethin' upside down about that girl that makes my spirit leap around inside of me. I just don't think it wise that you keep her too close." Millie seemed to look right through Darlene as though she had seen a ghost, and that "somethin' upside down" her mother described walked across Darlene's skin and gave her goose bumps.

Darlene shook it off. "Mommy, you're just imaginin' things. True, Mickey has changed a lot since we were little girls. Everybody changes. She gets high and she drinks, and she sleeps around some. But, she's still *our* Mick." Darlene tried to rationalize Mickey's behavior, more for her own benefit than for her mother's.

"Well, just mark my words, no good will come of that girl. She runs with a rough crowd, and there's an edge to her that's too sharp for my taste. But she's welcome here for the holiday. Maybe bein' around us will help her see how far off the path she is," Millie said.

There was a clatter at the back door. The company had arrived. The madness of the holiday had begun.

***

Darlene couldn't remember when she had cooked and cleaned and laughed so much. The past few days had been wonderful. Millie was right; Beth was a mess. She just wanted to drink and smoke cigarettes all day. She asked Darlene several times where she could get beer and if there were any pills to be had. Darlene knew better than to offer her last Lortab or her pot to Beth. Beth never stopped talking and would spill the beans in a hurry. It was Wednesday afternoon, and Darlene offered to take her to buy beer at the Gas 'n' Go. Of course, she got Millie's approval before making the offer. Millie said that would be fine, but only after Judy agreed.

"Beth, when Mickey gets here, which should be any minute, we'll make a beer and cigarette run. So, get your shoes on and brush your hair or whatever you need to do," Darlene said.

Dave was at his parents' with the girls. The plan was for him to drop the girls around five, and then he would be off to work third shift. Darlene and the girls would stay with her parents for the night so she could get up early to help cook. The girls were thrilled to have a pajama party.

Darlene and Beth were on the back porch when Mickey pulled in at 6:30. They jumped in the car, barely giving Mickey time to come to a stop. "Gas 'n' Go! We're makin' a beer run," Darlene said.

"Beer? In this house?" Mickey asked. "Seriously? Did Millie fall and hit her head?"

"Well, it's for Beth, and she has to be discreet with it. In a cup and not let the girls know she has it. Oh, sorry. Mick, you remember my cousin Beth, don't you?" Darlene asked as she reintroduced the two women.

"Hi," Beth said as she lit another cigarette. "You got somethin' better than this to smoke, Mickey?" Beth asked.

"All right, it's a party!"

"Girls, I hate to be Debbie Downer, but we can't go back to Mommy's smellin' like pot. The beer was pushin' the limits of everything Mommy had," Darlene said with hesitation.

"Buzz kill!" Beth said.

"Really! Buzz kill, and we ain't even high yet. Geez, Darlene," Mickey chimed in.

"Okay, okay, I know, but I will be the one to get beat on after you two leave on your merry way," Darlene reminded them.

"So, let's light up now and roll down the windows so the smell won't be so obvious," Beth said. "Look, I'm in the middle of a divorce and need to just cut loose for a while. I've had a rough couple of months."

"Okay," Darlene said. "We may freeze, but we'll be high and not care."

Mickey pulled a joint out of her purse and handed it to Darlene to light. The last thing Darlene wanted was to go home smelling like pot. She decided she would blame it on the other two and tell her mom she was just in the car with them. She hoped Millie would believe her.

When they got back in the car with the beer, Mickey pulled out a small brown vial from her purse. "What's that, Mick?" Darlene asked, hoping it wasn't coke.

"This is the bride. Beth, you do coke?" Mickey asked with an air of superiority in her voice that Darlene had never heard before. Her mother's words hung in her head.

A hardness and sharp edges.

"I've never had any. What does it do to you?" Beth asked as she leaned in between the two front seats to see what Mickey had.

"It makes you feel really good. Happy, full of energy, like you could fly," Mickey informed them. "You feel like Superman! I swear."

"How do you do it? Do you snort it?" Mickey nodded her head yes.

"That sounds horrible," Beth said. "Do I have to snort it? Is there some other way?" "Don't be a pussy. Just snort it. It'll drain a bit down the back of your throat, but it won't last long. It's worth it." She cut out three lines of the white powder.

"Mick, you only need two of those lines. I ain't doin' that stuff. It's bad enough I'm goin' back half stoned. Cocaine is the last thing I need to do." Darlene knew she sounded like a complete dork, but cocaine was so hardcore, and she was not about to get involved.

Mickey and Beth snorted their lines of cocaine. Beth coughed and hacked for about five minutes as the cocaine drained down the back of her throat. Darlene noticed that Mickey didn't seem to have the same issues and worried that she must have been doing this for a while. They returned to Darlene's parents' with the beer, and Darlene prayed that the smell of cigarette smoke covered the smell of pot smoke.

Mickey and Beth became fast friends, and it was obvious Darlene was the odd man out as the evening wore on. Mickey and Beth seemed to be in the same head space and were outside smoking together quite a bit. Darlene knew they were snorting more cocaine and went out to check on them during one noticeably long smoke break.

"Ain't you two freezin' out here?" She sat down on the top step.

"It is a little chilly. Our next smoke might not be as long. The bride has left for her honeymoon," Beth said.

"Well, not to fear. I can get more. I just need to go get it. I think we may need a pizza. Think the girls would like a pizza, Darlene?" Mickey burst into giggles.

"Mickey! You mean from that crazy man you told me about? I don't want my girls eatin' nothin' from that place." Darlene could not believe Mickey would even suggest it.

"Darlene, it ain't like he puts coke in the pizza sauce. The food is actually good. It's just if you want a little somethin' extra..."

"Ain't that stuff expensive, Mick?" Darlene asked. "We ain't got money for that kinda stuff."

"Well, I know Ray really well, if you know what I mean, and I think I can get us a hit for nothin'. We may have to pay for the pizza is all." Mickey had been hinting at some kind of relationship with Ray all night.

"Mommy's been cookin' for a week. She will completely freak if we say we want pizza. But you go right ahead and ask." Darlene knew she was fighting a losing battle and gave up trying to convince Mickey and Beth of anything that made sense.

Mickey and Beth concocted a plan to have the kids ask for pizza. Within twenty minutes, Darlene was driving to The Place with Mickey and Beth in tow. The girls had begged to ride along, but Darlene would not allow it and promised to bring them each a slushy in addition to the pizza.

They pulled into the parking lot, and Darlene was amazed at how crowded it was. There was barely room to park.

"There, around back." Mickey said. "We can go in the side door. I do it all the time. Everybody here knows me."

The three of them walked through the side door, which opened into the kitchen. The door was propped open with a case of tomato sauce. The kitchen was narrow and long and very bright. The stainless steel counters looked like they hadn't had a good cleaning in months. There were three women and one man making pizzas. Two of the women were adding toppings; the man was working the oven, and the third woman was boxing up the pizzas. They moved seamlessly and seemed to be having a lot of fun. There was one woman working the grill; she looked like someone's great grandmother and was moving at a very slow pace compared to the others. There was a young girl who looked to be no more than fourteen at the sink washing dishes. It was loud and hectic and hot.

The staff greeted Mickey, and she gave her order for the pizzas. She walked over to a cooler and took out three beers. She kept one for herself and handed one to Beth and one to Darlene, who stood just inside the door, away from the hot oven. From Darlene's spot, she could see into the dining room through a pair of swinging doors as the waitresses slipped in and out of the kitchen to pick up and deliver orders. Darlene was trying to catch a glimpse of what was happening on the other side, when the door swung open wide.

"Ray!" Mickey said, rushing over to the man. She whispered something in his ear; he nodded his head yes and rubbed Mickey's back, never taking his eyes off Darlene.

"Ray," Mickey said, "this is my best friend in the entire world, Darlene, and this is her cousin, Beth. We came to get a pizza and the fixin's."

"Well, it's a pleasure meetin' you ladies. Welcome to The Place. Come on out back to the office so we can talk. It's too damned hot in this kitchen to do anything." Ray led them past the grill and sink, through another door and a short, narrow hallway. On the left side was a stainless steel refrigerator and a large, white freezer, the type Darlene's parents had in their laundry room, but much bigger. On the right, the wall was lined with shelves holding Styrofoam containers, go-cups, plastic utensils and other supplies. In the corner was an old Coke machine, the kind Darlene remembered seeing at Akers' grocery store in North Matewan when she was little.

They entered an office that was twice the size of the kitchen. It was dark with paneled walls and only one window, which had a room-darkening blind pulled completely down.

There was a door with three deadbolt locks leading outside and another closed door at the far end of the office to the right. The room was messy, like a party had taken place the night before and no one had bothered to clean up. Beer bottles, whiskey bottles and full ashtrays littered the square coffee table and two end tables. In front of the door to the outside, the floor was covered in mud. But the smell was what hit Darlene hard in the face. It smelled like last night's pot and spilled beer and stale cigarette smoke.

Ray motioned for the girls to sit down, and Darlene took a seat on the couch next to Beth. Mickey sat in a chair next to the couch. Ray took his place at a wooden teacher's desk. She wondered if he had stolen it from the school next door. The desk had been pushed up against the wall across from the couch. Ray had his back to Darlene as he got something from the desk's center drawer. She watched his muscles move underneath his thin T-shirt. She was so intent on watching him that when he swung around, it startled her. She jumped and could feel herself blushing.

He smiled. She was terrified of him and fascinated at the same time. It puzzled her as to why a man his age would be selling drugs, let alone taking them. She had never encountered anyone like Ray. From what she had observed so far, he was full of energy, funny, and in control of everyone around him—even Mickey. Darlene didn't find him necessarily handsome. He wasn't like Dave, who was tall and lean from working hard every day in the mines. Ray was short and solid with thick muscles. He had a hard look. He smiled with his entire face, causing the lines around his eyes to become more pronounced. She liked his long wavy hair and the way it fell over his right brow. He had more gray than brown, and Darlene guessed he was closer to her father's age than her's.

She liked the way he looked directly at her when he spoke, almost as though he could read her mind. She was getting uncomfortable with Ray's attention, especially since

Mickey liked him. She wished she could just leave or wait in the car.

"You're about the cutest thing I've ever seen," he said.

Darlene could feel her face getting hotter and redder as Ray continued to look at her and—she felt—into her.

"Thanks."

No one since high school had told her she was pretty.

"You married?" Ray never took his eyes off her face.

"I sure am. I have two little girls, too." Darlene hoped a married woman with two little kids would be the biggest turn-off in the world and he would lose interest.

"Well, ain't that a shame. You ever find yourself single and in need of a man, or just in need of a man, you know where to find me." Ray was charming, and he sucked the air out of the room. Darlene was having trouble breathing.

"Ray, we gotta be gettin' back. The entire family's waitin' on the pizza, so we gotta scat pretty soon." Mickey suddenly was in a hurry to leave, and her tone had switched from superior to something else Darlene couldn't quite put her finger on, but it wasn't pleasant.

"Sure, sure, let me just cut this out and you can be on your way. The pizza should be done pretty soon." Ray cut out four lines and filled Mickey's little brown vial.

"Ray, we only need three lines. Darlene don't do coke. She's a little sissy Mary." Mickey laughed and slapped Darlene on the knee. But there was no humor on her face, and her eyes were hard.

A hardness and sharp edges.

Darlene felt that *somethin' upside down* walk over her skin again, and the goose bumps returned.

"You don't partake of the white lady?" Ray shot a quizzical brow at Darlene.

"No, not my thing." Darlene was embarrassed, but not quite sure why. She suddenly wanted to be home with Dave and his familiar, controlling ways. This scene was not what she was used to dealing with. She tried to hide her discomfort. Mickey's change of attitude had hurt Darlene's feelings.

"Well, darlin' we need to change that. You need to lighten up a bit. Life's short." Ray was convincing, and Darlene knew he would convince her if she stayed there long enough. He could probably convince her to do a lot of things.

"Well she won't, so let's not push the issue. Some people don't know how to have a good time, Ray." Mickey was pointing her strange mood directly at Darlene.

Ray, Mickey, and Beth snorted the cocaine laid out on the table. Mickey put her little brown vial in her pocket, they got the pizza and left. Darlene didn't say a word on the ride home. Mickey and Beth didn't shut up. No longer was Darlene concerned about smelling like pot; she was trying to sort out what had just happened. This stranger had slipped into her mind and lingered there. She was also trying to sort out the hostile mood that Mickey had taken when they were with Ray.

They arrived home with the pizza. Darlene felt as though they had been gone forever. So did her mother.

"Where in the world did you girls have to go to get that pizza? You've been gone for almost an hour!" Millie said.

"They were really busy, Mommy. It was packed. We barely found a place to park."

"They're always busy, Millie," Mickey said.

"It was a hoppin' little place, that's for sure," Beth agreed.

"Well, it better be good. The girls are starving," Millie said.

They ate the pizza, and it was pretty decent. Darlene was glad to be home and in the safety of her parents' house with her kids. She didn't want any part of Ray and his drugs or his lifestyle.

So why couldn't she stop thinking about him?

***

Mickey left Darlene's parents' house and returned to The Place; the real party wouldn't start for another hour or so. Lighting a cigarette, she pulled out onto the highway and thought about the evening. Millie had allowed beer in her house; that was a first. Snorting coke on Millie's back porch was a first and probably a last. Being jealous of Darlene was definitely a first, and Mickey feared it wouldn't be a last. She was surprised at herself for being jealous of Darlene. She had never been jealous of her. They had always been supportive and protective of each other. She knew Ray flirted with all women, and Darlene was tiny and cute—just his type. She felt guilty for being nasty with Darlene earlier at Ray's. She knew Darlene didn't want Ray, but she hadn't planned on Ray's coming on so strong to her. The Place was Mickey's territory, her world—the one thing over which she had control—and Darlene had shaken her grip on that world.

CHAPTER FOUR
Merry Christmas, Baby

"Always winter but never Christmas."
— C.S. Lewis, *The Lion, the Witch and the Wardrobe*

Thanksgiving was barely over when Darlene started preparing for Christmas. The girls begged her to put up the Christmas tree early, so it had been standing in the living room since the first of December. The girls were finally old enough to really get excited about the holidays. Darlene and her mother had shopped most of the fall for the latest toys and dolls and had them stored at her parents' house so the girls wouldn't find them.

Some days the anxiety was a giant monster sitting on her, ready to devour her completely with her next breath. She knew she had to make peace with the life she had and accept things as they were. Dave had his issues, and some days, most days, he drove her crazy, but she knew he was a good provider and father. She had not talked to Mickey since the night before Thanksgiving. She was afraid to take too many risks. Darlene enjoyed getting high; it provided a much-needed escape and calmed her in a way nothing else did. However, the visit to Ray's had rattled her. She didn't want any part of that kind of life, so she had flushed the little bit of pot, Lortab, and Xanax she had left.

Darlene was wrapping gifts for her parents while the girls had their afternoon nap. She was attempting to tie a fancy bow she had found in a magazine. Just as she finished the last loop, the phone rang. She looked at the caller ID. It was Mickey. Darlene took a deep breath and answered.

"Merry Christmas, Mickey!" Darlene tried to sound excited to hear from her friend, and in a way she was, but she was beginning to think her mother was right. Her friendship came with a price—one Darlene wasn't sure she could pay.

"Hey, girl. You ready for Christmas?" Mickey asked.

"Sort of. The girls insisted we put up the tree early, so that monstrosity has been standin' in the middle of the livin' room for two weeks already. They love it, though. They want to sleep under it so they can look up at the lights all night."

"They're too cute. How are things with you? You still good on pot and pills?"

Darlene took another deep breath. "Yeah, yeah. I'm good. Not much opportunity to smoke these days. It's just too darned cold outside."

"Oh, yeah, too bad you can't smoke in your own house. That sucks." Mickey's mocking tone was not lost on Darlene.

"I got a great Christmas party to go to and thought you might wanna join me. It'll be a lot of fun. Maybe I can get you to try some coke finally."

"Oh, Mick, I doubt it. I have so much to do with the girls, and Mommy has shoppin' or bakin' planned almost every day. It's probably not a good idea. But I'll see you after Christmas at Aunt Penny's for our gift exchange dinner?"

"Yeah, sure. Always. Let me know what time." Mickey was ready to hang up. "Hey, Darlene, if you change your mind about the party, let me know."

"Sure. Sure, I will. I'll see what time Aunt Penny wants us there and get back to you." Darlene felt a heaviness in her heart as she hung up the phone. There had been a shift between her and Mickey that night at Ray's. They hadn't talked about it and probably never would, but something had changed.

A hardness and sharp edges.

***

Three days after Christmas Darlene, Millie, Mickey, Amy, Renee and two of Aunt Penny's closest friends gathered at Aunt Penny's for their annual post-Christmas celebration. They had been getting together for as long as Darlene could remember. It was one of Darlene's favorite holiday events.

"Aunt Penny, this batch of punch is the best yet." Darlene filled her cup for the third time.

"Go slow there, sweetheart. There's quite a bit of rum in that new recipe. So, give me another scoop-full." Aunt Penny laughed and held her glass for Darlene. "Where's Mickey? I thought she said she was comin' today?"

"She should be here soon. You know Mick. She's probably runnin' a bit late." Before Aunt Penny could respond, Mickey came through the kitchen door with a shopping bag full of packages.

"Ho, ho, ho! Merry Christmas, everybody! Let's get this party started."

Mickey was in a great mood. Darlene wondered if it was the cocaine.

"I've missed you, little britches." Mickey's hug took Darlene by surprise. She should have known things would go back to normal with Mickey. They always did.

"Yeah, me too," Darlene said.

"Did the girls have a good Christmas? Did Santa bring 'em all they wanted?" Mickey asked as she hugged and kissed Amy and Renee.

"Santa brought those two all they wanted and more. They have more toys and dolls than they'll be able to play with in a year's time," Darlene said as they moved to the dining room table to fill their plates.

"I've got a special little gift for you, Ms. Darlene," Mickey whispered.

"What you got for me?"

"Well, it's somethin' I'll need to give you when we're alone."

Darlene knew what the gift was. Drugs. She was excited and nervous. She wanted the drugs as much as she didn't want them. It was just too tempting to turn down. Most days she just wanted to relax or escape from what her life had become. She loved her kids and would die for them, but she just needed a day off once in a while. It was a twenty-four-hours-a-day job. Dave rarely took the girls for the day, and if he did, it was only for a couple of hours. If he had time off, he always had other things to do. Her mother would take the girls any time Darlene asked, but Dave disapproved of throwing the kids off on someone else.

She just needed a day alone to go to the mall or the grocery store or just take a bath without the girls begging to join her or throwing dolls, crayons and Sponge Bob in the tub. Dave couldn't understand why any woman would want a day off from being a mother, and he accused her of not loving her children if she even hinted at needing time alone. Apparently his mother had never needed a break and never took one, and she had four kids. Maybe that explained why his mother was such a bitch.

The drugs provided a momentary escape of sorts, and it didn't hurt anyone. Dave didn't know and didn't need to know. She looked forward to enjoying Mickey's Christmas gift.

The party was great fun. They ate and laughed and exchanged presents. When it was time to leave, Mickey helped her carry the gifts to Millie's car. Darlene hopped in and turned the key to get it warm before they brought out the girls.

Mickey slid into the passenger's seat after retrieving a package from her own car. "Here ya go! Santa's best," Mickey said.

Darlene peeped into the gift bag. "What's in here?"

"Weed—good weed—no, make that *great* weed. It's an ounce and enough to last you for a month or longer at the rate you get to smoke it. There's twenty Lortab, fifteen Xanax, papers, a Bic lighter, and some pills you haven't tried yet called OxyContin. The Oxies rock. They're really hot, so take only one and see what happens. I think you will likey-like."

"Wow, Mick, I don't know what to say. Mick, this stuff is expensive. I can't take this from you. It's too much. Pot's expensive. Pills are outrageous. You can't afford this." Darlene was putting the red tissue paper back in the gift bag.

"No, don't worry. This is not a gift from me. This is a gift from Ray," Mickey said.

"Ray?" Her heart jumped. "Why?" Darlene had tried very hard to put Ray out of her mind and had succeeded. She hadn't thought of him in a few weeks.

"Well, he told me to take what I wanted and give it to you. He lets me have what I want. I'm his number one, so to speak," Mickey said with that puffed up pride she had displayed at Thanksgiving. So he had given the stash to Mickey, and Mickey had decided to give it to Darlene. She felt foolish for allowing herself to get excited over this strange man.

"His number one what? Girlfriend?" Darlene was more than a bit disappointed to think Mickey was his girlfriend.

"Hmmm…not really a girlfriend. I'm his number one delivery person."

"Delivery person?" Darlene felt ignorant because she had no clue what Mickey was talking about. "Pizza? You deliver pizza?"

Mickey laughed so loud Darlene was afraid her mother was going to come outside. "Pizza? Really? You can't be that dense, Darlene!" Mickey lowered her voice. "Drugs. I deliver drugs. I sell drugs to people who don't want to come to The Place. People in Williamson, Belfry and around."

"Mickey! Is that safe? Ain't you afraid of gettin' caught? You could go to jail!"

"Nahh…Ray's wired all the way up the line. Word is he even has Senator Steves in his pocket. So, no, I ain't too worried." Darlene had never heard Mickey so cock-sure of herself before. Something had changed.

"Senator Steves? Really?" Darlene's father and Senator Steves had grown up together and remained good friends through the years. Darlene had known him her whole life. He had started out in the prosecutor's office, then became judge and now state senator. He seemed like a straight arrow to her, but he was a politician.

"Well, he don't stop in and do the drugs, as far as I know. But he can be bought for the right amount of money. Between you and me, word is that Ray has somethin' on him. Like pictures with a stripper or somethin' from a party in Charleston years ago. They can all be had, Darlene. And it ain't just him. All the mucky-mucks at the courthouse are customers, too. They've set up a little drop box. They call Ray and tell him what they want. They leave money in the box. I go on certain nights and leave drugs and take the cash. The judge, the prosecutor and a bunch of lawyers in town— they're all customers. They're pretty much all coke heads or crack whores. So, no, I ain't none too concerned about gettin' busted."

Darlene wanted to know what else Mickey and Ray had going on and got up the nerve to ask. "So, do you like Ray? You know, like boyfriend-girlfriend?" Darlene tried not to sound too curious about Ray.

"Not really. Ray ain't attached to nobody. Ray has a lot of girls. It's just a matter of where you are in the peckin' order."

"Oh, I see." Darlene was glad it was dark so the disappointment would not show on her face. "Just be careful and don't get in trouble, Mick."

"Don't worry, Darlene. I'm fine and havin' the time of my life. I quit my job last week. I'm makin' so much money deliverin' for Ray that I don't need that job no more."

"Really? You loved that job! I can't believe you quit. Why not do both?" Darlene asked.

"No need. I make three times more with Ray and free drugs to boot, which I get to share with my friends. And I get to sleep in every day."

Mickey prattled on about her new gig. Darlene barely heard what she was saying. The news that Ray had lots of women had settled like a rock in her head, and Darlene wanted to smack herself for thinking he had liked her. She figured he looked at every girl that way. Still, he seemed to look into her, and she couldn't imagine he looked at everyone like that.

"Darlene? You in there?" Mickey's voice pulled her back to reality.

"What? Sorry. Too much of Aunt Penny's rum punch."

"By the way, do you want to go to a New Year's Eve party?" Mickey asked.

"Mick, you know that's impossible."

"Well, think about it. If anything changes, let me know."

"Be careful, Mick. I love you. Have a happy New Year."

She wrapped her arms around herself to keep warm as she watched Mickey pull away. Ray was walking through her thoughts. She couldn't stop thinking about him. And Mickey and Ray. And all those other women and Ray.

She was so absorbed in thinking of Ray that she completely forgot to take the drugs out of the gift bag and put them in her purse. She was about to walk into the house when she remembered that she had left it on the front seat. She ran back to the car and emptied the contents of the gift bag into her purse, folded up the bag and stuck it down into one of the shopping packages full of the girls' gifts.

***

Darlene was quiet on the drive home. The girls had fallen asleep the second they were buckled into their car seats.

"Dave's not home?" Millie asked as they pulled into the driveway. Dave's truck was gone and all the lights were off.

"I...I guess not. That's strange. Not sure where he could be." Darlene was actually relieved that Dave was not home. She would have time to stash the gift from Mickey and get Ray out of her head. "He said he was goin' to visit his cousin

Johnny to watch football or something. It's the playoffs. Maybe he's still there."

Millie helped Darlene carry the gifts and the sleeping girls into the house. Darlene made sure Millie's car had pulled away before she got the drugs from her purse and hid them in her tampon box.

She unpacked the Christmas gifts and put on her pajamas. It was almost eleven, and Dave was still not home. She checked the caller ID to see if he had called. The last call was from her mom earlier in the day.

Darlene decided not to worry and went to bed. As far as she was concerned, Dave was a big boy and would get home when he got home. She tossed and turned for about forty-five minutes and then fell into a fitful sleep. At 2 a.m., she was jolted awake when Dave slammed the front door. She went into the living room to tell him to quiet down before he woke the girls.

He was sitting at the kitchen table taking off his boots and mumbling to himself about eight hundred dollars and his cousin Johnny's friends. He was drunk. Really drunk. She could smell the Jack Daniel's and cigarette smoke before she entered the kitchen.

"Dave, keep it down. You're gonna wake the girls. Are you drunk?" Darlene had not seen Dave drunk since their first year of marriage.

"Fuckin' Johnny. Asshole took *all* my money. His stupid friends. A bunch of cheaters from Kermit. I'm his fuckin' cousin, man. That ain't right. What kinda cousin does that?" Dave's words were all jumbled, and he was angry.

"What are you talkin' about? Cheatin'? Cheatin' at what?" Darlene could not understand half of what he said. She stood in front of him with her arms folded over her chest trying to stay warm.

"Fuckin' Johnny and his friends cheated me out of eight hundred dollars tonight playin' poker." Dave's words came out slow and deliberate, and his voice grew louder and louder with each word.

"Eight hundred dollars? Are you kiddin' me? Eight hundred dollars? Dave, we ain't got eight hundred dollars to lose. How'd they cheat you out of eight hundred dollars?" Darlene was in shock and hoped it was just the Jack Daniel's talking and that $800 was a gross exaggeration.

"Well, we ain't got eight hundred dollars now!" Dave finally got his second boot off and threw it across the room; it bounced off the door. "Those mother fuckers took my money in a poker game. We's playin' poker, and they teamed up on me and took my fuckin' money."

"Tell me you're lyin' or you're too drunk to remember."

Darlene was dumfounded. Dave was never this irresponsible.

"Nope, I may be drunk, but I 'member. Those assholes took my money. *All* of it. They took *my* money." Dave pounded his finger into his chest. "*My* money, Darlene."

Darlene was pacing back and forth now, feeling sicker with each step. "Dave, we can barely afford all this stuff we bought for Christmas, and you went and lost eight hundred dollars in a poker game. What's wrong with you?"

"Fuck…you…Darlene. I work. I make the money 'round here, not you. You don't do a damn thing but whine and complain about bein' a mommy and a wife. You got it pretty damned easy. So shut…the fuck…up. I'm goin' to bed." Dave stumbled down the narrow hall of the trailer to the bedroom.

Darlene sat in the chair Dave had just vacated. The smell of whiskey and cigarette smoke lingered. She was too stunned to cry. She was angry that he had lost eight hundred dollars. She was angry that he felt justified talking to her that way. She wanted to slap him and tell him what an asshole he was, but she knew there was no point in arguing with him when he was like this. He would just get louder and wake the girls. She couldn't believe he had lost eight hundred dollars in a poker game. She locked the door, turned off the lights and went to the bathroom. She took her tampon box from the top shelf, took a Xanax and went to bed.

The girls came in and woke Darlene at eight. She was still a little groggy from the Xanax but managed to make the girls' breakfast and get a few of their new toys and dolls out for them to play with. Dave was still sleeping when Darlene went in to check on him at eleven.

Darlene was feeding the girls lunch at noon when she heard Dave go to the bathroom. She held her breath and hoped he would go back to bed. She was angry and wasn't sure what she should or could say to him.

Dave came into the kitchen and sat down at the table with Darlene and the girls. "Got coffee made?" He held his head in his hands. "Advil, too."

Darlene just looked at him. "Coffee's in the pot, and the Advil are in the medicine cabinet in the bathroom, where they always are."

"Get me three Advil and a cup of black coffee. I feel like shit."

"Dave, watch your mouth in front of the girls. You're the one who visited your good friend Jack last night. Get your own coffee and Advil. I'm tryin' to feed the girls their lunch."

"I'll get the coffee, you get the Advil," Dave said.

Exasperated, Darlene flounced up to get the Advil. It was always what Dave wanted. Always.

She returned to the kitchen with the bottle and placed it on the table in front of him. "When the girls go down for their nap, we'll talk about last night."

"Darlene, there's nothin' to talk about. Besides, I feel too bad to talk. I just wanna lay on my couch and watch TV."

And he did just that, for most of the afternoon.

Darlene cooked dinner and tried to read a book. She was disgusted with Dave and surprised. He was so hateful toward Mickey and anyone who partied, drank or used drugs, but here he was staying out all night and losing $800 in a poker game. At Christmastime no less—a time when he should have been with his family. Eight hundred dollars was more than he had allowed her to spend on herself or the girls in the past three years. She was angry at him, and the guilt she had been dragging around over the drugs stashed in her tampon box was slowly seeping away. She was trying to decide how to talk to him about the money he lost, when he woke up and started barking orders.

"Darlene? Where are you? Bring me a Coke and more Advil. My head's killin' me." He never moved from the couch.

Darlene was in the bedroom, and her stomach started churning when she heard him call her name. She made her way to the living room. "You've been sleepin' for four hours. The girls have had to play in their room all afternoon. Why don't you go get in the bed, so they can play out here?" She handed him a Coke and the bottle of Advil.

"'Cause, I like layin' here so I can watch TV. They can stay in their room. It won't hurt 'em. Hand me the remote."

"Dave, we need to talk about the money you lost." She wanted to throw up. "What were you thinkin' and why were you drinkin'? I thought you hated that stuff now." It had taken her all morning to work up the courage to confront him. She was certain he would play the switch-a-roo game and turn this around to be her fault. She started biting the nail on her left thumb.

"Darlene, I'm a grown ass man, and I work every day. I can do whatever the hell I want. If I want to get drunk every day, I will. So shut up about it. Hand me the remote and move out from the front of the TV."

"If I went out and got drunk and spent *eight* dollars you would have a fit, let alone *eight hundred dollars*. We ain't got that kinda money, Dave." Her stomach was rolling now, and she knew it was a matter of minutes before she would be making a dash to the bathroom.

"That's different. *You* don't work. *You're* the wife. I'm the *man*, Darlene, and I will do what I damned well please." He never moved except to put out his hand for the remote.

She threw the remote at him and ran to the bathroom. Before she even got halfway down the hall, she made up her mind to call Mickey first chance she got and tell her she would go to the New Year's Eve party with her.

Dave spent the rest of the evening on the couch and came to bed sometime during the night. Darlene put the girls to bed and made a trip to the tampon box for another Xanax.

Dave went to work the next afternoon with no mention of the $800 poker loss.

***

As soon as Dave left for work, Darlene called Mickey. The party was going to be in Williamson at one of the two bars in town. Dave had signed up for a double that day and would leave for work around noon. He wouldn't be home until eight the following morning. Mickey would pick up Darlene at 7:30 p.m., and they would plan to be home no later than two. Darlene's next call was to Brooke, the fifteen-year-old neighbor who had offered to babysit a dozen times. Darlene decided to take the girl up on her offer. Darlene thought of asking her parents, but her mother would never agree if she thought Darlene was going out—especially with Mickey.

On New Year's Eve, as soon as Dave left for work, Darlene jumped in the shower while the girls took their afternoon nap. As she washed her hair, she started having doubts about going out. For the rest of her shower she imagined everything that could go wrong. What if Brooke had boys over, or Amy fell and hit her head, or one of the girls got sick? She decided to call Mickey and cancel. She was combing out her hair, when the phone rang.

"Hey, Darlene. This is Johnny. Dave left for work already?"

"Yeah, Johnny. He left around noon. He's workin' a double tonight." Darlene wanted to ask Johnny about the eight hundred dollars Dave had lost earlier in the week, but she decided not to bring it up.

"Well, darn. I was gonna tell him we're playin' poker tonight if he wants to stop by. Let him know I called if he comes home early. Otherwise, we'll just see him for the regular game tomorrow night."

"Oh, is he plannin' on playin' tomorrow night?" Darlene could barely breathe, and her voice sounded tight.

"Yeah, tonight's a special night, it bein' New Year's Eve and all. But we play pretty much ever' Saturday. He sure lost big the other night. Not like him. He usually quits before he loses that much."

"Yeah, he was pretty upset about losin' to those Kermit boys. So, he plays with you every weekend?" Darlene thought she must have misunderstood Johnny. He had a way of twisting things and not speaking plainly.

"Just about. We been pretty regular for the last few months, anyway. Well, tell him I called."

"I sure will, Johnny." Darlene wanted to throw the phone across the room. Any guilt or concern she had about going to the party had vanished quickly during her chat with Johnny.

"That son of a bitch. Son of a bitch! So every Saturday night when he's supposed to be with his parents or just hangin' out with Johnny watchin' football, he's at Johnny's playin' poker and losin' money?" Darlene was speaking to her reflection in the bathroom mirror. "Fuck you, Dave!" Darlene had no way of knowing how much money he had lost over the past six months. No wonder he was such a jerk about buying the girls toys for Christmas. "Bastard!"

Darlene was determined to go to the party now. Even if Dave came home before she left, she was still going. She'd had enough. He treated her like she was his personal slave and would not allow her to have friends or do anything without him or the kids, while he was out every weekend playing poker and drinking.

Brooke showed up on time, and Darlene gave her instructions, which included her parents' telephone number, to be used only in case of an emergency. She told Brooke she would call and check in from time to time and that she planned to be home no later than two. The girls were allowed to stay up until midnight, and then they had to go to bed. She kissed the kids goodnight and explained to them that they could not tell Daddy. It was their little secret.

Mickey showed up as scheduled, and they left for the party. Darlene felt good; she was wearing a new pair of jeans, a sweater Aunt Penny had given her for Christmas and new earrings her mother had given her. She thought of Ray as she was dressing and wondered if he would think she looked nice in her new jeans. Darlene tried to hide her disappointment when Mickey informed her they would not be stopping at Ray's to get "supplies" for the evening. She had stopped by earlier and had a bag full of stuff to "dispense" at the party.

Mickey stopped at the old Montgomery's parking lot.

"What we stoppin' here for?" Darlene asked.

"You're gonna do some coke before we get this party goin'." Mickey cut lines out on a CD cover.

"Oh, Mick, I don't know. I'm happy just smokin' pot and takin' a Lortab or two. Really. I don't think I wanna do this. It seems pretty hardcore."

"Come on, girl. It's just coke. It ain't like you gotta stick a needle in your arm. It's easy to do, and it won't make you crazy or loopy. It'll make you feel like Superman…or Supergirl, in your case. Trust me. You'll love it!" Mickey had cut out two good size lines and took out a straw from the cosmetic bag where she kept her private stash.

"Okay, this is what you do. Put the end of the straw in your nose. Hold the other nostril with your finger and just sniff it in. You might want to take a couple of sniffs. Once you have it in, tilt your head back, and just sniff deep, like you have a runny nose." Mickey demonstrated. "Whatever you do, don't breath out when you have your face close to the coke or it will go everywhere."

Darlene decided to do it. Not think about it. Just do it. And so she began her journey with the white lady. Mickey was right on all accounts. It burned a little the first time, drained down the back of her throat, and she felt amazing.

"Mick, I feel like Mighty Mouse."

Mickey laughed so hard she nearly ran off the road. Darlene provided her best Mighty Mouse impersonation, placing her hands on her hips and thrusting her chest out. "Here I come to save the day!"

***

Darlene had a great time at the party. They snorted coke about three more times that night, and she truly felt like a different person. She was happy and laughing and had tons of energy. Darlene had called home a couple of times, and Brooke reported that all was good. The girls had fallen asleep around ten.

Darlene hated for the night to end. She had barely thought of Dave and all the reasons she had been so angry at him earlier. She was so wound up that Mickey instructed her to take a Xanax when she got home so she could sleep.

At the edge of the yard, where the pavement turned to dirt and gravel, Darlene's good time turned to terror. All the lights were on in her house and Dave's truck was in the driveway.

"Oh, Mickey, I'm fucked. He's gonna kill me. This is gonna be ugly." Darlene started getting a sick feeling in her stomach. She wanted to throw up.

"Darlene, Darlene. You want me to wait? Want me to go in with you?"

"You crazy? Seein' you'll make him really crazy. No, I need to face the music. I'll call you when the dust settles." Darlene reminded herself why she went to the party in the first place. Dave was the one out gambling every Saturday night he had free. She went to a party. So what? She would just stand up to him for once. If she could.

She met Brooke at the foot of the porch steps. "Darlene, I'm sorry. I didn't know what to tell him. He got home about fifteen minutes ago and totally freaked out when he saw me and realized you's gone. I just told him you went to a New

Year's party. He told me to get my shit and get out of his house, and then he started throwin' stuff." Brooke zipped her jacket and ran home, and Mickey drove away, leaving Darlene alone to face the rage of this man she called her husband.

Her fear started as a tiny gravel in her stomach and grew with every shallow breath until it was a giant monster ready to devour her from the inside. Each step seemed like one inch closer to the edge of the abyss. When she reached the door, she realized she still had the small vial of coke Mickey had given her. It was tucked into her makeup bag, and she prayed he didn't search her purse.

"Where the fuck you been?" Dave was in a tirade, and the girls were awake and crying in their room.

"I went to a New Year's Eve party. I ain't been gone that long."

"With Mickey? That piece of shit. I should've known. You been doin' this behind my back for years, ain't ya? Tell me the truth, you little whore."

"Stop calling me a whore. I'm your wife! For the record, this is the only time I been anywhere without you or the girls since we got married. You're the one sneakin' around playin' poker every Saturday night and losin' all our money. Don't try to deny it! Johnny called today and told me all about it." Darlene was trembling, but the coke had given her a newfound bravado. She had never stood up to Dave, and she had no idea how he would react.

"*Our* money? Did you say *our* money? That's *my* money. I'm the only one who works around here so you can lay on your lazy little ass all day and do nothing. I can do whatever I want, when I want. You're the one layin' out all night with your whore friend." Dave clenched his fists and paced back and forth.

"I'm your wife, Dave. I want to work. You are the one who told me I can't go back to school, so I can finish my nursin' degree. You don't want me to be a nurse. You won't let me work. Hell, you won't even let me out of the house."

"Oh, no. Let's get this straight. You quit school with only one semester left. Don't blame me for that."

"I quit because I had a sick baby that never slept and a hateful husband who bitched at me all the time. Studyin' and stayin' focused was impossible."

"Well, you should've thought about that before you got yourself pregnant."

"I didn't plan to get pregnant."

"And why did you get pregnant? Oh, yeah, because you's runnin' 'round with Mickey and stayed high all the time and forgot to take your birth control pills. You decided to marry me and have babies so I could take care of you, 'cause when it gets right down to it, you're a lazy whore, Darlene. Just like Mickey."

"Fuck you, Dave. You know exactly what happened. You were drivin' me crazy. You couldn't stand the thought that I was gonna leave here and go to Marshall, and you made sure I was miserable. I got high just to get the fuck away from you. Yeah, I screwed up and shouldn't have let you get to me. I'd give anything if I could change things. But you *loved* it when I got pregnant. It was exactly what you wanted."

"Yeah? Maybe so. But you still quit. So don't blame me. Now you want me to pay for you to make up a bunch of classes and finish so you can quit again? I don't think so. You thought you were so damned smart and was gonna be a nurse. Thought you's better'n ever'body else. Well, I guess you got put in your place, didn't ya? Little Miss High-and-Mighty got cut down to size."

He was quite smug. He knew where all her buttons were, and he jammed his fist into each one of them with each hateful word.

"Just stop it. You treat me like a prisoner. I never leave the house, Dave, unless I'm with you or the girls." Darlene was feeling very brave. She had come this far, so no backing up now.

"So, you decide to lay out all night at a party with God only knows who and what kinda people. What kinda mother are you? Leavin' your little girls here with some stranger. Some teenager barely old enough to know how to open a pop, let alone babysit. You think it's okay to lay out all night with that whore and that bunch she runs with?"

"I wasn't out all night. I was only gone for a few hours. You are such a hypocrite, Dave! You're the one that goes out and loses money at poker every Saturday. You're the one that came home drunk last week and laid on the couch all the next day with a hang—"

She didn't even see him move across the room. She didn't see him raise his fist. She *did* feel the left side of her head hit the wall as his fist hit the right side of her face.

She slid to the floor. She barely had time to think about what had happened when Dave picked her up and slammed her back into the wall. The room blurred, and he sounded like he was far away. She was having trouble breathing. Then she realized he was choking her.

Dave had his hand around her throat as he held her against the wall. "You fuckin' little cunt. Who do you think you are, talkin' to me that way and questionin' what I do with *my* fuckin' money. I'll show you who's the boss around here. Your place is right here doing whatever the hell I tell you."

He released her and she melted to the floor like a rag doll.

"You ever sneak out again or even so much as talk to that fuckin' whore, and I *will* kill you. Do you understand me?" He kicked her thigh for good measure before he stormed off.

***

Darlene woke up on the floor by the door where he left her. She couldn't move. When she came to, her head hurt and her throat was sore. She couldn't see very well. Her right eye was swollen shut from the punch. Her right thigh throbbed.

She pulled herself up and sat leaning against the wall for a few minutes. She was surprised to see her bloody right hand. She felt around to see what was bleeding. It was her nose and mouth. She slowly stood up and limped to the kitchen table.

She sat down and tried to remember what had happened. The only thing she was certain of was that Dave had beat the shit out of her.

The house was quiet, which was good. She was glad everyone was asleep. The clock in the kitchen said it was 5:22. She must have been out for three hours or more. She eventually made her way to the bathroom. She washed her face and assessed the damage. She had an eerie calmness when she looked in the mirror. The entire right side of her face was swollen and bruised. Her right eye was completely shut and very red, blue and black. Her nose had dried blood all over it, and the right side of her top lip was bruised and almost as big as her eye.

She couldn't understand why her throat and neck hurt; then she saw the bruise in the shape of Dave's fingers and thumb wrapping around both sides. She couldn't put any weight on her right leg. She pulled her jeans off and saw the bruise on her thigh, where he had kicked her with his boot.

She rinsed her face and began crying as she splashed the warm water on her bruised and beaten skin. "Oh, dear, God. Please help me. I don't know what to do. I love my kids and I even love Dave, but I can't keep doin' this. I can't keep livin' like this. What is wrong with me? Am I just a bad person? Am I that messed up?" Her prayer was barely a whisper.

Does God hear whispers?

Darlene fell asleep on the couch wondering how she would explain the bruises to the girls. What would happen next? Would Dave divorce her? What would her parents say when they saw her face? They were supposed to go to her parents' for lunch today.

Dave woke Darlene a few hours later. "You need to go get in the bed. Don't let the girls see your face like that." He wouldn't even look at her.

Darlene had not slept much, and her entire body ached when she tried to sit up. She had nothing to say to Dave. She didn't want to speak to him. She didn't want to look at him.

"I'll take the girls today. Call your parents and tell 'em you have the flu or somethin'." Seems Dave had thought of everything. Everything to cover what he had done and to make him look like the hero again. Always the good guy.

Darlene went to bed. Dave got the girls dressed and left the house around noon. She called her parents and told them she was sick and wouldn't make it for lunch. Her mother insisted on bringing food or medicine or something to help Darlene feel better. She convinced her that she was fine and Dave would stop by and pick up a plate of food for her.

The ringing phone woke Darlene in the afternoon. Her throat was sore and her voice was raspy from the choking. "Johnny, Dave's not here. He's probably at his mommy's."

"Well, tell him were gonna be startin' a little earlier tonight. He can have extra time to try and win his money back. That boy lost his ass again last night." Johnny was chuckling.

Darlene was fully awake now. Dave didn't work last night? "Last night? He played poker last night? He must have started early, 'cause he was home early."

"Oh, yeah, he stopped in after work and got here around nine o'clock. We had quite a crowd here. Your boy held in there for a while. Too bad he lost again. I'd say he lost about $350. Anyway, just let him know we're gettin' an early start tonight, if he wants to stop by."

Darlene felt sicker and angrier than she had all day. Dave had lied to her about working a double shift? He said it was a maintenance night and he had volunteered to work. What a liar. He never lied about work. Or did he? She never saw his paycheck. She just assumed that he was working. Maybe he always lied about working overtime and was really playing poker. She couldn't remember whether he had smelled like cigarette smoke and whiskey. She crawled out of bed, shuffled to the bathroom and dug through the laundry basket until she found the work clothes he had taken off the night before. Sure enough, in addition to the typical smells of the coal mines, there was the smell of cigarette smoke and whiskey.

"That fuckin' bastard had been playin' poker and drinkin' again," she muttered to herself. In a daze from all that had happened, she couldn't wrap her mind around this. He had lost at poker and took it out on her? The fact that she had been out with Mickey was just the excuse he was looking for to make this her fault.

***

Darlene's face stayed black and blue for a week. The bruises had turned a lovely shade of pale purple and green. It was like the spring landscape, changing colors nearly every day. The swelling had gone down, but her lip was still busted. It was this day her mother decided to stop by unannounced.

"Dear, Lord, Darlene, what happened to your face, honey?"

"Nana, Mommy was in a car wreck with Aunt Mickey." Amy's little voice repeated the lie Darlene had told her.

"A car wreck? Darlene why didn't you say somethin'? When? What were you doin' with Mickey? Was she drinkin'?" Millie examined Darlene's face.

"Amy, you and Renee come sit on the couch and watch TV. You can talk to Nana later." Darlene carried Renee to the couch and covered them with a blanket.

"Mommy, there wasn't no car wreck. Dave did this. Perfect, little Dave." Darlene poured two cups of coffee and sat at the kitchen table with Millie. "Stop lookin' at me like that. I didn't *do* anything. I went out New Year's Eve with Mickey, and Dave was home when I got back. He beat the shit out of me. It looked much worse.

"Dave did this to you? That son of a bitch. What did you do, Darlene?"

"He said he was goin' to work for a maintenance thing and would have a double shift. But, he didn't. He went to Johnny's and played poker after work. He never planned to

71

work all night. He was lyin' so I wouldn't bitch about him losin' money in a poker game. So, he played poker, lost his ass—again—got drunk on Jack Daniel's—again—came home pissed, and took it out on me. Simple as that. My bein' with Mick was just more fuel for his fire."

"Lord, Darlene. Why do you keep runnin' with that girl? She's been nothin' but trouble for you since high school. Why on earth would you go out with her? I just don't understand what you're thinkin'."

"Mommy, this is not my fault." Darlene pointed to her face. "He did this, and he was not one bit sorry. He knew what he was doin'. He left me on the floor for hours. *Unconscious!*" Darlene started tearing up. "He hit me with his fist, he choked me, and then he kicked me with his work boots. What about him? Why is this *my* fault?"

"I know, honey. I know, but you gotta try to keep peace. He *is* your husband. Oh, Darlene. What are you gonna do? Is this the first time he's hit you?"

"No, remember, he hit me before we got married and he's slapped me around a few times since. Oh, and the best part is that he's been goin' to Johnny's every Saturday night playin' poker and loses most of the time. That's where he was the night you dropped me off after Aunt Penny's party. He lost $800 dollars that night and came home drunk and angry. But, *that* seems to be okay. He can do whatever the fuck he wants, and because I'm the woman, I have to just suck it up and take it? No. *No!*"

"Is he cheatin' on you?"

"I wish he would cheat on me. I just wanna leave, Mommy. I can't take much more of this."

"Oh, Lord. Darlene, you ain't got no choice but to stay with him. Where will you go? You got two little girls and no job. Besides, they ain't no jobs around here for you to get."

"Well, I can't stay here. I'm gonna lose my mind. I talked to Rachel this mornin', and she said I could move there, to Tennessee. I could work at Elaine's restaurant until I get on my feet. Elaine's husband has a bunch of rental properties, and I could live in one of them real cheap. The girls love the lake, and we would do good there, Mommy. We would do real good there." The tears flowed down her bruised face. "I got to get out of here. I've been thinkin' that I would just pack up what we need and go. Not tell Dave. Just go. He would never think to look in Tennessee."

"Darlene, you can't just up and take that man's kids and leave the state. He *would* kill you, then. If you want to leave, you do it the right way and divorce him and then leave."

Darlene's heart sank. She knew her mother was right. Dave would eventually find her and kill her and take the girls.

"Darlene, you need to just work this out and try to fix your marriage. Your father will kill him if he finds out Dave hit you like this. But you know how your father feels about Mickey, too."

"I'll try, Mommy. Dave hasn't even talked to me in a week. Just barely speaks or grunts when he wants somethin'. He won't even look at me, 'cause he's ashamed of what he's done. He acts like he's so concerned about his children. If he was, he wouldn't beat their mother like this."

Millie left, and Darlene felt even more defeated. She had no clue what she was going to do. She made a trip to the tampon box and took half a Lortab. She still had the Oxies but was reluctant to take them, since she had no idea what they would do to her. She didn't want to pass out and leave the girls roaming around the house. She would save them, but not for long.

The year was definitely not getting off to a good start. She hoped it would get better. She had nowhere to go but up.

CHAPTER FIVE
Hell Broke Loose

"All things truly wicked start from innocence."
— Ernest Hemingway

Darlene thought winter would never end. It either snowed or rained nearly every day in January and February, and she had never felt so low. Her mother made a point of taking her and the girls out at least once a week. They would go to Walmart, the mall, to Aunt Penny's or just to her house for the day. Getting out once a week certainly helped, but Darlene was still in the gray ditch. She couldn't shake it. Things with her and Dave were not getting any better. They weren't getting any worse, but it was still not good.

He stopped going to the poker games through January, but in mid-February he announced he was going to play poker, and he started going every Saturday. He would come in around dawn with no apologies or discussion. That was just the way it was. They settled into a routine, with very little communication.

The girls felt the tension and became very clingy to Darlene. They rarely wanted to be with Dave. His anger and frustration filled the room, and the girls reacted with a manic energy that resulted in a fuss between the two of them or whining to Darlene. By the first of March, Darlene was exhausted from the entire ordeal. Dave took no responsibility or even seemed to notice the change.

Darlene had lost five pounds in the past month, and her nerves stayed in a twist. She had diarrhea nearly every day. Everything she ate just passed straight through. Her mother insisted she go to a doctor, who gave her one prescription to help with diarrhea and one for depression. She took the pill for her stomach, and it worked most days. The anti-depressant lasted for two weeks. It made her feel even more sad and anxious.

She still had the vial of coke Mickey had given her the night of the New Year's Eve party, but she refused to use it. It would only make matters worse. She thought about flushing the coke, but it was expensive, and she decided to give it back to Mickey (if she ever saw her again). The pot had long been gone. She had just a few Lortab left and the Oxies.

Saturday night rolled around, and Dave took off for the poker game around seven. Darlene was left alone with the girls. They ordered a pizza and settled in to watch TV. The girls quickly fell asleep, but Darlene was unable to drift off. She decided to give the Oxy a try and took half of one. She felt fabulous and had energy she hadn't had since high school. She cleaned house and baked a cake. This is what the anti-depressant should have done. She felt great. She had only five Oxies, so she decided to use them sparingly.

She finally went to bed around two. She didn't care if Dave ever came home. It was nice not to worry about his being there and making her miserable.

***

In early April, Darlene and Millie took the girls to buy their Easter dresses. They had been gone all day Saturday, and Millie dropped them off around four. The girls ran into the house, excited about showing Dave their new outfits. He was sitting at the kitchen table and was in a dark, angry mood. Darlene could not imagine why he was angry. Her mother had paid for the dresses. She was home at the time she told him she would be. And he had a poker game to go to that night.

He showed mild interest in the girls'. Darlene took the them to their room and told them to stay there for a minute, while she and Daddy talked.

"What's wrong now? Why are you mad this time?"

"You're somethin' else, Darlene. Somethin' else." He sat at the table, coiled like a snake ready to strike.

"What are you talkin' about, Dave? Just say it. I haven't done anything."

"Oh, really? You been seein' Mickey again?"

"For the love of God. We back to that again? No. You know I ain't. When would I see her? I never leave the house."

"Well, if you ain't seen her, where did you get this?" He threw the vial of coke and the remaining pills at her.

"Where did you get that?" The words were like nails coming out of her throat.

"You know where I got it. In your tampon box. It fell off the shelf when I was lookin' for a light bulb. Your stash started rattlin' around when I picked up the box. What's in that little bottle? Coke? You a fuckin' coke head now?"

"Dave, Mickey left it in my purse New Years Eve and I forgot all about it. I intended to give it back to her. You can see it's all still there. I ain't done any of it. Do I seem like someone on coke to you? People on coke feel good. I don't feel good. I'm fuckin' miserable."

"Well, I don't know what people on coke do, Darlene. I don't hang out with coke heads. Is this what you were doin' with her?"

"She left it in my purse, Dave. I didn't do it. I don't want to do it. I don't like stuff like that. You can believe me or not. You won't believe me. You never do. Nothin' I do pleases you. I can't do nothin' right enough for you."

"Well, if this is the kind of life you want, go get it. I ain't puttin' up with this shit. You're way out of control, Darlene."

As he got up and came at her, she put her hands up in front of her face.

"What's wrong with you? Ohhh…I should hit you. But I ain't. You ain't worth the energy it would take. Besides, I don't ever want to touch you again. Your nothin' but a filthy whore, just like your fat friend." He walked to the door.

"Where you goin'?" Darlene could barely breathe.

"Away from you. I can't stand to look at you." He slammed the door and went out.

Darlene picked up the drugs and ran to the bathroom and threw up. Amy opened the door of their bedroom and peeked her little head into the hallway to see what was wrong.

"Nothin', baby. Just go back in your room. Mommy'll come get you in a minute."

Darlene threw up two more times. She flushed the drugs along with the contents of her stomach. She rinsed her mouth, brushed her teeth, and washed her face. Some part of her wanted to cry…thought it should cry. She couldn't find the emotion to make it happen. She was numb. Empty.

Darlene moved through the evening with no thoughts of Dave. She bathed the girls and brought them to bed with her. The girls drifted off to sleep, and she lay there just listening to them breathe; she was overwhelmed by how much she loved her babies and how much she wanted to protect them and keep them safe. To keep them safe from anyone who wanted to steal their dreams, control them, own them. She would fight to make sure they had a better life, more options, more freedom to be and do what their hearts truly desired. She wanted them to get out of this place, send them to college. She wanted them to have extraordinary lives, careers. The life she cheated herself out of. The life and dreams she left on the side of the road. The ones she abandoned for a life with Dave and what seemed like the right thing to do at the time. She now knew it had been the easy way out.

***

Darlene called her mother the next morning to ask if she and the girls could come and stay for a while. She told her mother everything that had happened with Dave. She packed their clothes and the girls' favorite toys, and her mother came to pick them up that morning. The girls were excited to be going to Nana and Poppy's for a sleepover. Darlene left a letter for Dave on the kitchen table.

Dave—

I don't know what to say other than I'm sorry. I'm sorry that our marriage is broken. I think we both know that too many things are wrong for this to mend anytime soon. I do love you and have loved you, but I'm miserable, and you're miserable. I feel like a prisoner. I sit here day after day and I have nothing to look forward to. I don't have any friends. I know you hate Mickey, but we both know that you would hate anyone I was friends with. You won't let me work. I'm unhappy. You're unhappy. The girls know something is wrong, and this is not good for them. They are my first concern. I don't want them to see us fighting and arguing and you hitting me. That's no way to raise them.

I don't know what we do next. I want to make this work, but something needs to change. Lots of things with you and me.

We have gone to Mommy and Daddy's, and you can call us there. I'm not sure what we do from here, but I know that we can't keep living like this.

I love you,
Darlene

***

At eleven the next night, Darlene was surprised to see Dave at the back door. "What are you doin' here so late? Why didn't you call? The girls have been wonderin' where you are." Darlene closed the kitchen door and stepped out onto the back porch and stood facing Dave.

"What'd you tell 'em?"

"That you went fishin'." Darlene shuffled nervously from one foot to the other. Left, then right. Left, then right again.

Dave sat down on the steps and Darlene sat next to him. They sat not looking at each other. Not touching.

"Darlene, I don't know what you think this is all about. Don't know what you think you're doin' or why you think *I've* done somethin' wrong. I go to work, I come home, I give you and the girls a place to live. You got it pretty good. I guess that ain't enough for you."

"Dave those things are good, and I appreciate it. I do. But, there's nothin' wrong with me wantin' to go to work. You get to go out and work and do whatever you want. I don't. I feel trapped at the head of Rutherford Holler. What happens when the girls go to school? I'll be there all day. Alone."

"Yep, I guess you're right. Well, do what you want. Go back to school. Get a job. Run around with Mickey. Do all the drugs you can. I don't care anymore, Darlene. It's probably best if you and the girls just stay here with your parents for a while. I need to figure out what we're gonna do."

"*You* need to figure it out? Don't you mean *we* need to figure it out?" Darlene was starting to get angry at Dave's attitude of being in control. "This is just what I'm talkin' about, Dave. You act like I don't have a say-so in our marriage or what we do or don't do. Everything is what *you* want and what *you* think is best." Darlene started to cry.

"Well, dammit, Darlene, I *am* the husband and it's my job to make sure we stay on track. You ain't in no shape to make decisions. You're high most of the time and runnin' around like you're a single woman. You think I'm gonna let you decide what we do? That's just crazy." Dave was looking at her now as if she were a feeble-minded child.

Darlene could feel her throat tightening as she fought back the tears. The words were sticking in her throat, but she managed to get them out. "Dave, I am not on drugs. I am not gettin' high every day. I do not see Mickey every day. Hell, I haven't seen Mickey in months." Her voice was tiny and tight. "You're the one who goes out and drinks and loses money at poker every Saturday when you're supposed to be watchin' football or NASCAR. So don't go throwing stones at me."

"Don't you dare question where I go and what I spend my hard-earned money on. That ain't none of your business. I'm the one who works. Not you." His voice was getting louder.

Darlene could see her mother's shadow as she looked out the kitchen window. "Dave, you're gonna wake the dead. Keep your voice down."

"Ya know what, Darlene? I'll keep doin' what I damned well please. I'm goin' home. To *my* home. The one *I* pay for. You and the girls can just stay here, and I'll let you know what I decide, 'cause it *is* up to me."

With that, Dave stomped back to his truck and left.

Darlene sat on the steps and listened as Dave's truck rolled over the dip between the driveway and the highway, to the roar of his big tires on the asphalt as he pulled away and the gears shifting as he picked up speed around the curve— then silence. She could hear a train in the distance as it pulled around the bend toward Lynn. It was a chilly night, and she could see her breath. She wondered how she could see her breath when she could barely breathe. She was alone. Alone, but the voices in her head were loud—her parents, her kids, Dave. She could hear her father's disapproval and anger that she and Dave were not getting back together. He always sided with Dave. He always thought the woman had no choice. Her mother had lived that way her entire life. Her girls would have so many questions she wouldn't be able to answer. Her mother would wring her hands and worry. Dave would just keep calling all the shots.

She started to cry. Soft at first and then sobs. The kitchen light went out. She sat on the steps until her feet were nearly frozen to the second step. She dried her eyes and wiped her nose on her sleeve. She quietly slipped through the back door and crawled into bed with the girls.

CHAPTER SIX
From the Pot to the Fire

"The road goes on forever, and the party never ends."
— Robert Earl Keen

A month had passed, and Darlene and the girls were still at her parents' house. She had gone home several times to gather up more of their clothes and personal items. Dave was still not speaking to her. He took the girls on Saturday afternoons and Sunday mornings for church. Other than that, he didn't spend much time with them. She had heard through his cousin's wife he was still playing poker every Saturday night and had lost quite a bit of money. He was drinking again almost every night he didn't have to work.

Darlene had been laying low. She had no desire to go out and do much of anything. She visited her Aunt Penny and went to church with her parents; that was the extent of her activities. She moved through the days like a lost kitten.

In early May, Dave called. "Darlene, I think you oughta know I filed for divorce today."

"What? You did what? I suppose talkin' about this was not somethin' you thought we should do? You just up and filed?" The room became a smear of light and dark as tears flooded her eyes.

"Nope. No reason at all. You got what you wanted, and I got what I wanted. Way I see it, you and the girls can stay right where you are, and I'll keep gettin' 'em every Saturday."

She had not heard him like this since before they got married. He was spewing his anger and hatred through the telephone. "I'll give money to your parents for helpin' out, but I ain't givin' you a damn thing, Darlene. Not one red cent. So don't even think about askin' for nothin'. You had it made, and you done gone and fucked it up."

She reckoned it was true, that at a person's core, they never really change all that much. "Dave, what am I supposed to tell the girls? They won't understand." Darlene had to sit down before she fell down.

"Well, tell 'em their mommy's a drugged out whore for starters. Tell 'em their mommy wanted to do drugs and didn't want a home. Tell 'em whatever you want, Darlene."

"Dave, are you sure you wanna do this?"

"Yep. I wanna do this. I'm sick of you and your whiney little ass. I want a woman that appreciates me and my hard work. My lawyer says you should be gettin' the divorce papers one day this week. You should probably come tomorrow and get the rest of your stuff. I want it outta here."

She couldn't believe it was happening this fast.

"Oh, and Darlene? Fuck you."

The phone went silent. Sad and scared, Darlene sat at the kitchen table crying.

***

The divorce proceedings were uneventful. Darlene's attorney tried to get her spousal support in addition to the child support, but since she had abandoned the home, she would get nothing. Dave's attorney turned out to be a ruthless, cut-throat sort and threatened to drag Darlene through the mud if she protested too much. The fact that Dave had hit her was irrelevant since it was her word against his; she hadn't filed anything with the police and had no evidence. Darlene and the girls stayed with her parents, and Dave sent a check to Darlene's father every week for child support. Darlene's dad gave the check to Darlene's mom, who deposited it into their checking account and snuck $25 to Darlene.

Darlene needed a job, and her father was trying to get her a position at the State ABC store. Darlene wasn't sure about working in a liquor store, but it was a good job with good benefits that would allow her to provide for the girls, and it was close to home. Her parents agreed to let her and the girls stay there for as long as they needed. Darlene felt trapped and free all at the same time. She was free of Dave's control but now was under her father's control. At least it was a step in the right direction. She knew her father had her best interests at heart, even though he sided with Dave on the divorce and blamed her for letting her marriage fall apart.

"The girls are confused about why we don't still live with Daddy, but for the most part they think we're havin' just one long pajama party at Nanna and Poppy's." Darlene took another cigarette from Mickey as she joined Darlene on the back steps. Darlene looked at her cigarette after she lit it. She was surprised she was smoking. Something she had found so distasteful only a few weeks ago now seemed to bring her a mild comfort. She savored the idea that it would drive Dave nuts if he knew she was smoking and, as she exhaled, smiled at the thought of his conniption fit.

"Girl, I don't know how you put up with his shit as long as you did." Mickey shook her head and ground out her cigarette on the side of the step.

"Well, I still have to put up with it. He calls every time he sends a check for the girls to make sure I ain't gettin' any of the money. I hear daddy talkin' to him and informin' him that 'Darlene don't get a dime of that money, Dave. You can rest assured of that. She'll have to work. I won't put up with her layin' around here.' Blah, blah, blah. Daddy's almost as bad as Dave about some things." She took another drag off her cigarette.

"Your daddy's always sided with Dave and believed everything he says."

"Yeah, they are two peas in a pod when it comes to me. Daddy always thought my ideas of goin' to school were far-fetched, and the other day I got the speech about a woman's place is in the home raisin' the kids and takin' care of the house. Then he actually told me I chose to marry Dave and I should have tried to make it work, even though he beat the shit out of me and would do it again. It feels like you and Mommy are the only ones on my side, Mick."

"I'm always here for you, Darlene."

"Hopefully Daddy can get me the liquor store job. It'd be better than nothing'." Darlene folded over and rested her chin on her lap, playing with her toes as she fought down the anxiety rising in her chest. She didn't want Mickey to see how scared she really was. Everything was so uncertain now.

***

Her father managed to get her the job at the ABC store in Matewan. She was grateful for the position, even though the work was boring and the manager of the store was a bitch most of the time. The manager had wanted the job for her friend's son, but Darlene's dad had more political pull and had won the battle. Most of the patrons smelled like sour liquor and cigarettes.

Darlene's days were filled with going to work, helping her mother with chores, and taking care of the girls. Because she wanted to finish nursing school, she planned to save her money and start taking classes in the fall. Right now she needed to prove to her parents, mostly her dad, that she wasn't the person Dave had portrayed her to be. Part of this included not spending too much time with Mickey. She had offered Darlene more Lortab and pot, but Darlene turned it down. She really needed to prove herself to her parents.

She decided to stay with them as long as she needed to. She would save every penny and find a place for herself and the girls to live. Once she moved out, the child support would have to come to her, or her father would have to give it to her to help pay rent. She could make it work. She had to make it work. She could not live like this forever.

***

The heat of summer moved in. Darlene worked, rarely going out. If she did venture out it was with her mother and the girls or, occasionally, with Aunt Penny for lunch.

Thirty minutes before closing time one Friday night, Darlene was taking inventory for the Monday morning stock up when the door buzzer announced someone had entered. Darlene looked up as the door closed.

"Mick!" Darlene left the inventory list on top of a case of Smirnoff and went over to hug Mickey.

"Well, I figured if you won't come out with me, I'll just come in here and drag your sorry ass out." Mickey sat on the corner of the desk and twirled her car keys around her thumb. "What time do you get out of here?"

"Oh, Mick, I can't. I need to get home. I'm just not ready to go out and…" Darlene's voice trailed off.

"And? And what? We're just goin' to Ray's to get a pizza and drink a beer. Nothin' fancy. My treat."

Ray. Darlene hadn't thought of him in a while. Now that Darlene was a single woman, she could think of Ray without any guilt. Unless, of course, Mickey was dating him.

"Ray's? Well, if it's just for pizza, sure. I can't stay out late, Mickey. My parents will have a cow if I'm out all night." Darlene called her mom and told her she was going out to have a pizza with Mickey and would be home by midnight.

After locking the front door of the store, Darlene freshened her makeup and fluffed her hair in the ladies' room. She wanted to go home and change but knew the girls would cry and she would change her mind about going. No, it was best just to go straight from work.

Darlene barely heard anything Mickey said on the way to Ray's. She was too nervous and was running through possible scenarios in her mind. What if he had a girl there? What if he and Mick were dating? She told herself not to get her hopes up, but she still had butterflies in her stomach.

The Place was hopping when they pulled in. There were about fifteen people lined up outside to put in an order and another twenty in line to pick up an order. Darlene wondered why she and Dave had never come here with the girls. Although it had a reputation of being a hangout for thugs and druggies, Darlene thought everyone here looked like everyone else in Matewan. No one was fighting or smoking pot. It looked like everyone was just having a good time. There were lots of teenagers, lots of twenty-somethings, and some people even had their kids here. There was outdoor seating, and all the tables were full. The parking lot was packed.

Darlene and Mickey entered through the back door into the kitchen, just as they had on the previous occasion. Darlene looked around for Ray. He was nowhere to be seen. Mickey introduced Darlene to everyone as they walked through the kitchen into the back room, where Ray had his office and private space. Mickey knocked three short knocks on the office, and Ray barked through the closed door, "Yeah, who is it?"

"It's Mickey. Open the door, you deadbeat. I gotta surprise for you." Mickey winked at Darlene.

Darlene was about to ask Mickey what the surprise was when Ray opened the door and Mickey pushed her through. "Happy birthday, Ray."

Darlene didn't know what to say or how to act. Of all the scenarios she had played out during the short drive here, this was not even on the radar. She was mortified that Mickey would do this to her, and she could feel her face burning red.

"Well, well, well. Looky here! Mickey, this is probably the best birthday present I've ever had. Please, do come in." With his hands on his hips, Ray stood aside to let them enter, all the while not taking his eyes off Darlene.

"Happy birthday to me!" Ray said. "Darlene, you are lookin' mighty fine this evening." He wrapped her hair around his finger. "I sure like these red curls. Damn, you are a cute little thing."

Mickey introduced Darlene to the other people in the room, but Darlene could barely pay attention—she was so aware of Ray and the fact that he was watching her every move. She felt his eyes roaming over her body, and she was certain she was blushing from head to toe like some love-sick school girl. The room was suddenly very warm, and she thought her heart would explode out of her chest, it was beating so fast. She was thrilled and terrified, noticing again how much older he was. Mickey had told her that Ray had spent five years in prison for selling drugs and attempted murder of one of his drug suppliers. She attributed his hard look to his time behind bars. She didn't find him necessarily handsome, but powerful and in control, which she found quite sexy.

Sitting on the sofa was Sally something—Johnson, Jones—she couldn't remember. Darlene knew Sally from high school. She had been one year behind Darlene and Mickey. She seemed so out of place here, even more than Darlene felt. So innocent and backward, but there she sat lighting a giant red bong full of pot.

The other girl sitting beside Sally, Darlene remembered from high school, as well. Her name was Louise, and everyone called her Lou. She had been a year ahead of Darlene and Mickey and was, as far as Darlene could remember, a total bitch. Judging by her icy glare directed at Darlene, Lou appeared not to have changed. She always thought she was the prettiest girl in town and hated anyone who took the attention away from her. Even though she was with a man, and they were both wearing wedding rings, she was probably interested in Ray. Anyone new who entered the scene would be met with the same icy stare.

Sitting in the recliner with a girl from Delbarton was Gabe, a friend of Darlene's from high school. He, too, had been a year behind her and Mickey. He lived in the back alley and had always been around when they played in the neighborhood. He was a nice kid and had been a good friend growing up. Darlene was happy she had at least one friend in the room besides Mickey.

Ray sat beside Darlene on the loveseat and put his arm around the back. He was sitting very close, and Darlene could feel the heat from his body. He smelled good—a mixture of cologne and pot and whiskey. Mickey put the last lip-swirl on a very large joint, lit it and passed it to Ray. He took a hit and passed it to Darlene. The last thing she wanted was to go home smelling like pot, but here she was, and she wasn't going to look like an idiot in front of Ray again. Besides, she deserved to have a good time. She needed to relax and enjoy herself. She needed the attention Ray was pouring on her. Dave hadn't paid any attention to her since they got married. Ray made her feel beautiful, and he liked her hair. She was thankful she had gotten up too late to straighten it.

"Little Darlene, Mickey tells me you finally got a divorce?" Ray looked down at her with a playful grin on his face.

Darlene wondered if she was still able to flirt without looking like an idiot. His gaze was so intense—hell, everything about him was intense—she had trouble putting two words together. Her stomach was a bundle of nerves, but they were good nerves. She could feel her face getting warm as the heat rose from her chest. A small gasp escaped her throat, and she found her voice. "Yep. I'm a free woman." She tried to relax and hoped the pot would kick in soon. She needed it to take the edge off.

"Well, that sure is good to know."

She had noticed the tattoos on his left hand when she was there at Thanksgiving with Mickey and Beth but hadn't had the nerve to ask about it then. It was 13 ½ with a hangman's noose beside it. As he passed a joint to her, she noticed it again and found the courage to bring it up.

"I got that in prison. It's 13 ½—a judge, a jury, and a half-assed lawyer. The hangman's noose is just 'cause I liked it."

The night wore on, and Darlene reluctantly snorted coke and smoked more pot than she had ever seen before. A lot of people came and went, and around eleven, Zip came in all jacked up on coke. At first Darlene was not even sure it was Zip; he was heavier and meaner looking than she remembered. She hadn't seen him in years.

Growing up, he had been a tall, super-skinny kid; everyone called him Zipper. The joke was that he was so thin that if he turned sideways and stuck out his tongue, he would look like a zipper. This stuck with him through eighth grade. Then the summer between eighth and ninth, he grew. A lot. He filled out his lanky frame, becoming a brute. Then he started playing football and was the Matewan Tigers' hero. He was invincible. He was so fast; everyone just started calling him Zip. Marshall University recruited him and offered a full scholarship. Other schools had courted him— WVU, University of Kentucky, Tennessee, Texas A&M— most of the Division 1-A schools. He settled on Marshall so he could be close to home. His mother was not well, and he needed to be able to get home on short notice.

The NFL scouted him during his senior year. Two weeks before finals, he was on his way to class when a car ran a red light and hit him as he crossed the street. His left leg had been severely damaged, and there were a few weeks when it was doubtful he would get to keep it. Eventually he had to drop out of school, and he came home to Matewan. It took a year for his leg to mend. During that time he was on a lot of pain killers, and he developed a nasty habit of taking them long after the physical pain had ended. The drugs helped ease the disappointment of not going on to play professional football, which clouded everything else in his life. Now here he was serving as one of Ray's goons.

Darlene had always liked Zip. She noticed a dark edge to him now—probably the drugs.

Zip had two girls with him that Darlene didn't know and wouldn't get to know because it was late, and she needed to leave. "Mick, I hate to be a party pooper, but I gotta go. I'm sure Mommy and the girls will be wonderin' where I am."

"Are you Cinderella?" Ray twirled her curls around his finger. "You turn into a pumpkin at midnight? Tell you what, I'll have the kitchen make you a pizza to take home to your girls, and then you can go. But you gotta promise me you'll come back tomorrow night. This birthday party will last all weekend, and it won't be the same without you here. Mickey, you be sure and bring this sweet little thing back with you."

"Sure thing, Ray." Mickey winked at him.

Judging by Ray's attention and Mickey's reaction to it, Darlene thought she must have been way off base about Mickey and Ray dating. It was obvious now that they were just good friends. Mickey respected him and was devoted to him, but there was nothing romantic between them. Darlene was glad there was nothing going on, because she loved the attention Ray was giving her, and she wanted more. And, as a bonus, she caught Lou's glare more than once.

Darlene got home at half past eleven. The girls were still up and thrilled that Darlene had brought them a pizza. Darlene put the box on the table and ran into the bedroom to change her clothes before her mother had a chance to smell the pot on her.

***

Lou was having a great time. She just wished Doug wasn't there. Tomorrow night he had to work, so she could get a little cozier with Ray. Five years of marriage to Doug had been about four years and six months too long. She would have left after the first year, but then she got pregnant, so she stayed. It crossed her mind over the years to divorce him. She just wanted to be free to date and run around when she wanted. Doug had a good job, which meant she didn't have to work, definitely a plus. He worked hard, and they had a nice home and a new car. If she left, she would have to give all that up, so she had resigned herself to staying.

Then she met Ray. She could have Ray; she knew she could. Then she would have whatever she wanted. He had lots of drugs and lots of cash. She had been hanging out at The Place for a year now, but Ray still kept her at arm's length most of the time. Probably because Doug was always with her. She just needed to spend more time with Ray without Doug tagging along; this weekend would be the perfect opportunity.

The party had just started; they had all done a line of coke as soon as they arrived. She was enjoying herself. Then there was a knock at the door. She watched Ray as he moved to the door. He was a no-nonsense sort and always on guard. With that much cash and that much dope, she couldn't blame him.

He shouted through the door, "Yeah, who is it?"

It sounded like Mickey who answered. Lou didn't care too much for Mickey, but she acted like Ray's guard dog, so Lou tolerated her in order to stay close to Ray. She kept it friendly, but Mickey wasn't a girl's girl.

Lou was expecting Mickey, but Darlene entered, then Mickey. Darlene? What on earth was she doing here? Lou had heard that she and Dave had split up, but she never imagined she would see her here. It made sense to see her with Mickey, though; those two had been thicker than thieves in high school.

Darlene had not been one of Lou's favorite people back in the day. She was cute, popular and a cheerleader. Three strikes. Here she was now, not a cheerleader, not so popular, but still cute. Ray sure seemed excited to see her. What was that about? How did they know each other? She hadn't been divorced for a hot minute. Why was she here? Other than the Mickey connection, this wasn't any place she would ever expect to see Darlene.

Now Ray was playing with her hair. Darlene sure looked like a fish out of water. She looked quite uncomfortable. Good. Maybe she wouldn't stay too long.

***

Gabe couldn't believe Darlene was actually in the back office at The Place. She was a good girl and real smart. Why was she here? He wanted to talk to her, but Ray was hovering over her like a Black Hawk helicopter, and Gabe knew she was hands off. He would wait until another time when they could talk. He just wanted to catch up and see how she was doing since the divorce. He also wanted to find out what she was doing here. He wanted to let her know what she was getting into.

***

Mickey dropped Darlene off and headed back to The Place. She had been disappointed when Ray had asked about Darlene earlier in the week. She had mentioned to him a couple of months earlier that Darlene was getting a divorce. It had been an off-hand comment when she was on her way out to meet Darlene at Aunt Penny's. When he asked her to bring Darlene for the birthday party, she hesitated and gave him a dozen reasons why Darlene wouldn't want to hang out with that crowd. He had insisted, and she couldn't say no to him.

Now she regretted saying anything. She loved Darlene, but she also loved Ray. She wanted Ray for herself. Hell, the way Ray went through women, Darlene wouldn't be around for too long. Besides, naïve and innocent Darlene wouldn't be able to take too much of Ray's lifestyle, anyway. So Mickey decided to just live with it and wait for it to fall apart.

CHAPTER SEVEN
Cocaine Crazy

"You know, a long time ago being crazy meant something.
Nowadays everybody's crazy." — Charles Manson

The following night Darlene and Mickey returned to Ray's. Darlene told her parents she would be spending the night with Mickey to watch movies and just hang out. The girls were with Dave for the weekend. Millie didn't like that she was with Mickey but agreed that Darlene needed a night away and told her to enjoy herself. Darlene felt horrible about lying to her mother but knew she couldn't tell her the truth, and she wanted to stay out past midnight. She wanted to act like an adult and be able to stay out all night if she wanted without someone shaming her and treating her like a disobedient child.

She went to Mickey's after work. She changed clothes and freshened her makeup, and they returned to Ray's. The party continued. The same crowd was there—Lou (without her husband), Gabe (without a date), Sally, Zip (with two new girls) and Mickey. This was a typical weekend for them, and they all seemed to be very comfortable with each other. Everyone was nice to Darlene. Everyone except Lou. She barely spoke to Darlene, and when she did, it was some snide comment about her clothes, her hair or her divorce.

Darlene wanted to talk to Gabe. They had not seen each other since just after she got married. Gabe had been a good kid. He played football in high school with Zip, but he was not as good as Zip and not as smart. For Gabe there were no scholarships or offers to do anything after high school. After a couple of hours, she got her chance.

"Hey, Gabe, how you doin'? I didn't expect to see you here."

"Well, Darlene, I sure never expected to see you here. Ever! How'd you get mixed up with this crazy bunch? Sure don't seem like your kinda crowd." Gabe passed her a joint.

"Mickey's the connection. I had no clue this place even existed until she brought me here last year for pizza. How about you? How did you get hooked up with Ray? Mickey tells me you work for him now?"

"Yeah, I been here for a little over a year now, I guess. I do odd jobs, whatever Ray wants me to do."

***

Gabe didn't know how much Darlene knew about the drugs or Ray's business, and he wasn't going to be the one to tell her. He figured he would let Mickey or Ray do that. The length of time he had been here was enough for him, and he would love to just get out. He was afraid of Ray and really afraid of Zip. He was crazy. Gabe wanted to warn Darlene to run while she could, just back out of it now before she got in too deep. Ray had a way of sucking people into his world and never letting them go. He wished he had known this when he came looking for work.

Right out of high school, Gabe had gotten a job driving a coal truck and was glad to have the job. It paid well, and he had insurance and other benefits just like the miners. Things were going well for a few years. Then he got his second DUI, lost his license for a year and lost his job for good. That was when he went to Ray and asked for a job. He sold himself as a bodyguard and drug mule. Ray took him in and paid him $500 a week to start and a little extra when they made a big haul, plus all the drugs he could do. Rule was he could not get high when he was with Ray, on a drug run, or if Ray needed him to serve as bodyguard. He also had to be available 24/7 and do whatever Ray told him. No questions asked. Gabe had agreed and thought it would be a fun, easy job.

Gabe never considered what the "no questions asked" really meant. Then Ray asked him to beat up some tiny punk from Beech Creek who had not paid for his drugs. Gabe was sick to his stomach when he punched the kid. Gabe knew Ray was testing his loyalty and would make it much worse for him if he didn't do as instructed.

There were other things Ray made him do that really turned his stomach, but he did what he was told to do. He took the money and the drugs Ray offered and kept looking for a way out. Gabe hated to see Darlene get mixed up in this mess.

***

Ray invited Darlene back for the next weekend and asked if he could call her. She was embarrassed to tell him she was living with her parents and it might not go over so well if a strange man were to phone. She wanted to live her life as she pleased and not be treated like a fourteen-year-old child, but as long as she was under her father's roof, she had to play by his rules. As strict as he was, it was still better than being with Dave. She told Ray he could call her at work, but only on shifts when she was there alone, and he could always get in touch with her through Mickey.

***

She danced through the next week. She hadn't felt this good about herself or her life in a long time. She had a man interested in her. Not just any man, but a powerful man with lots of money and lots of drugs and lots of attention just for her. Sure, he wasn't someone she wanted to spend the rest of her life with, but for now, it was fun, free and exciting. If she were honest, it was also a bit dangerous, and she liked that. She had never really walked on the edge. Besides, a summer fling might do her good. She needed to have some fun before she started back at nursing school.

Darlene spent every spare moment with Ray for the rest of July and all of August. She really liked him, and he seemed to dominate her every thought and action. She was glad she had continued taking her birth control pills, because after the second week, they were having sex. She never dreamed she would be having sex with someone new this soon. She was barely divorced and barely knew Ray, but she felt comfortable and safe with him. He made her feel special and beautiful and sexy. She thought about all the other women Mickey had mentioned at Christmas, but she had no evidence they were still around.

"How come we always make love here in your office? Why don't we ever go to your house?" Darlene asked one afternoon.

"I just need to be here a lot. It's convenient. Why? You don't like my office bedroom?" He gave her a sad face.

She kissed him. "Of course, I do. As long as I'm with you, that's all that matters." The fact that she had never been to his house kept needling Darlene, but she pushed it away and ignored it. She thought maybe taking her to his house was too much of a commitment, so she dropped it. She didn't want to rock the boat.

"What are you doin' next Wednesday and Thursday? Can you call in sick or somethin' and go with me to Columbus? I gotta go on business and would love to take your sweet little ass with me."

"Oh, Ray, I don't know. I don't know how I could swing it. The girls are startin' school in a couple of weeks, and I gotta take 'em to buy clothes and supplies. Besides, my parents would freak." She really wanted to go with Ray and feared losing him if she had to keep putting him off because of her parents' disapproval.

"Well, you're a big girl. Figure it out. I want you to go." He got up and got dressed. He was very matter of fact about her going, as though she didn't have a choice. He had spoken and she would go. After he got dressed, he pulled $300 out of his pocket and tossed it on the bed. "Here, this should buy a lot of pencils for school."

"Ray, I can't take money from you."

"Yes, you can. Take it. Then figure out how you can go with me to Columbus."

"I'll try." Darlene got up to get dressed. They smoked another joint, and then she left.

Lying to her parents had been hard enough these past two months. She couldn't imagine what sort of story she would tell them in order to be gone for two whole days in the middle of the week. The more she thought about it, the more her stomach ached, and she ran to the bathroom when she got home.

***

Darlene concocted a story to tell her parents about visiting Mickey's sick cousin in Lexington. Of course, Mickey would have to keep a low profile and not be anywhere her parents would see her. Darlene was disappointed when Ray informed her there was no need to worry about Mickey being seen; she would be joining them. Not just Mickey, but Zip, too. Ray needed Mickey to ride shotgun while Zip drove. She needed to do it with him a few times, before Ray could trust her to make a run on her own with Zip or Gabe. Darlene was relieved that Mickey wouldn't be running up and down the roads and potentially blowing her cover, but she was also disappointed that she wouldn't get to spend the time alone with Ray.

Zip drove, as Ray, Mickey and Darlene snorted line after line of coke all the way to Columbus. Darlene could barely remember the drive down Tolsia Highway and then up Route 23 into Columbus. They arrived at the hotel, and Ray checked in while Darlene and Mickey waited in the car with Zip. When they got to the room and Mickey and Zip went in with them, Darlene realized Ray had gotten only one room. It was a suite with two full beds and a sofa and a small kitchen area. Why were they sharing a room with Mickey and Zip?

They snorted a line of coke and then walked across the street to the bar to wait for Sammy, Ray's drug connection. Darlene liked being in Ray's inner circle. Everyone was so afraid of him, but here she was getting to know about his business.

The bar was small and the lights were dim. Filling the air was the smell of stale cigarette smoke and wet bar rags left out overnight. The booths were worn and old. A handful of people sat at the bar watching ESPN. Other than that, they had the place pretty much to themselves. Darlene figured this was why Sammy chose this spot in the middle of the week. It was empty.

Ray told the bartender they would be sitting in the round booth at the back of the bar, and they needed drinks and menus. When the waitress brought menus, she took their drink order. Ray had a beer, Darlene and Mickey had margaritas on the rocks and Zip had a Pepsi. After they finished their first round of drinks they ordered food and waited for Sammy. Mickey had met Sammy once at The Place and said he was a scary Puerto Rican who always travelled with two or three goons.

It was only four, and Darlene felt as though she had been awake for days; the coke had her really wired. She tried to eat but was so wound up that eating was the last thing she wanted to do. She started biting her fingernails.

"Hey there, baby, don't bite your nails. I hate when you do that. It's disgusting. Stop!" Ray pulled her hand away and laid it on the table. "What's wrong? You nervous? Too much blow?" He handed pills to Darlene and Mickey. "Here. Take two of these. It'll calm you down. It's Xanax. It'll mellow you right out, baby. Shame to waste all that coke, but you need to relax. Sammy'll freak if he sees you like this, afraid you'll draw too much attention. If you can't calm down before he gets here, Mick'll need to take you back to the room." He pushed his beer toward her and told her to take the pills.

Being the obedient girlfriend, Darlene took them. Mickey slipped her pills in her pocket for later.

Darlene could feel the meds calm her down. She went from wound up to yawning in a space of about twenty minutes. Ray told her she could have another pill later when it was time for bed.

They ate and waited. After about an hour, Sammy entered with his goons, just as Mickey said he would. One in front and one in back. The one leading the way was Mexican or Cuban or something south of the border—lean, tall, muscular and bald. Bringing up the rear was a mountain—at least six feet, seven inches—and solid, the biggest black man Darlene had ever seen. He looked like the guy from *The Green Mile*. Sammy was in the middle and, just as Mickey described, Puerto Rican, not quite six feet tall and a lot older than she expected. He was skinny—almost scrawny—with a mean, hard look. Sammy also had a six-foot blonde in very little clothing clinging to his arm. She was pretty, in a cheap, stripper sort of way. Her fake boobs were two sizes too big for her thin frame and were pushed up and spilling out of her hot pink bustier. Beneath a micro-mini skirt, fish net panty hose led to a pair of the most amazing hot pink stilettos Darlene had ever seen.

"Sam-Bo! Good to see you, my man." Ray stood up and gave Sammy that half-hug-thump-on-the-back-thing guys do.

"Good to see you, Ray. I see you have some lovely ladies with you today. Who is this green-eyed angel?" Darlene liked his accent, but she didn't like the way he looked at her. He made her skin crawl, and she hoped she never had to be alone with him.

Ray whispered something to Sammy, and they both laughed while looking appreciatively at Darlene. She could feel her face burning from embarrassment. The blonde smiled and winked at her.

Ray, Sammy and the blonde slipped into the big round booth, and Sammy and Ray whispered. Ray ordered more drinks and food, and the goons stood at either end of the dining room to keep people away from the booth.

After Sammy and Ray had talked and they had eaten, they all left the bar and went back to the hotel. *The Green Mile* guy stood outside the room and watched the elevator and stairwell exit. "South of the Border" brought in a huge duffel bag full of coke and pills. Zip hovered in the corner, close to Ray. Ray handed over a smaller duffel bag full of cash. The deal was done, and Sammy and company left.

The Xanax had started taking its full effect on Darlene, and she felt like lead. Ray told her to take another Xanax and go to sleep. Darlene crawled into bed, and Ray stuffed the duffle bag under the blankets with her. Darlene could hear Mickey and Ray talking and laughing. Zip never said anything. She fell into a deep sleep within minutes.

Darlene woke up hours later to find the room dark and everyone gone. She felt disoriented, a little woozy and very thirsty. Her mouth felt disgusting. There was a faint glow coming from the bathroom and a sliver of light coming through the window curtains. Her eyes adjusted, and she realized where she was. She sat up in bed and felt the duffle bag of drugs beside her. She wondered where Ray, Mickey and Zip were. She turned on the light beside the bed and swung her legs over the edge of the mattress. She was more than a little woozy now and decided not to stand up too fast. The Xanax was still working on her.

She looked at the clock; it was 3 a.m. She couldn't believe she had slept nearly six hours. Assuming everyone was across the street at the bar, she decided to go over and find them. She stumbled into the bathroom and brushed her teeth and hair and fell into the chair. She was putting on her shoes when she heard Mickey and Ray laughing as they made their way down the hallway. Darlene had one shoe on and stumbled over to the door. She looked through the peephole. Ray and Mickey were laughing hysterically as they tried to get the key in the door. Zip was behind them, watching. Jealousy pinched her as she watched Mickey and Ray holding onto each other. Mickey seemed to have a little secret with Ray that Darlene couldn't figure out. It felt as though they had a private joke or story.

"Find your center," Mickey said and grabbed Ray's crotch. They both leaned against the door.

Ray grabbed Mickey's breasts and pretended he was tuning in a radio station. "Come in Tokyo," he said, and they both laughed again as Mickey tried to get the key in the door.

Darlene didn't understand how they could so freely fondle each other. Why would they do this? Have they been sleeping together all this time? Is this their private story?

A hardness and sharp edges.

With only one shoe on and the other in her hand, Darlene opened the door, and the two of them nearly fell into the room, still laughing. Zip walked in behind them.

Ray grabbed Darlene and kissed her. When she pushed him away, he barely noticed. He stumbled to the bed and curled up with his duffle bag of drugs and passed out fully dressed.

Mickey fell into the other bed, and Zip went to the sofa. Darlene was so angry she took off her shoe, threw both shoes across the room and got into bed next to the duffle bag, with Ray on the other side. She soon feel back to sleep.

Darlene barely spoke the next morning. They went to breakfast, and the others talked about their night out at the bar across the street. Apparently they had had a great time but missed Darlene. Ray assured her that Zip had been to the room several times to check on her and the drugs. She brushed off their questions about her bad mood as too much coke and Xanax. She was mad and quiet on the ride home.

***

Mickey had known Darlene was pissed the second she had opened the door the previous night and knew she was still pissed on the ride home. Good. She didn't need to get too comfortable in her relationship with Ray. Mickey loved Darlene and didn't want her to get hurt by Ray. But more importantly, she wanted Darlene to understand that Mickey's relationship with Ray was much deeper than anything he would ever have with Darlene. Ray wanted Darlene just for sex, and that was all it was. A cute little thing to have hanging around to feed his male ego. Mickey was surprised it had lasted this long, but Ray seemed determine to keep dating her, and Darlene was getting more comfortable with the drugs and Ray's lifestyle. In time, it would fall apart. Mickey settled in to ride it out.

***

When Darlene started seeing Ray, she had many reservations. Dating a drug kingpin was not what she wanted to do with her life. If Dave found out, he would convince himself and her father that she had been using drugs for years. He would take her kids away and never let her see them. She knew this, but it was not enough to convince her to stop seeing Ray. She planned to end the relationship before it got too serious. She just needed to keep it quiet until then, and Dave would never find out.

The whole drug scene was not her thing. It was scary. People like Sammy were scary. When she started seeing Ray, Darlene had reasoned that she was young, newly divorced and needed to have some fun. What could it hurt to date him through the summer? But, summer melted into fall, and suddenly it was Thanksgiving again. She had spent nearly all her time with him for the past five months. She was afraid she would lose him if she didn't make time for him when he wanted her. It felt like a trap—a different trap than she had been in with Dave, but a trap nonetheless. She knew turning over her life and choices to someone else was taking the easy way out. Again. It was a well-worn path in her life, and she knew where most of the land mines were buried and could navigate her way around the chaos. She knew how to mold herself to fit Ray's expectations.

Navigating her parents, especially her father, was another story. It became harder and harder to invent excuses for being gone so much. She had missed a couple of days of work to go to Columbus with Ray and had gone in late a few times due to hangovers. Her father would have a fit if he found out she was skipping work to be with Ray. In fact, her father would have a fit if he knew she was anywhere near Ray for any reason. She knew she was playing with fire but continued on her path anyway. The fire made life exciting, and she deserved some excitement.

The girls spent weekends with Dave (or Dave's parents), so this left her free to do what she wanted. Her weekends were typically fueled with cocaine binges and parties at The Place. Sunday nights always ended with a Xanax.

She ignored that annoying little voice circling in her head that kept demanding she look a little closer at the situation and her relationship with Ray. She was having fun and making up for lost years with Dave. The voice could wait. *A hardness and sharp edges* seemed to just be something crazy her mother had said once about Mickey and certainly didn't apply to Ray.

Aunt Penny came home from Myrtle Beach Thanksgiving weekend. She had been living there part of the year with her new boyfriend, John, whom she had met through an online matchmaking service. John had retired to Myrtle Beach to play golf and enjoy the warm weather. Aunt Penny was in love.

The night before Thanksgiving, Darlene was helping her mother and Aunt Penny bake. Darlene had told Ray she couldn't come out no matter what. She wanted and needed to be home with her mother and her girls. Dave would get the girls Friday morning, and she wanted to spend this time at home. She was exhausted from months of cocaine and partying. She never got to rest anymore, and she needed the calm of her mother's kitchen and baking.

"Darlene, honey, you look so thin. You're not big as a minute. Are you eatin'?" Aunt Penny grabbed Darlene around the waist and shook her head at Darlene's tiny frame. "Are you doin' okay since the divorce?"

"Aunt Penny, I'm fine. I just stay busy, and liftin' those boxes of booze keeps me lean and mean." Darlene flexed her biceps. She, too, had noticed how thin she was becoming and assumed it was the cocaine.

"Are you dating? You need to get out and date. You're a beautiful young woman. There are plenty of men who would love to take care of you. Of course, there are no men around here that you would probably want. You should plan to come visit me in Myrtle Beach this spring. You would certainly meet a lot of nice young men there. You could work on your tan and let me fatten you up a bit."

Darlene desperately wanted to tell Aunt Penny about Ray but knew she would disapprove and would tell her mother. So she kept silent about the relationship and agreed that she would come to Myrtle Beach in the spring.

Thanksgiving provided Darlene a comfort she hadn't realized she'd missed, and she ate more than she had in months. She had not used cocaine all week and suddenly had a ravenous appetite. Dave picked up the girls Friday morning, and Darlene went to work.

Darlene had just finished her lunch when she looked up to see Ray coming into the store. Her boss, Faye, had gone out to run errands. "What are you doin' in here?" She tried to control the panic in her voice.

"I came to see my favorite girl." He leaned against the corner of the checkout counter and smiled at her.

"Well, I better be your *only* girl, and you need to leave. *Now!* Faye will be back any minute, and she is a nosey old coot. So, go." Darlene shooed him away.

"Well, now, maybe I want to buy some liquor. I need some JD. Where might I find that, miss?"

"Back shelf, left side, bottom. Hurry up!" Ray turned to get the JD. Darlene was standing at the cash register waiting for him when Faye returned. Darlene thought she was going to throw up right there all over the counter.

"Hi, Faye. How was your lunch?" Darlene's voice was suddenly very small and tiny. She could barely breathe.

Ray came over to the cash register with the bottle of JD. Darlene rang him up and took his money. Her hands were shaking so badly she dropped his change; it fell on the counter, and a quarter bounced off onto the floor.

"Thank you, sir." Darlene handed him his change.

Ray picked up the bag and smiled at Darlene. "Thank *you.*"

Darlene took a deep breath and tried to act normal, but she felt very sick. She wiped the counter and began tidying behind it to keep her hands busy.

"That man is a disgrace. Trash! Surprised to see him in here. I understand he's more into drugs than alcohol." Faye didn't try to hide her distaste for Ray as she watched him get in his car and pull away from the liquor store.

"Who? Him?" Darlene was surprised that Faye would even know him.

"Yes, him. Do you know who he is? He's a drug dealer. Been in prison for drugs and attempted murder. He owns that pizza joint in Red Jacket. The Place. It's a place all right." She shook her head. "I don't know why his wife stays with him. She's a bigger fool than he is."

There was a roar in Darlene's head as Faye's words came rushing at her. "What? His…wife? He's married?" Darlene could barely get the words out. How did she not know this? Faye must be mistaken. "Are you sure?"

"Oh, yes, I'm certain. He dated my friend's daughter for a while, and his wife caught them together and nearly beat the girl to death." Faye looked up at the ceiling and started counting. "That was about seven months ago, 'cause it was right around Easter. Yes, he's a real son of a bitch, that one."

Now Darlene felt really sick. Her stomach was not going to calm down. She excused herself and ran to the ladies' room. She threw up her lunch and began to cry. So this is why they never went to his house and why he only invited her to the restaurant on certain days. It all made sense now. Why hadn't she asked if he was married? She should have paid attention. She felt like such a fool. She had opened the store that morning, so she had only a few more hours to work. She washed her face and reapplied her makeup and went back to work.

Darlene managed to get through the shift, but she was in a daze. Her thoughts were running in all directions. She was mad one minute, confused the next. Overall, crushed. She had spent most of the shift in the ladies' room either throwing up or having diarrhea. She told Faye she thought she had the flu or food poisoning. Faye insisted she stay home the next day if she was still throwing up. Darlene knew it was not out of concern for her; Faye didn't want to get it, if it was contagious.

***

After work she drove straight to Mickey's house. She walked in without knocking. "Why did you think it wasn't important to tell me Ray was married? What part of that did you think was information I shouldn't have?"

Mickey looked up from the joint she was rolling and just sat back on the couch and started laughing. "You can't tell me you didn't know." When Darlene shook her head no, Mickey laughed that much harder.

Darlene started to cry.

"Oh, shit, Darlene. I'm sorry. I didn't mean to laugh at you. Honestly, I thought you knew. Ever'body knows he has a wife and kids. It ain't some big secret. This is a small town. Ever'body knows everything. I can't believe he never said anything. Why did you think he would only see you at the restaurant?" Mickey lit the joint. "Oh, Darlene. Damn, girl. I thought you knew."

Darlene sat down on the couch and bent over with her face in her hands. The tears were an uncontrollable flood.

"Darlene, I can't believe you fell for Ray. He's not the kind of guy a girl should get all emotional over. He's bad news. He goes through women like socks."

"Well, now is probably a little late to be dispensin' your wise relationship advice, Mick. Yeah, I fell for him. I'm crazy about him. What am I supposed to do now? Stop seein' him? I don't want to stop seein' him. But I can't date a married man. A married man with kids! I was so afraid of Daddy findin' out I was datin' Ray because of his lifestyle and the fact that he's been in prison. I was ready to deal with that. But, this? No way. Daddy will disown me. How am I supposed to tell my girls Mommy's boyfriend already has a wife and kids? Oh, Mick, this is fucked up."

Mickey passed the joint to Darlene. "Girl, I don't know what to tell you. We'll figure it out. One thing I do know is that Ray won't let you just walk away. He's a little possessive of people he thinks are his."

"What do you mean, *his*?"

"The last girl he dated broke up with him after Connie confronted her, and Ray beat the shit out of her. He made Connie take the rap for it, because he was afraid he would go back to jail."

"Who's Connie? His wife?"

"Yeah. I don't know why she stays with him. Maybe just too afraid to leave or too dumb to leave. She has anything she wants, so maybe it's the money. Who knows? She sure seems dumber than a box of rocks."

Darlene was torn about what to do. She felt stupid for not even considering the idea that he could be married. How could she be so naïve? She didn't want to stop seeing him, but knowing he was married changed everything. She justified the drugs, because this was how he made a living, and he was not forcing anyone to buy them; people came to him of their own free will. Besides, she liked the parties, free drugs, the nice things he bought her, the trips out of town. Most off all, she liked dating someone in control. Someone that everyone else was afraid of. Ray made her feel pretty and special, and he included her in his life. She wasn't ready to walk away from that.

"What will people think of me, Mick? Now that I know he's married? If I decide to stay with him, will people think I'm dumber than a box of rocks?"

"No. People don't think that of the mistress. You get to have all the fun, use all the drugs, take the trips, and be his girl. People'll think you're cool and not to be messed with. Look at Lou. She's so damned jealous of you, she can't see straight. She knows not to mess with you, though, because she knows Ray will go off. No. You're good. Don't worry about it. If you want to keep datin' Ray, keep datin' him and don't worry about what people think. Fuck 'em."

Darlene knew Mickey was right. She should not worry about what people thought, and she didn't for the most part. Her father was another story altogether. He would be livid that she was dating Ray. She would just have to find a way to deal with her father. She wanted to be with Ray and was willing to suffer her father's wrath. He would come around eventually.

***

Darlene waited a few days before she confronted Ray. She was nervous. His temper only needed a small spark to turn into a consuming rage. She wasn't sure what to say to him. She didn't want to break up with him, and she didn't want to anger him or threaten him with an ultimatum. She had seen him turn on other people who tried those tactics, and he exploded, beat the shit out of them, and then tossed them out on their ass. She put a lot of thought into what she would say to him.

When Darlene entered the back office at The Place, she was nervous and apprehensive. Her stomach was in knots, and she felt a little sick. Ray was on the telephone and hung up when she entered.

"Damn, baby. What's wrong? You're as nervous as a whore in church, and you're bitin' those damned fingernails again." He swiveled around in his desk chair, pulled Darlene down onto his lap, and put his cigarette out in the ashtray. "Somebody do somethin' to you? You need money? You need a little somethin' to calm you down? You need to get laid? Tell me."

"Ray, I'm fine. I think." Darlene's eyes filled with tears and she swallowed hard before she continued. "Ray, why didn't you tell me you were married?"

He sat silent for a moment just looking at her, almost puzzled. A grin formed at the corner of his mouth. "Baby, I thought you knew. Everybody knows I'm married. It ain't no secret. I don't hide the fact that I got a wife and kids. You really didn't know? In this small shit hole of gossip, you really didn't know?"

"No. I really didn't know. You don't wear a ring. You never talk about her. I assumed you were divorced. I guess I should have asked."

"What you gonna do about it now that you know?" His smile had been replaced with a hard line, and his eyes had turned dark. Darlene had seen this look before, just before he punched someone.

She was quick to let him know that she was not wanting to break up. "Well, I don't know. Nothin', I guess. It just changes things, sorta."

"How?"

"Well I guess there's no chance we'll ever live together or anything like that. I certainly can't tell my daddy about you. Can't take you home for the holidays. I guess it changes my expectations is all."

"Well, darlin', we might not be able to live together, but I can certainly give you a place to live, and I can come and spend the night. It'll be our little love nest."

"When my daddy finds out about you, you'll have to give me a place to live, 'cause he'll pitch me out with the trash."

Ray laughed and promised her he would take care of it when and if she needed a place to live.

"There's one more thing, Ray. I don't want your wife beatin' me up like she did that other girl. Do I need to worry 'bout that?"

Ray's playful mood slipped away and he grabbed Darlene's chin and forced her to look at him. "Who told you she beat somebody up?"

"It don't matter Ray. Like you said, it's a small shit hole of gossip and people talk." Darlene knew he would confront Faye, and that would be a disaster.

"Tell me, Darlene." He wouldn't let her go.

"It was some old biddy who came into the store. She was talkin' with her friend about goin' to get a pizza at your place and the other one started tellin' her about your old girlfriend and how your wife beat her up. I don't know who they were."

"Well, it better not of been any this bunch here sayin' that shit. One thing I won't tolerate is these losers talkin' about my business."

Darlene stayed for a little while and then told Ray she needed to leave. She had to work the next day, and the girls had school. She felt betrayed and stupid, but she had made her choice to stay with him—a choice that took her further down that path than she ever thought she would go.

***

Christmas came and went with little fanfare. The girls enjoyed having two Christmases but didn't understand why Daddy couldn't be with them for Christmas and why they couldn't all go home together. Dave bought the girls the toys and dolls they had put on their Christmas letter to Santa, but they had to leave them at his parents' house. The only things they could bring home were the new clothes he gave them.

Ray gave Darlene $500 and a diamond necklace for Christmas. She was thrilled, but she had to hide the necklace from her parents and couldn't spend the money all at once;

her parents would want to know where she got that kind of money. They knew she could pay only for basics right now. She stashed the $500 with the other money he was always giving her. She now had $975 saved for a rainy day. At this pace, she might actually be able to get her own place in a few months.

***

New Year's Eve was a wild night at The Place. Darlene had to convince her parents she would be safe and not driving. She hated lying to them. She told them she was just going out with some old friends from high school and that was partly true—she knew Mickey, Gabe, Zip, Lou and Sally from school.

The Place was hopping that night, with customers at the front end, in the restaurant, and with the inner circle in the office. The cocaine, pills and booze flowed, and everyone was having a great time. At midnight they all walked outside and shot guns in the air. Gabe had brought fireworks and put on quite a display until he caught a tree on fire. The spigot to the water hose was frozen, so the tree continued to burn. Calling the fire department was out of the question, because the cops would also come. They all stood outside and watched the tree burn. Eventually it flittered out. Gabe was banned from all future pyrotechnics.

Darlene spent the night with Ray at The Place. She got up around noon and walked into the office. The only people there were Mickey, Gabe and Zip. Darlene had not realized the sofa was actually a sleeper. Mickey and Zip were passed out on that, and Gabe was unconscious in the recliner. The office smelled like pot, sweat, cigarettes and beer. It looked much worse than it smelled, if that were possible.

Darlene started cleaning up. She needed to get a shower because she was supposed to work that afternoon until closing. Head pounding from all the champagne she'd had the night before, she looked for headache medicine in the bathroom and found none. She then looked in the desk.

The center drawer had nothing useful—a gun, a note pad, pens, pot, papers, a couple of lighters and a book of matches from a strip club in Columbus. The drawer on the left was locked, but she knew it contained files. Tax files, bank statements, stuff to do with The Place. There were three drawers on the right. The top drawer had pens, Post-it notes, rubber bands. Darlene opened the second drawer and there was another gun. The gun didn't catch her attention, but what was underneath it did. She pushed the gun aside with the back of her hand.

There were pictures of naked women…*girls* actually. About a dozen pictures, and judging by the shoes they were wearing and the clothes scattered around in the background, Darlene presumed they were taken recently. There were three girls, and she didn't recognize any of them. They looked to be about nineteen years old. If that. They were in various stages of undress, and in several pictures, the girls were kissing each other. One picture showed two girls sitting on Ray's lap. Naked.

The pictures were disturbing because the girls looked so young. But more than that, the pictures looked rather recent. She had accepted that he had a wife and kids and had lied about that, but this was too much. Hearing him moving around in the bedroom, she shoved the pictures back into the drawer and closed it. She was afraid of what he would do if he thought she was snooping. Even though she was looking for Advil, he would never believe her. She hurried back to the bathroom and jumped in the shower. She tried to convince herself the pictures were taken before he met her. Even though the clothes he was wearing in the one picture looked recent. She would have to look at them again to be sure, but she was not about to look back in the drawer. This was not the lifestyle she wanted. What was she doing here? Another new year had begun on a sour note.

***

Her current arrangement with Dave was that he got the girls three weekends a month, and she got them all week and one weekend a month. However, Dave's weekends were actually his parents' weekends. Dave had the girls during the day, and then they went to his parents for the night. He played poker or worked at night. Mostly poker.

Anything for parents at the girls' school, Darlene and Dave both attended. School resumed in January. Amy had begun talking back to the teacher and starting arguments with the other students, so Darlene and Dave were asked to attend a parent-teacher meeting. The meeting was on a Saturday morning. Darlene couldn't understand why they scheduled these things on weekends. The night before had been a typical Friday night of partying, and Darlene had been up most of the night doing coke. She woke up late and showered and drove like a bat out of hell to get to the school for the 10:30 meeting. She was ten minutes late, and Dave was waiting for her in the office, scowling.

"Where the hell you been? You can't even make it here on time for your own daughter?"

"Oh, relax, Dave. I'm here. I overslept." Darlene sat down and jammed her hands into her jacket pockets. She felt like shit and wasn't in any mood for Dave's snarky attitude.

"Looks like more than over-sleepin' to me. You look hung over. You been out drinkin' all night?"

"Man, some things never change, do they? No, I've not been out drinkin' all night." Which was true, she had not had a drop to drink. Just a boat load of cocaine, and she was nervous and shaking.

"Why you shakin' like a leaf on a tree then? You need a drink? A pill?" He shook his head in disgust. "Yeah, you're right, Darlene. Some things never change."

The teacher described Amy's behavior and how out of character her recent actions were. She had been a great student all year until after the Christmas break. Darlene and

Dave explained that they were divorced now. Amy had not been taking it too well, and Christmas had been especially hard for her. She wanted her parents to get back together. The teacher gave them some information to read about depression in children and the effects of divorce.

Darlene left the meeting and went to work. She read the information the teacher had provided. She should have paid more attention to Amy. The signs were all there. Darlene realized she had been too busy these past few months, running back and forth to Ray's to pay enough attention to her children. She was a mother, and Amy and Renee were her first priority. She had felt like a prisoner with Dave for so long that being free to go and do as she pleased had been a relief. Freedom. It had been fun. But she needed to come back to reality and focus on making a better life for her kids. It was time to stop the drugs and partying and get away from Ray. She loved him, but he was no good for her. More important was the fact that he was no good for her kids.

A few customers came, and she dried her tears and pulled herself together. Once the store cleared out, she called Dave and asked if she could keep the girls that night, but he refused.

"Why? You feelin' guilty now? Wanna make yourself feel like a good mommy by spendin' a Saturday night with your kids? Darlene, it's Saturday night. Why don't you just go back to Red Jacket and be with your drug-dealin' boyfriend?"

"What? What did you say?" Darlene couldn't believe he knew about Ray. How did he know?

"You heard me. I know what you're up to, Darlene. Jeff told me all about it."

"Jeff? What does Jeff know about me?" She didn't remember ever seeing Jeff at The Place. Was he there? Buying drugs? How did she miss him?

"He said he saw you at The Place, that drug den in Red Jacket. He was there last night gettin' a pizza for his kids, and he says he saw you goin' in the back door. Ever'body knows what goes on there, Darlene. Drugs! That is where all the druggies hang out."

"Dave, I don't know what Jeff told you, but I will tell you this. He better not be tellin' anything he sees at The Place. Those people don't mess around."

"You threatenin' me, Darlene? Threatenin' my family?"

"No. Dave, listen to me." Darlene softened her tone. "This is not a threat. I'm just tryin' to tell you. These are not people you want to be spreadin' tales about."

"Sure sounds like a threat to me. What you gonna do? Have your drug-dealin' boyfriend beat me up?"

Darlene was losing patience with him. "Whatever. Jeff's a liar. What was he doin' there? Buyin' drugs? Good reliable source you have there, Dave. Be sure you have the girls back tomorrow at noon." She hung up on him. "Jackass!"

CHAPTER EIGHT
Judgment Day

"It is better to risk saving a guilty person than to condemn an innocent one." — Voltair, *Zadig*

"No, Your Honor, I do not have a job." Darlene stood before the judge, answering his questions. Her attorney stood next to her.

"Yes, sir, I have attended college and need just one semester to complete my nursin' degree at Southern."

The judge called her attorney and Dave's attorney to the front, and Darlene sat down. While they whispered, she looked around the courtroom. The bailiff, an overweight young man, looked as though he could barely breathe in his too-tight shirt. He carried a gun, but Darlene doubted he would be up for much of a chase. She hoped he was a good shot. The judge sat on his throne. A U.S. flag hung on the right and the state flag on the left. His glasses were sitting on the tip of his nose as he read something Dave's attorney had handed him.

Darlene managed a sideways glance at the other table where Dave sat. With their attorneys out of the way, she had a clear view of him. He looked good. Better than she remembered. Next to Ray, he looked really young. Healthy. She knew it was not fair to compare them; Ray was twenty years older, and he had lived a rough life. Years of drug use. Two packs of Marlboros a day. Five years in prison. No, any comparison was unfair to Ray. She couldn't deny that Dave did look good. She had heard through the Matewan rumor mill he had been dating some woman from Delbarton who had a kid of her own. How had they ended up here? Enemies, fighting over their children. It wasn't supposed to be this way.

She was grateful to get to sit for a minute. Her new shoes pinched the pinky toe on her right foot. She placed her hands in her lap. Her new dress was soft, and she was glad her mother had insisted on buying it. It was blue with little yellow flowers, and modest. When she came out of the dressing room, her mother noted it was good for court and church—her passive way of telling Darlene she needed to go to church. Darlene had pulled her long red curls into a ponytail and tied it with a ribbon that matched the dress. She had gone easy on the makeup, wearing a bit of powder, blush, mascara and clear lip gloss. No eye shadow, and she had skipped the dark eyeliner she normally wore to accentuate her green eyes. She admitted to herself she looked fresh and sweet.

"Darlene, you must wear somethin' with sleeves to cover up that nasty tattoo on your arm. What on earth were you thinkin'? What provoked you to get a dirty tattoo? And for God's sake, get that bar thing out of your ear." Her mother's view of tattoos and piercings was that they were dirty and nasty. Darlene now wondered herself what had possessed her to get the first tattoo and piercings. She and Mickey had gone to Columbus with Ray for business again. Ray and Zip had gone to meet Sammy and some new guys for a drug deal and gave the girls $300 for food and drinks. Lunch and drinks at the bar across the street from the hotel seemed like a great idea. After lunch and several shots of tequila, they had stumbled next door to the Dragon Maiden Tattoo and Piercing Parlor. That had resulted in her first tattoo—an angel on her ankle—and several more piercings in her ears, five in all. In each ear. On the next trip, she got the tattoo on her arm.

Now as she glanced over at Dave, she wondered if he thought she looked nice and lady-like in her new dress. She certainly felt pretty and loved the new clothes, even if the shoes did pinch her toes. Dave sat staring straight ahead, never looking in her direction.

The attorneys returned to their tables, and the judge told her to stand again. Her attorney placed his hand on her elbow and helped her up. She stood there wringing her hands, listening to her lawyer prattle on about her "good qualities" and her dedication to her children. She had begged Dave to settle this without going to court, but he wouldn't discuss it. Now here they were with strangers deciding the fate of their children and whether she would be allowed to continue to be a mother. It was unfair that this old, angry, balding man in a black robe, a man who knew nothing about her, or Dave, or their kids, was going to make a decision that would affect the rest of their lives.

Her father knew the judge and had tried to talk to him about the case. Her father knew everyone in Mingo County involved in politics. His knowing people had gotten her out of a jam the previous month when she put her car in a ditch. She had been at Ray's partying all night. A few too many Lortab and half a fifth of vodka (with cranberry juice) later, she was relatively numb. It was 6 a.m. and the party was winding down. Finally. People were passed out on the couch, in chairs, on the floor.

She had needed to get home and shower, having to be at work by ten. It was hard to keep her eyes open, but she needed to for just six more miles. She would be home in ten minutes and could sleep for a couple of hours before work.

She remembered approaching the curve, but not much after that, until she hit the ditch. For a few seconds, she thought she was dreaming. She decided to walk back to Ray's. It was closer than home. She grabbed her purse and was locking the doors when she heard the pop of the siren and then saw the blue lights. The West Virginia State Police pulled in behind her.

She mumbled under her breath, "Shit, really? This is so not cool. Where did they come from?" It was hard to stand up without weaving. Perhaps she had hit her head in the crash? Maybe she had a concussion? She presented this conclusion to the cops. They were not interested in her self-diagnosis and decided that instead of an ambulance she needed a breathalyzer. She found this notion to be absurd; she had stopped drinking hours ago. She really needed to sit down, and without grace, she fell into the side of her car and slid to the ground.

She took the breathalyzer right there on the side of the road in Red Jacket. Sure enough, her blood alcohol level was .09. She couldn't believe it and accused the cops of rigging it. How could she be drunk? She had stopped drinking at three.

After booking, she got one phone call. As much as she hated for her father to find out about this, she had no choice. He was the only one she knew who could and would get her out of jail. He came and paid her bail, but he swore it would be the last time. She needed to get her life together and be more responsible.

After the accident, Darlene missed three days of work. Well, three more days of work. Then she was fired. Those three days of missed work, the DUI, and all the other missed days of work and coming in late nearly every Friday and Saturday for two months had been too much. If her father had gone to bat for her, she could have kept the job, but he was done. The accident and DUI were the final straw for him. He informed her that she was responsible for finding her next job. He would not risk his reputation again.

She also had to come clean about where she had been and who she had been with. Everyone knew Ray's reputation and the rumors about the drug dealing. She didn't come right out and tell her parents she was dating Ray, but they put it together. Her father didn't speak to her for two weeks after that.

If today's custody hearing hadn't involved the kids, his grandkids, he wouldn't have tried to help with this mess.

The rap of the judge's gavel echoed off the marble floor and walls and jolted her to attention. She didn't understand what he had actually decided. As her attorney was packing his files into his briefcase, she tugged on his arm, confused.

"What just happened? What does that legal mumbo-jumbo mean? I don't get to keep my kids? Dave gets to keep my kids away from me?"

"Yes and no. Dave has sole custody of the kids, and you get visitation rights. But you must be accompanied by one of your parents or someone else whom Dave deems acceptable. I am very sorry, Darlene. The evidence was just too overwhelming. The testimony from Dave's cousin was just too damning. Plus, the DUI and the car wreck last month, coupled with the fact you were fired, didn't help any."

"Jeff? That stupid oaf? He's a dirty liar. I admit, I ain't no angel, and I was there, but he is a liar. He didn't see me staggerin' in with two men. I was alone and straight. That's the truth," Darlene said as she recalled Jeff's version of what he saw at Ray's.

Jeff had never come to the back office. As far as she knew he was actually at the front to buy food. His testimony said he saw her staggering in the back door with two men. Jeff's testimony made it sound as though she was crazed on drugs and out of her mind. Ray had threatened to have Zip beat the shit out of Jeff and dare him to say anything. Darlene begged him not to. She was afraid it would make the custody battle worse. So now that Jeff was testifying in court about the goings on at The Place—truth or not—she was certain Jeff would meet Zip's fist very soon.

"If gettin' stoned makes me a bad mother, then half the damned county should have their kids taken away." Her voice was getting louder, and several people turned toward her as they filed out of the courtroom.

Darlene cried in her mother's arm while her father talked to Dave at the back of the courtroom. Darlene wondered what they were saying. Her father sided with Dave on everything. At that moment she really needed her father to be there for her. As usual, he was disgusted with her.

"When do I get to see my kids? I want to see them today. I want to tell them what's goin' on. I don't want Dave and his crazy mommy tellin' my babies I'm a bad mother. Mommy, we need to go to Dave's right away. Right now."

"Darlene, there are rules to your visitation," her attorney started explaining as he put his hand on her shoulder. "You can't see the kids on the spur of the moment. You need to make an appointment with Dave first and—"

"An appointment? An *appointment*? Are you serious? What're you talkin' about?" The lawyer's words were like a bolt of electricity. "An appointment to see my own kids?" She fell into the seat as her father came up to them.

"Darlene, Dave will take care of Amy and Renee. You don't need to worry about them," her father said in a stern tone.

She stammered through the tears. "That ain't the point, Daddy. I want to see my little girls, my children. Today! I want to explain this mess to them so they will understand it from me. *Me!* Not Dave, not you, not Mommy, but me. I don't understand why I don't get a choice as to when I can see my own children! What did I do that was so horrible? Nothin'! Dave's mommy is crazy. She takes Valium every day and gossips and hates everybody. Dave drinks and gambles and beats women. That's supposed to be a stable environment for my little girls? They're just little girls, five and six years old. They need their mommy. Please, dear Jesus, let me see my babies."

Her father's voice was icy. "Darlene, you already made your choices. You chose to go down a path that was sinful and wrong. Look at you! I don't even know who you are anymore. Tattoos, piercin's, drinkin', runnin' around with an ex-con who sells drugs. Little girl, your choices are what got you in this mess." He turned to Millie and told her he would be waiting in the truck and she needed to hurry up because he wouldn't wait long.

Darlene put her head on the table and sobbed. *Permission? An appointment? To see her own kids?* This was more than a little messed up. This was the worst day of her life. Finally she followed her mother out to the truck. The ride home was torture. Her father told her to stop crying and stop talking about how wrong the situation was. It was her own stupid fault. She supposed he was right. Her life was a disaster. She went straight to her bedroom and stayed there for the next three days, crying all day and all night. By the second day, she had cried until she was sick, and her mother found her in the bathroom at 1 a.m., throwing up what little bit she had eaten the previous day.

"Darlene, you can't keep doin' this to yourself. You need to get up and pull yourself together."

"Mommy, I just don't know what to do. What am I gonna do? I miss my girls. My life is a wreck. Daddy hates me. I don't have a job. What am I gonna do?" Darlene cried as she slumped onto the floor against her mother.

***

After three days of crying, Darlene decided to get out of the house. It was a beautiful, early spring day, and she wanted some sunshine and fresh air. She wasn't sure where she would go; she just wanted to drive. She hopped in her beat up Civic, rolled down the window, and lit a cigarette. Sitting at the end of the driveway for a few minutes, thinking about her destination, she realized her destination today was a lot like her life—directionless. She had no more of a plan for her life than she had for the drive.

She looked through a box of cassettes in the back seat and settled on a compilation of Merle Haggard's best that her mother had made for her the previous year. A live version of "I Can't Stop Loving You" started out the journey. She turned right out of the driveway towards Matewan. She sang along with Merle, "*...they say that time heals a broken heart...*" Darlene fought the urge to cry, realizing Merle may not have been the best choice for music. Perhaps something a bit more upbeat would have been better. The music fit the mood of the day, however, and she sang along, "*…so I'll just live my life in dreams of yesterday…*" as the wind tossed her hair and blew cigarette smoke around her face.

Darlene thought about going to Mickey's and getting stoned but decided that was the last thing she needed that day. Besides, she just didn't want to talk to anyone. She wanted to be alone with her thoughts or no thoughts. Just Darlene and Merle out for a drive. The cassette continued and Darlene kept singing, "Sing me back home, before I die."

***

Weeks passed, and Dave still wouldn't let Darlene see the girls. She was losing all hope. Dave was now as distant as a random stranger. He told Darlene the kids needed to adjust to her being gone before she could visit. He didn't want to confuse them anymore than they already were. She knew he was brainwashing them to hate her. His mother would make sure of it.

Each morning she confronted a mountain of anxiety and spent the days climbing over it. She had chewed her nails into bleeding nubs. Her stomach stayed in knots and most every meal resulted in puking or diarrhea. She had no other goal than to get her kids back. She was standing on the edge of a cliff of desperation and was sick of hearing Dave say no to her about visiting.

She would just go see them. She didn't need Dave's permission. She carried them for nine months. She gave birth to them. She earned the right to be their mother; he had not earned anything. *He was suddenly the hero because he worked and pretended to be a saint? No!* These were her little girls and she was going to see them.

She got up early and drove to Dave's parents' house, where he and the girls had been living. It was seven, and she looked a mess; she had jumped out of bed and put her hair in a ponytail without even brushing it. She had been up all night again, crying. Her face was red and swollen, and the smell of cigarettes clung to her. But she was straight. She had lost nearly ten pounds—ten pounds she didn't have to lose. She hadn't had any drugs or alcohol since the judge gave her kids to Dave and told her she would have to make an appointment to see them.

What bullshit that was.

After several knocks, Dave's mother opened the door and stood on the other side of the screen looking at Darlene like she was a nasty beggar. In that instant, Darlene realized how she must look, and she regretted not taking the time to shower and get dressed before coming here. Panic grabbed her from behind as she realized her kids would also see her looking like this and think the same thing she knew Dave's mother was thinking. They would not want to go with this ratty looking woman on the porch. Now who was the stranger? Her plan, if she really had one, to take the girls or at least talk to them, vanished.

"What are you doin' here? I got half a mind to call the police. Dave ain't here, so you need to leave."

"Betty, I just wanted to check on my girls." Darlene absent-mindedly tried to smooth down her hair. She gave up and jammed her hands in her jeans pockets.

"Well, you can't see 'em. They're sleepin'. It's barely seven, Darlene. What were you thinkin', comin' here all hopped up on drugs this early in the mornin'?"

"I'm not on drugs, Betty! I've been up all night cryin' over my babies. I've spent the last month cryin', actually. You're a mother. You must understand how I feel. I love my girls, and I just want to be a mother to them."

"I know nothin' about how you feel, Darlene. I'm a mother and you…you're a whore. A doped-up whore. So don't even compare our motherly instincts, 'cause you ain't got a clue, girl, what it takes to be a good mother and wife."

"I know I look a mess right now, and I don't want my girls to see me like this, but I just want to know they're okay.

Dave won't take my calls. He won't talk to me. He won't tell me nothin'. I'm sick wantin' to see my babies."

"They're fine, Darlene. They're loved and cared for in a way you could never provide. So go home and don't come back here, or I will call the police. Stay away or you'll never see these girls again. I'm their mommy now. Not you." She slammed the door in Darlene's face.

Darlene shuffled back to the car, crying. She felt as though she had been slapped. This could not be happening. They couldn't shut her out of her children's lives, could they? How on earth did this spiral out of control so fast and so completely? She got in the car and put her head on the steering wheel and sobbed. She looked up and saw Dave's mother looking out the window, shaking her head in disgust.

Darlene pulled onto the road into the path of an oncoming coal truck that was not about to slow down. She swerved to get out of its path, barely missed it, and ended up going in the wrong direction. She needed to turn around; instead she went to Mickey's.

Mickey was still sleeping, and Darlene pounded on the door for a good five minutes before her friend woke up and let her in. Darlene sat on Mickey's couch and cried for a full hour about her kids. She called her mother to tell her where she was and what she had done. She promised to be home soon.

The morning passed; the tears stopped flowing. Mickey's consolation consisted of several joints, two Lortab, and a couple of shots of vodka. Mid-afternoon, Millie called to see when Darlene planned to come home, and soon Millie was there to force Darlene home.

The next day there was hell to pay.

***

"Why would you hang out with Mickey, when that friendship is what got you in this mess in the first place? What are you thinkin', Darlene? You were doin' so good.

You'd been straight and sober for over a month. Ever since the custody hearin'."

"Oh, Mommy, it ain't that big of a deal. I left Dave's after his dear mother told me what a piece of shit I was and wouldn't let me see my girls and I was…she told me I wasn't their mother anymore, that she was! That ain't right, Mommy. That is some messed up shit."

"Darlene, you had no right to go there. And please stop usin' that foul language."

"I went to Mickey's because I needed a friend. I needed someone I could talk to."

"Well, with friends like that you don't need no enemies. That girl ain't no good, Darlene, and you need to stay away from her. She'll lead you to a no good end."

CHAPTER NINE
Home is Where the Drugs Are

"I am tangled up in contradiction. I am strangled by my own
two hands. I am hunted by the hounds of addiction."
— Andrew Peterson, Ben Shive, Andy Gullahorn, *"Hosanna"*

The custody hearing had taken a toll on Darlene. It had been
more than a month, and she still meandered through the days
and cried through the nights. Apologies to her parents had
become a mantra she repeated over and over. Her father
barely spoke to her, and she doubted their relationship could
ever be made right again.

She felt herself sinking back down into the gray ditch,
unable to see a way out. The shame of everything her life had
become was strapped to her back like a dead, rotting body.
The stench permeated her being, hanging in the air around
her. She hated herself and everything she had become.

She had lost her job, lost her kids, her parents were mad
at her, and she was about to lose Ray. It wasn't that she didn't
want to spend time with Ray and party with the gang; she
wanted things to go back to some kind of normal, if that life
could be labeled normal. But she needed to fix the mess that
had become her life and thought it best to stay clean for a
little while, in case she needed to take a drug test for the
custody issue or for a new job. Ray wasn't happy but said he
would be patient—for a while.

Ray couldn't understand why she wanted to work anyway.
He was ready to give her anything she needed—money, a

place to live, a car. Whatever she needed. Darlene didn't want to be dependent on him for everything, but now she feared she might not find another job. There weren't a lot of jobs in Mingo County for a young woman with no education and no experience—at least not any that paid well and had benefits. She was screwed, and she knew it. Her path grew narrower every day.

It was mid-April, and Darlene had been checking the want ads in the newspaper fervently. Nothing—nothing she was qualified for anyway. She decided to just go and apply in person at several places. Maybe applying in person would have a better impact if they could see her and talk to her face-to-face. She dressed as she had for the custody hearing—same dress and little makeup. She made sure her tattoos were covered, as her mother had recommended, and she set out early on Thursday morning. She put in applications at Food City, the Bank of Mingo, every store in the mall, Walmart and K-Mart. They all took her application, but no one was hiring. Walmart indicated they might be hiring in six to eight weeks.

Her last stop was the hospital. A tired, bored, overweight, mad-at-the-world woman took her application and informed her they were not hiring either. She glanced at Darlene's application, then informed her that even though she had attended nursing school, without finishing, she was wasting her time and the hospital's time by pursuing a job there. Hospital policy was to hold the applications for six months, but Darlene was certain the old biddy tossed her app as soon as she was out the door.

Her ever-faithful companions, disappointment and defeat, escorted her to her car. She was able to hold back the tears and anger until she was alone outside. The anger was at herself for being stupid and for letting Dave dictate her life for five years. Not finishing nursing school right away was a big mistake, and it was her mistake to live with. She had been stupid for allowing herself to get pregnant, which derailed her dreams and plans. She was smarter than this. When did her life go over the cliff? When did she become this stupid girl?

Which turn was the wrong one? Or were they all wrong? The drowning feeling was returning, only this time she was awake; the more she tried to find solid ground on which to stand, the more she got sucked down into the muck and mire of her life.

She sat in her car and cried for a long time. Maybe it was too late to turn her life around. There seemed to be so many obstacles in her path—money, a job, drugs, Ray. Maybe Ray was right; she should just let him take care of her. But then what? What happened if he broke up with her? Then she would have nothing and even fewer options. Did she want her claim to fame to be that she was the drug king's whore?

"Oh, sweet Jesus, help me. Help me out of this mess. Show me what to do. I need you." She laid her head on the steering wheel and cried. Her prayers had become more frequent and desperate since the custody hearing, but there seemed to be a stone wall between her and heaven.

On the way home, rain began to fall. Between the rain and tears she had a hard time seeing through the windshield.

Arriving in Matewan late in the afternoon, she drove past her parents' house. She wanted to see Ray. She missed him, but she also needed to get high. She just wanted to forget about everything. Maybe Ray *was* the answer, at least for a little while. He could give her money and would probably even give her money for school.

Mickey, Gabe and Lou were there. Everyone was surprised to see her. She had told Ray she would not be back until Friday. Lou seemed especially annoyed at her arrival.

"Baby, look at you all dressed up." Ray kissed her.

"How was the job hunt?" Mickey asked as she passed her a joint. "You find anything? Here, this might help. Hopefully, you didn't find a job that requires a drug test."

"Nobody's hirin'. It was rough and discouragin'. A wasted day. I really don't want to talk about it. I just need to kick back for a while. First, I need to call Mommy and let her know I won't be back right away." Darlene used the telephone in the bedroom and called Millie.

The afternoon became evening with people coming and going. Zip showed up later with two very young girls, and Darlene wondered if these were the two shown in the pictures she had found in Ray's desk drawer.

Later, it was just Darlene, Ray and Mickey. Darlene was still bummed and nervous about not being able to find a job. Mickey gave her two Xanax. She had taken Xanax before to come down off cocaine. Tonight she needed something to take the edge off. With the Xanax, Mickey offered a shot of vodka. And then another shot. And then another. And then another Xanax. After a liter of vodka between the three of them, Darlene could barely walk, but somehow she managed to get in her car around ten.

She didn't remember leaving Ray's. She didn't remember the drive home. She did remember she was barefoot when she left Ray's. She couldn't find her shoes and in a belligerent tirade accused one of Zip's girls of stealing them. Who would want to steal her shoes? Her feet were so small, who could wear them?

By the grace of God she made it home safely. Then she went off the rails.

***

Darlene had trouble remembering most of the details, but she would never forget the aftermath. What she did remember was coming in drunk. Her father hated when she was high or drunk, and she had the bad judgment to be both that night. She had fuzzy recollections of her father yelling at her about being high and how much he hated Ray. He blamed Ray and Mickey for her current troubles. Darlene reasoned, as best she could, that he had no right to bring Ray into their argument and told her father so—just before she tried to slap him. This led to more screaming from both of them, while Millie tried to calm the storm. Darlene remembered her father calling her a worthless, drugged up whore and adulteress, maybe not in that exact order. The last thing Darlene remembered was throwing a half-empty bottle of vodka across the living room. It was intended for her father's head but hit the fireplace mantle instead and shattered, throwing vodka and glass on the wall and carpet. At that point, her memory went completely black.

She must have eventually passed out. When she woke up the next day around noon, she went into the kitchen. Her father was sitting at the kitchen table with his .38. He told her to have a seat. She slowly sat in the chair across from him. His right hand was flat on the table beside the .38 and six bullets. He looked at her with a mixture of disgust and pain.

"I want you to look around this house—our home—and see all the damage you did last night. Then I want you to look at your mother and see what you are doin' to her. She's a wreck, and her hand is probably broke where you hit her. Then I want you to pack your stuff and get out and don't ever come back. If you try any of that crazy stuff you pulled last night, I will load this gun and shoot you. I won't tolerate your drugs and crazy ways anymore, Darlene. You gotta get outta here before you kill us."

"Where's she gonna go, Bill? She'll get destroyed." Millie's face was red and swollen from crying all night.

"She can go live with that low-life boyfriend of hers. She seems to like him so much. If he can give her all the drugs she wants, he can certainly put a roof over her head. I really don't care. She just ain't stayin' here. Besides, she's already destroyed anything that was the Darlene we knew and loved."

"Bill, she'll get destroyed with that man."

"That ain't our problem no more, Millie. We can protect you from a lot of things in life Darlene, but we can't protect you from yourself. You made your choice. You chose to do drugs and put them and that man before your kids and family. So, now you're free to go live that life. You're killin' us. Look at your mother. She's a nervous wreck constantly worryin' about you. Last night was the last straw. You won't do this to us. I won't let you."

Darlene was still a bit high and groggy and not totally sure of what she had done. Snippets of it floated at the front of her mind before dashing away and hiding behind the fog just out of reach, keeping her from grabbing them. When she started to apologize, her father told her not to bother; it wouldn't help matters. She stood and walked into the living room. Looking around, she was horrified at what she saw.

A hardness and sharp edges?

It looked like a tornado had blown through the living room. She must have thrown anything she could get her hands on—pictures, mirrors, a chair. Her grandmother's antique mantle clock was on the floor, shattered. Her mother had prized that clock and took pleasure in telling people the base was pure mahogany and had come all the way from London, England, via Chicago. It had been a gift to her grandmother from a lady in Chicago, for whom she had worked as a housekeeper. Darlene's great grandparents had moved to Chicago briefly to find work after they were married, but they eventually returned to West Virginia. Millie loved that clock. The mirror above the fireplace was shattered. Pictures were smashed. The antique rocking chair was on its side, and the right arm was in splinters. As Darlene walked through the room, she stepped in something wet; the broken bottle of Smirnoff was on the floor.

Crying, she stuffed her clothes into garbage bags to the mournful sobs of her mother. Darlene had never felt so defeated. What had she done? What on earth had caused her to do this? She tried to remember the night before and could only remember being with Ray and Mickey. Mickey had given Darlene Xanax. She took two of them. Or was it three? Then they decided they needed to have a few drinks and opened a bottle of vodka. After that, it was sketchy. She was not sure how she got home or why she would even go home. Obviously she had done it, and obviously it had turned very ugly.

The last thing she wanted was to hurt her parents. She loved her parents. She also loved getting high; she loved Ray, and she loved the life he offered her. She packed her things and went to Ray's.

***

"I need a place to stay. My daddy kicked me out." Darlene sat on the sofa in Ray's office and cried uncontrollably. She told him about the disaster she had created in her parents' living room. Nothing he said or did helped. But he was expecting a customer from Pikeville. It was a $10,000 buy, and he told Darlene she'd have to wait in the bedroom at the back of the office until the deal had gone down and everyone left.

She stayed in bed crying the entire day. She tried calling her mother, but there was no answer. She assumed they were avoiding her. What if they never spoke to her again?

She could hear Ray and the guys from Pikeville making their deal. There was a lot of laughing and negotiating on price. She could hear the voices of Ray, Mickey and others she didn't recognize. She assumed Zip was there; he never spoke, but he was always present for a big deal.

Darlene was losing hope fast. She was circling the drain and feared there was no way to stop her descent. She loved her parents so much and would never intentionally do anything to hurt them. But she had hurt them and was disgusted that she couldn't even remember what she had done. And that scared her. As much as she loved them and would never consciously hurt them, she had hurt them terribly. She vaguely remembered the fight, but certainly not the rage and destruction of what she had done to her parents' house. She never wanted to use drugs again. She despised herself and what she had become and realized she had hated herself for quite a long time. She wanted to die. She had nothing to keep her here. Her kids had Dave, and he had made it clear the girls didn't need her. They would forget about her soon enough. Better she die now and they remember her as something good, before they found out the truth later and hated her forever. Ray? Ray would have her replaced before he got home from the funeral—if he even went to the funeral.

There were enough pills in the bedroom to do the job. She was used to taking two Oxies at a time, so if she took fifteen or twenty, that should do the trick. Or she could get the gun from Ray's bedside table and shoot herself. She wasn't sure she would have the resolve to use the gun, so she returned her focus to the pills.

Then she thought of her mother. Her mother would be devastated. Her mother would never get over it. They might as well dig the grave both deep and wide; it would kill her mother. Thinking of her mother made her cry that much harder. Made her hate herself that much more for even contemplating the thought of hurting her mother more.

Darlene sat with her head on her knees. What was wrong with her? What had happened to her? She was divorced, homeless, and dating a married man who also happened to be the local drug lord. She spent most of her days high or thinking about getting high. How? How did this happen? She rolled over and cried herself to sleep.

***

She stayed at Mickey's place for a couple of weeks while Ray found her a place to live. He owned a few trailers and rental properties around town and just needed to kick someone out. He found her a place in North Matewan, a trailer he owned in the back alley, about a quarter-mile from her parent's place and a mile from the girls. The people he kicked out had left it a mess. She and Mickey spent a week cleaning it up. It took a lot of bleach, a lot of paint, and some repairs to holes in the walls. After they cleaned everything, Ray had new carpet and tile put in and let Darlene pick out all new furniture. She had never been so happy with a home. Maybe she *could* start over. Her new place was clean; it had a small yard and two bedrooms, so the girls could have their own room—if she ever got to see them again. She decorated their room in all their favorite colors. Ray gave her money to buy everything she needed—furniture, dishes, linens, curtains, everything. She was glad to finally have a place that was hers.

***

It had been weeks, and her parents would still not answer her calls. She called every day, sometimes two and three times a day. She tried to stay busy cleaning and decorating her new place.

After four weeks of not talking to her mother, she couldn't take it any longer and decided to go visit at lunch time, when she knew her father was at work. She walked in the back door through the kitchen. She and her mother had spent many afternoons in this kitchen talking, laughing, sharing, gossiping, giggling. This was their nest.

"Mommy! Mommy, it's me. Where are you?" Dolly Parton was playing in the living room and her mother was singing along "...*Jolene, Jolene, Joleeeeen, please don't take him just because you caaaaan.*" It must be cleaning day—Dolly blasting and the house smelling of a mixture of bleach and lemon Pledge. Her mother came into the kitchen, startled to see Darlene.

"Oh, honey, what are you doin' here? Your daddy'd have a fit if he knew you's here. You need to go, honey, before he gets home." Millie went into the living room and turned off the music.

"Mommy, please. I can't take it anymore. Why don't you answer my calls? I miss you, Mommy. I really, really miss you." Darlene started to cry. "Please don't make me leave, Mommy. I need you. I need for you to forgive me and love me again. I can't live without you, Mommy." Darlene hugged Millie tightly.

"Darlene, honey, I do love you. I will always love you, and nothin' will ever change that. You are my only child, and I would lay down and die for you. But what you did here that night is just unforgivable for your father. He's more than mad, and I ain't too sure he'll get over it."

"Mommy, please just let me stay for a minute and talk. I just need to be with you. I'm sorry. I'm so incredibly sorry for what I did. For everything. I love you and Daddy, and this is the only home I've ever known. You can't just shut me out and not ever speak to me again." Darlene sat down at the kitchen table and cried.

Millie went to her, wrapped her arms around her and held her head close to her chest. "Oh, baby. I love you. You know I love you and always will. You are my life. I will always be here for you." She took Darlene's face between her hands and turned it up to her. "But your daddy is another story. I don't know if he'll ever get over this. He loves you, but you went too far this time. Too far. Lord, your father would have a fit if he thought you's here. I can't stand to see you like this. If you come visit, it has to be when your daddy ain't here. So, you need to call first. If I don't answer, assume he's here, and I'll call you back when he's gone." Millie kissed the top of Darlene's head and sat down at the table with her.

Millie made lunch, and Darlene told her all about her new place. Millie promised to come visit. She wrote down Darlene's new telephone number and promised to call every day.

Darlene was glad she had gone to visit. She couldn't have taken one more second with her mother mad at her. Her father was a different story. It seemed he had been mad at her for years for one reason or another. She would just have to be patient.

***

It had been three full months since the custody hearing, and Dave finally agreed to let Darlene start seeing the girls. Visitation was based on Dave's rules, and there was no getting around them for now. He made it difficult for her at every turn. She could see them only at scheduled times, and it had to be at her parents' house with at least one of her parents present. She could not take the girls to her house for any reason. She could attend school functions, but she had to be accompanied by one of her parents. The custody rules were solid. Dave's lawyer had been cut-throat and had connections with the judge. Darlene's lawyer had tried to appeal the custody decision but was denied. He said they should wait a little while—six months to a year—and try again. A year seemed an eternity to Darlene.

Spending time with the girls was the most important thing in Darlene's life now, and she made certain to be straight and happy and on time for her scheduled dates with them. She got them every other Saturday, but no sleepovers. The routine was simple; her mother would go to Dave's parents', pick up the girls and bring them back to her house. Darlene would be there with gifts. They would do whatever the girls wanted to do. Movies, pizza, shopping, their choice.

Although Darlene's father didn't want her in his house again, he agreed to allow her there for the few hours she would spend with the girls every other Saturday. It was difficult, and the girls didn't understand why things were like this. She prayed Dave and his mother weren't trying to brainwash them against her.

***

Mommy Cat had been a birthday gift to Darlene from her grandmother. For the first few years, Darlene called the cat Princess, but then after Princess's third litter of kittens, she was just Mommy Cat. Darlene's dad was not pleased with having a cat around the house. In his mind, cats were useless creatures. They couldn't guard the house. They didn't fetch. They didn't get excited when you came home. They ate, meowed and slept. Over time he had grown to accept Mommy Cat, but he had never cozied up to her the way Darlene and her mother had.

Mommy Cat had many litters of kittens, all of which Darlene's dad insisted they give away. They had no trouble finding takers. Most people liked them to keep away mice.

It had been a few years since Mommy Cat had had a litter of kittens, and Darlene and Millie assumed she had passed that season of her life or she was just too tired to leave the back porch in search of a mate. So they were both surprised when they started noticing the pregnancy signs—a droopy belly, restlessness and her desire to come inside.

Amy and Renee were very excited about the impending birth of new kittens. They begged to take one or two of them home. Of course, Dave said no, not under any circumstances could they bring a kitten home. The girls were crushed, but Darlene promised they could keep the kittens at her parents', or she would take them home with her and bring them with her on their weekend visits.

The vet said Mommy Cat's age shouldn't present any problems in delivering the litter, but she might be more needy than usual and the kittens might be underweight, if they survived at all. Darlene prepared the girls for the possibility that none of the kittens would make it.

Mommy Cat's weight didn't help the situation. She had weighed in at a hefty eighteen pounds before getting pregnant, and she gained another four pounds during the pregnancy. Darlene and her mom kept a watchful eye on Mommy Cat and waited with great anticipation for the delivery. When the day arrived, Mommy Cat gave birth to three beautiful kittens. Two of them were twins looking just like their mother, and the other one was all black with bright green eyes.

The first two days were nip and tuck as all three kittens struggled to stay alive. Mommy Cat became distressed and then disinterested in the two that looked like her. On the third day, the twins died. After that, Mommy Cat began to shun the black kitten. Darlene's heart broke for the little guy. The girls loved him and were disappointed they couldn't hold him yet.

"Mommy, I don't understand why she's being so mean to the little kitty," Amy said. "She won't even let him feed. He's so little."

"I know," Darleen said. "He ain't much bigger than a jelly bean."

"Poor little Jelly Bean," Renee said. "We gotta find a way to make her feed him."

Eventually Mommy Cat relented and let the kitten feed. Darlene decided to take Jelly Bean home with her and take care of him as soon as he was ready to leave the nest. She promised the girls she would bring him with her every time they came to visit. He was part of the family now and loved being the center of attention.

When he was ready and strong enough to travel, Darlene took him home with her, stopping at the grocery store to buy him toys and kitten food. The first night he slept under the blanket right on top of her chest. Jelly Bean's love was unconditional; as he purred contentedly, they both fell asleep. She woke up the next morning and couldn't wait to introduce Jelly Bean to Ray. Later that afternoon, she packed Jelly Bean and a small fleece throw into a little cloth bag before setting off for The Place. Ray was in a dark mood when she entered the office. Jelly Bean was content and sleeping in the bag.

"I have somethin' that will put a smile on your face." Darlene opened the bag and told Ray to peek inside.

"What is it?" he asked and looked in the bag. "What is that? A cat? I hate fuckin' cats. Get that damned thing out of here." He punched at the bag, and Darlene jumped back.

"Stop! You'll hurt him. He only weighs two pounds. He's a newborn. Don't be so mean." She had seen Ray's nasty side before but never directed at her or something she loved.

"Get the fuckin' cat out of here, Darlene. Now!" Darlene knew he wasn't playing. She made sure Jelly Bean was okay and took him out to the car.

As the night wore on, Darlene went out several times to check on Jelly Bean. He was fast asleep each time. Ray became less angry, but he was snorting a lot of coke. Zip came in with a crew of young girls, and the party really got started. After a few hours, Ray started picking on Darlene and her lack of drug experience when he met her. Then he told Zip she had a cat in the car.

"Zip hates cats more than I do. He's probably drowned more cats than most people've seen." Ray took a hit off a joint. "Hates 'em."

Zip chuckled as they discussed a bag of kittens Zip had thrown into the Tug River during the past summer. Horrified, Darlene slipped out and went to her car to check on Jelly Bean. She would not put it past Zip to get the little guy and torture him just to impress his gaggle of tramps.

When Darlene checked the bag, Jelly Bean was a little ball of black fur, curled up and fast asleep. She wanted nothing more than to start the car and go home and snuggle with the little guy. A quiet night in front of the TV with a pizza and Jelly Bean sounded wonderful. But she knew Ray would have a fit if she left. The party was just starting. She was also afraid if she left now, he would hook up with one of Zip's tramps, and the thought of that made her decide to stay as long as needed. She would come out and check on Jelly Bean every hour or so. Just to be sure Zip didn't bother him, she locked the car doors and put the key in her pocket.

Darlene knew Zip was capable of anything. He hurt people just for sport; she could only imagine what he would do to a defenseless little kitten.

Zip was polite enough to Darlene, but he kept his distance. He did whatever Ray wanted and was paid in cash and all the drugs he could do. It was more than money and drugs, though; it was almost like worship on Zip's part. Being Ray's number one henchman gave him the illusion of power, and he thought he was invincible. He rode shotgun on most of the drug trips and was always around when Sammy came to town. When anyone got on Ray's bad side, Ray sent Zip to take care of them. Ray was afraid to go back to jail and wanted to keep his hands clean, so Zip was his go-to guy for beatings and shaking up anyone stupid enough to cross Ray. Everyone knew it, and everyone stayed away from Zip.

Zip had a revolving door of women, nothing more than drug babes, who hooked up with him for the ensuing drug fest. It was certainly not for his charming personality or stimulating conversation. He barely said four words any time Darlene saw him. He seemed to be a step off all the time, but when Ray wanted something, he was a different person. He had actual conversations with Ray and made sure Ray got what he wanted.

Darlene had decided after the first few weeks of dating Ray to just speak to Zip and go on. She tried to have a conversation with him a few times, but he just mumbled his response and walked away. At first Darlene thought he was being rude, but then she realized Zip had changed since his accident.

The scary Zip had come out to play one Saturday night when two young guys from Belo came in to buy drugs. Kids, probably no more than nineteen years old. One was tall and skinny with flame-red hair. The other was a little chunky, nerdy-looking kid, the brains of the outfit. They had been sent by a friend of a friend. Ray didn't know them; Zip didn't know them. No one in Ray's circle knew these guys. Ray was paranoid about strangers and being set up; he thought everyone was out to set him up. These two fools thought they could just walk in and lay their $100 on the table and walk out with weed and coke. They thought it would be that easy. They had no clue what they were walking into. Darlene thought they were just innocent kids looking to get high. Ray thought otherwise.

Ray questioned them: "Who sent you? Why are you here? How did you find out about me?"

Nerd kid answered all the questions. Red just stood there, looking more out of place by the minute. They rattled off some names of people who told them where they could get hooked up with some weed and coke. Ray pretended he didn't recognize these names, never heard of them. Nerd kid offered to call them, if that would help.

Ray laughed at them. Maybe he didn't know who sent them. Maybe he did. Either way, what happened next scared Darlene to her core.

A hardness and sharp edges? No…this was evil.

Zip grabbed Red and threw him into the wall; the boy dropped to the floor with a thump. Zip held a knife to Nerd kid's throat and told him he better be coming up with some better names of who sent them. The Belo kids were terrified. Nerd kid wet his pants, standing right there in the middle of the room with the knife to his throat. Zip was determined to beat them into admitting they were lying, even if they weren't. He punched Nerd kid in the face and something snapped. Most likely his nose and probably a few teeth.

Red was still trying to stand up, and Zip kicked him in the stomach, in the face, in the groin, in the ribs. Both kids were bleeding…a lot. They were crying and begging. Finally, Red just lay there, staring at the wall, not moving.

No one in the room breathed. They all sat, not moving, afraid they would be next if they said anything. Zip was going for Nerd kid again and Darlene couldn't take it anymore. She jumped up and begged Zip to stop. He ignored her as always. She turned to Ray and told him to do something, to stop Zip before he killed them. Finally, Ray called off Zip, as he would a junkyard dog on the attack.

Red was still not moving, his eyes just fixed on the wall, with tears and snot and blood running down his face. Nerd kid begged for his life. "Please don't kill us, please don't kill us."

Darlene started to help them, but Ray grabbed her arm and told her to stay put.

When Zip had his fill, he picked up the kids one at a time and tossed them out the back door. There was a puddle of blood and piss where the kids had dropped on the floor. She tried to watch from the window to make sure they got in their car. Again Ray held her back and made her sit down and mind her own business. She was dumfounded and scared. She had never witnessed anything so brutal, and the frightening part was that it was just for sport. Ray needed to make an example of some pitiful, innocent fool from time to time. The Belo kids were victims of their own bad timing and innocence.

Ray made Gabe clean up the mess on the floor, and the party continued as though nothing had happened. Just another Saturday night at The Place.

The images had haunted Darlene for weeks. She knew if Ray would do this to a stranger for no reason, he would do worse to anyone who crossed him. She was glad she was on his side. All the same, she would keep Jelly Bean away from these crazy cat-haters.

CHAPTER TEN
Motor City Shakedown

"…fools detest turning from evil." — Proverbs 13:19

Darlene packed her overnight bag; she was going with Ray to Detroit to make a drug run. She had never been to Detroit and was excited. It was going to be a long ride, and Mickey and Zip were joining them.

Zip drove; Ray rode shotgun. Mickey and Darlene were in the back. They'd both had a line of coke before they left. Ray was becoming more paranoid with each drug run they made and would no longer allow alcohol or pot in the car during runs, in case they got pulled over. It was too hard to hide, and cops could smell it. They could do all the coke they wanted and all the pills they needed. And so they did.

It was an eight-hour drive, through Huntington, then on to Columbus and north to Detroit. It seemed like a lifetime to Darlene. She was wired up on the cocaine, and being trapped in the back seat of Ray's Suburban was not the best situation. She could barely sit still. They seldom stopped—gas and restroom twice, and once for food.

She asked Ray about the Detroit connection, but he wouldn't provide a lot of detail, saying it was some people he knew from prison. He had maintained the contact over the years, and now they were doing business together. Unlike with Sammy, who dealt mostly in cocaine, the shopping list for this trip consisted of OxyContin, Vicodin, Lortab and

Xanax. More and more people were wanting pills, and there was more money to be made.

When they arrived, they went to their hotel and checked in. It was 3 a.m., and they were exhausted. They were planning to meet Ray's friends in the afternoon, when they would get the stuff and head home. Ray instructed everyone to get some sleep, especially Zip, who needed to drive them home and be ready if anything bad went down.

Eight hours of cocaine had Darlene wound up. When they got to their room, they smoked a couple of joints, and Ray gave her two Xanax. She was reluctant to take the Xanax, afraid she would black out again as she had the time she destroyed her parents' living room. Ray assured her it was the Xanax and vodka combination that had sent her over the edge. Darlene was glad Ray had gotten separate rooms for Mickey and Zip.

Darlene had never seen Ray so jumpy and nervous. He had never bought from these people and didn't trust them. Also, he was nervous about driving eight hours back to Matewan with $30,000 in pills loaded in the back of the Suburban.

The Detroit dealer showed up at the hotel as scheduled and made his way to Room 314. There were three of them, and they were scary-looking characters with guns and grills and facial tattoos. Ray greeted the one he knew, and waited for him to introduce him to the other two thugs. They discussed the quantity, the money and the best way out of town. Ray checked the pills and had Mickey check also. Zip stood in the corner leaning against the wall near the bathroom. Darlene sat in the chair not saying anything. The Detroit-Three counted the money.

After the deal was done they discussed the next run. Ray preferred to meet half way or have them bring the pills to him. This was a long trip with too many chances for something to go wrong. With a few tense moments of haggling, the Detroit-Three agreed to deliver the next load to Ray in Matewan.

After the deal was done the Detroit-Three left. Zip, Mickey and Ray took their bags and went out the back door to the car while Darlene went to the front desk and checked them out. Constantly checking the side view mirror and looking around to make sure they weren't followed, Ray was a ball of nerves until they were out of the city limits. Once they were on the Interstate, he started to calm down. There was no drug use on the way back and very little conversation.

What conversation did take place on the ride home centered on how to do this more efficiently. Ray refused to drive eight hours to make a deal. If they wanted him to sell their stuff, they needed to bring it to him or he could hire mules to make the run. He had shopped around; he knew the price the Detroit boys offered couldn't be beat, and they could provide the quantities he needed.

Zip told him about the people running to Florida to get prescriptions filled and then bringing the pills back and selling them. The competition was heating up with everybody trying to sell pills. Ray's strategy was just to be a better businessman than the local thugs with a few hundred pills to unload. He would move mass quantities and lower the price in hopes of killing the competition. Then Ray wondered why he couldn't send his mules to Florida, get fifteen or twenty prescriptions each, which should make the price per pill cheaper. He was concerned he couldn't find enough mules he could trust to do the job.

The problem was that everyone was on pills now, and no one could be trusted to make it from Jacksonville to Matewan without consuming the merchandise before they got back. Cocaine was quickly being out-paced by pain pills. Seemed like most people were just one prescription away from being an addict. Opiates were certainly easier to get and cheaper than cocaine. And a lot more addictive.

OxyContin was hillbilly heroin, and people were doing all sorts of crazy things to get it. Home robberies were common. The users would check the obituaries for funerals, case the house when everyone left for the funeral, and then rob the house for any drugs the dying person may have left behind.

Elderly people and those dying of cancer were prime targets. The druggies would stalk the cancer patients as they left the oncologist's office, follow them home and rob them. They had OxyContin and morphine patches and typically couldn't fight back.

Zip's cousin had been arrested in Charleston for stealing a bottle of OxyContin from someone's house. His cousin and his girlfriend had been hitting every real estate open house in town. They'd pretend they were interested in buying. Then they would hit the bathrooms and bedrooms, looking for prescription bottles; when they found pills they would empty the bottles into his girlfriend's purse. They had a pretty good thing going until they got caught. The last house they visited had nanny-cams set up in nearly every room. They had been arrested within a week.

The ride home from Detroit seemed longer than the ride up. Darlene was anxious to get back to her new place and be alone. She longed for the quiet of her home and her new clean sheets. She missed Jelly Bean.

***

Even though Ray was reluctant to go back to Detroit, he made one more trip a few weeks later. He needed cocaine. Sammy couldn't deliver, and the Detroit-Three could; they just couldn't bring it to him. So he and Zip made the trip alone. Ray and Zip returned from Detroit around 1 a.m., with Ray insisting again this would be his last trip to Detroit. If those punks wanted to sell to him, they would have to bring it to him. The trip was too long and too risky. He wouldn't take the chance again.

Darlene had never seen so much dope. The haul consisted of five kilos of cocaine and 2,500 Oxies. The risk of going to Detroit was high, and he was determined to make it worth the effort. He had been prepared to buy five kilos, but the Detroit guys didn't have that much and couldn't get it.

Once they got inside the back office with the drugs, they locked the doors into the restaurant and to the outside. Ray insisted they try the goods and cut out five lines, one each for himself, Darlene, Mickey, Zip and Gabe. Then he cut another and then another.

Ray wanted to move the stuff as soon as possible, so they got out the scales and prepared the production line. He had almost $60,000 wrapped up in the stuff and wanted to get his money back quickly. It was August, and he planned to triple his money before September. With any luck, he could move it in a couple of weeks. Business was booming.

They cut the cocaine with something called procaine. Darlene had no clue what the stuff was, but she, Mickey and Gabe had gone to the head shop in Charleston earlier that day to buy it. She had never helped prepare the coke and was impressed with the production and exactness Ray insisted on. They weighed out a certain amount of cocaine and then added the procaine, then bagged it up: 1/4 grams, 1/2 grams, grams, and eight-balls. It was a big job, and they worked all night to complete the task.

When it was all bagged up, they loaded it into Ray's safe. It was noon the next day before they started winding down. They all took a few Xanax and smoked a lot of pot and eventually went to sleep—Ray and Darlene in the bed, Zip passed out on the couch, Mickey in the recliner and Gabe on the loveseat.

***

Ray had Zip, Gabe and Mickey get the word out on the street that there was a new load available. It was Friday night, and within hours there was an onslaught of activity in the restaurant and the back office.

The back office was full of people, the regular gang and a slew of customers. Darlene was busy going back and forth to the office to bring out the coke and pills. Ray was getting nervous about the number of people in the office and tried to keep it to no more than two customers at once. Ray was always paranoid, but nights like tonight made him more anxious than usual.

Over the previous few months, Ray had been moving larger quantities of drugs. In turn, his paranoia was increasing, and he was taking ever more precautions to ensure his security. In addition to drugs, he had purchased new guns from Sammy a couple of months earlier. Ray had guns stashed all over the office and kept a 9mm strapped to a shoulder holster he wore all the time. He kept a .38 in the desk drawer, a semi-automatic rifle in the bedroom, a switchblade in his boot and several guns in his car. Zip also carried a Glock at all times. Gabe carried a .38, and Ray insisted Mickey start carrying a .38. Ray had shown Darlene where all the guns and knives were stashed, and he showed her how to use the guns. Ray hoped she never had to use them because she would probably end up shooting herself in the foot.

Ray had new doors installed to the office. The back door was made of steel with a reinforced frame and an industrial-type lock that consisted of a bar that went over the width of the door and locked into a slot. There was a deadbolt at the top of the door and one at the bottom. The door from the office into the restaurant was also made of steel and had a deadbolt at the top and one at the bottom. Ray had security cameras installed all over the place—the restaurant, the back office, the bedroom, outside. He was able to monitor anyone coming and going 24/7.

Since Ray started dealing with the Detroit-Three, he was on edge more than usual. He didn't trust them and was concerned they might take him for a stupid hillbilly and try to rob him. He insisted they come to his turf for future deals. He needed to be in control of the situation.

With his increased paranoia, he was using more cocaine. Every morning started with a line of coke and five, 10mg

Lortabs. This was almost always followed by a cocaine afternoon and evening. Now that he was using cocaine daily, he needed more pills to sleep and had also become impotent. He had started trading coke for Viagra and Trazodone. Initially, the Trazodone helped him come off the cocaine binges and get some sleep. But now that he was using daily, he needed Trazodone every night. He took the Viagra every day he knew Darlene would be there. He convinced himself it was just the cocaine that created the need for the Viagra and *he* wanted to have sex. He would never admit he was impotent and feared losing his young little thing if he didn't keep her happy in bed.

Ray was glad to be back from Detroit. He hated that nasty city. He had spent a few summers there when he was a kid. He and his mother went for the month of June from the time Ray was in third grade until sixth grade. Ray figured out later that his father sent them away for a month so he could be with his mistress.

The man who was Ray's prison connection was about 50 years old. The two men knew some of the same neighborhoods, but none of the same people. Ray trusted the guy enough to do business with him, but the kids working for him seemed like trigger-happy street punks trying to be cool and establish their street cred. They were thugs, and Ray didn't like them and certainly didn't trust them.

He made it clear this trip would be his last, and they would need to bring any further deliveries to him. He was the customer. He knew it was a matter of time before they tried to rip him off. He would show them just what a stupid hillbilly he was when he went all Mingo on them. He still needed their drugs, but he would be in control of the situation from now on. They had the pills he needed. He would get all the cocaine from Sammy. He and Sammy had an understanding.

He had another $60,000 invested in this run and wanted to move it fast. Selling eight-balls was not the way to go. He wanted to sell big quantities. He wanted his operation to be a hub for anyone wanting to buy mass quantities of coke and pills. He had big plans, which included controlling everything from the tri-state area and south to the Georgia-Florida border. This nickel-dime stuff was too risky. There were too many people showing up all at once. He needed to get a handle on it. Having more than three buyers in the office at once made him nervous. It was Zip's job to get this under control.

He took Zip into the bedroom. "Man, you gotta get these people outta here. There's too many people. Half of 'em I don't even know. This is gettin' outta hand. Other than the regular crew, I don't want no more than five people at a time, and they need to come in, buy what they want, and get the hell out. Take care of it."

***

Zip agreed with Ray. It *was* getting out of hand. Most of the people in the office were just looking for a free line of coke and thought they could stay all night and get high on Ray's dime. Not so. He was going to kick them all out. He left the bedroom and went back to the office. He looked around and told those who had already purchased to get out. Then he stood at the door and monitored who went in and who went out. When he opened the back door, he was surprised to see a line of people—eight thick. This was crazy.

Darlene was talking to several of the people he was trying to push out the door. She was inviting them to stick around, and he was trying to kick them out. She was such a user. She was with Ray for drugs and a free ride. She didn't *do* anything. She didn't work, she didn't sell, she didn't do anything 'cept blow Ray and get high. She had worn out her welcome, and Zip figured she had lasted a lot longer than most and would be gone soon enough.

CHAPTER ELEVEN
Something Borrowed, Something Blue

"Three things cannot be hidden: the sun, the moon, and the truth." — Buddha

Dave wanted the girls to be with him for Labor Day weekend. Actually, he insisted. He said it was important, and unless Darlene wanted to miss her visit this month, she needed to switch. First, she had to deal with Ray. Ray was going to Columbus the weekend before Labor Day to visit Sammy. He needed to load up on cocaine for the Labor Day weekend, and he was furious that Darlene wasn't going with him.

"What's wrong with that son-of-a-bitch ex-husband of yours? Why does he get to call all the shots where your kids are concerned? I've half a mind to kick his ass."

Darlene knew this really meant Zip would kick Dave's ass. "Ray, no. Please don't say stuff like that. I'd never get to see my girls if you did anything to him. Just leave it be. You can just go without me. This way, we can spend Labor Day weekend together, and I can be here to help out. You know it'll be crazy busy."

"Yeah, I guess you're right. I still don't like it, and I don't expect it to happen again."

Darlene felt pulled in all directions—her kids, her parents, Dave's demands, Ray's demands. She couldn't please everyone; she kept trying, but it was getting harder and harder. Everyone wanted something she couldn't provide. Everyone had expectations she couldn't deliver.

The girls came the Saturday before Labor Day weekend. Dave dropped them off at Darlene's parents' and said he would be back at eight to pick them up. Darlene could get them again on Sunday after church, but they had to be home by seven. More of Dave's rules and regulations. She nodded at his demands and herded the girls inside.

It was a rainy day, so they decided to stay in and make pizza and cookies. The girls were placing green peppers and onions on the cheese. "Mommy, you should see our dresses for the weddin'," Renee said.

Amy shot Renee a stern look and elbowed her. "We ain't suppose to say nothin' about that. We agreed we wouldn't hurt Mommy's feelin's."

"About what? What weddin'? Who's gettin' married?" Darlene asked.

Renee dropped her eyes and started tearing up. "I'm sorry, Mommy. I wasn't supposed to say nothin'. I'm sorry if I hurt your feelin's."

"Oh, baby. It's okay." Darlene went over and kissed Renee's cheek. "My feelin's aren't hurt. Who's gettin' married?"

The girls looked at each other and would not look at Darlene. "Girls? Come on. You can tell Mommy." Darlene's heart was pounding hard. Certainly it wasn't what she thought.

"Well, Mommy, if you promise not to get upset," Amy said.

"I promise."

"Daddy and Caroline are gettin' married next weekend. That's why we had to switch our weekend with you," Amy said.

"Me and Amy are in the weddin'. We get to be flower girls. Our dresses are real pretty, Mommy." Renee wanted to tell Darlene all about their dresses and the wedding.

"Oh, really? When did this happen? How long have they been plannin' this?"

"Just a little while, Mommy," Amy said. "Not long at all."

Darlene went to the refrigerator to get more cheese for the pizza. "Well, good. Good for Daddy." Darlene wanted to run from the room and cry, but she had to just put that aside. The girls would be crushed if they thought they had hurt her feelings.

"So, you'll be livin' with Daddy and Caroline?"

"Yep. We get our own rooms. Daddy bought a new house," Renee said.

"Wow, that's excitin' stuff. Where's the new house?" Darlene choked out.

A house? He bought that bitch a house? I lived at the head of a fuckin' holler in a used trailer, and he bought her a house?

"Taylorville. So, we'll be changin' schools. I ain't too excited about that. I won't get to see any of my friends or anything, Mommy," Amy said.

"Oh, baby, you'll make new friends. You'll still have the same friends at church. It'll be excitin'." Darlene wanted to throw up.

"Well, maybe. I don't like Jeremy *at all*. He's a bully and mean," Amy said.

"Jeremy? Is that Caroline's son?"

"Yep. He is a total jerk face," Renee said as she placed cheese on the pizza.

"Hmm…I see. Well, I'm sure your daddy will take care of him if he gets outta hand."

"Mommy, why can't we come live with you? If we live with you, we won't have to change schools. We can make pizzas and cookies every night. We can help with Jelly Bean. Please?" Amy asked.

"Baby, hopefully you can real soon. We just gotta wait a little while."

"Caroline can't cook, Mommy. She's a terrible cook!" Renee covered her eyes with her hands and shook her head.

This news made Darlene smile. She knew if she was good at anything, it was cooking. Her mother had taught her well.

She had known this day would come; she hadn't expected it to come so soon. Married. He was really getting married and would raise *her* girls with another woman. *They* would provide the nurturing, loving home for her girls that she wanted to provide. He was such a coward. He couldn't tell her himself; he knew the girls would tell her, and he let them. She didn't care that Dave was getting married, yet a heavy disappointment settled in her heart. She had played the story over and over in her mind where she herself had lived happily ever after with Dave and there were no more beatings and no more drugs and no more controlling. But that story was a lie, a fantasy. They had made their choices; she just wished they had considered the girls before destroying everything. Now she had to live with the reality that this woman—this stranger—would be helping raise her girls, would be with them every day and experience those things that only mothers should share with their daughters.

At eight sharp, Dave pulled in and blew the horn. Darlene went out alone to talk to him about his upcoming nuptials.

"Dave, the girls tell me you're gettin' married? Don't you think you should have told me this before you dropped the girls off? I was completely caught off guard."

"Oh, well, I didn't think I had to clear it with you, Darlene."

"That's not what I mean, and you know it. They had questions I couldn't answer, and I was totally unprepared for the news. They were worried about sayin' anything and hurtin' my feelin's, so when they told me, it was a bit uncomfortable."

"Well, poor you. Sorry if my new wife makes you uncomfortable."

"You're such a jackass—uncomfortable for *them*, not me! You just can't help it, can you? You think everything revolves around you. I don't give a shit what you do, who you sleep with, who you marry, what women you beat on a regular basis. What I care about is my girls, and I don't want them thinkin' they can't talk to me about important things in their life—like their daddy gettin' married…and to a woman who can't cook to save her ass."

"Well, if they have questions about it, they can ask me. I'll take care of it."

"Whatever, Dave. You'll always be a jackass! I'll get the girls." Darlene threw their bags in the truck and went inside. She kissed Amy and Renee goodbye and told them she would see them after church.

***

Ray was pissed that Darlene had kid duty. He expected and needed her to go with him to Columbus. Why this weekend? What was that stupid ex-husband of hers up to? Why did he need to change weekends? Ray thought about having Zip teach him a lesson and would have, but he didn't need that heat coming down on him. He would let it go this time.

Darlene would be with her kids Saturday and Sunday. Ray decided to leave for Columbus early Saturday morning and return the same day. He would take Zip and Mickey with him, and they would be back in time for the evening rush.

They made the trip in record time. Ray wanted to get what he came for and get the hell back to Mingo County. Not liking to take a back seat to anybody—especially Darlene's ex-husband—Ray was in a foul mood. He was king, and he expected to be treated like one. He was good to that little bitch, and she needed to treat him with respect. He would let it slide this time, but she would pay.

They had been back for about an hour when Lou came in. Mickey had gone home to shower and change clothes, and Zip was in the restaurant eating. It was just Lou and Ray in the office. He had admired her big tits for quite some time now. She didn't have much of anything else that excited him, though. Her face was okay. Her hair was too short, and she had no ass. She had been coming on to him for a year. Problem was she was always with her husband. But not today. Here she was all by her lonesome.

"Hey, Ray. Where is everybody?"

"Mickey went home, Zip's eatin', Darlene's with her kids this weekend."

"Oh, really? Well, good. I'm glad to finally have you all to myself."

Ray told her to have a seat. He locked the back door, went into the restaurant and told Zip to make himself scarce for a bit.

He returned to the office and Lou. She was wearing a red tank top and no bra. Those tits sure looked good. He was mad at Darlene, and this was a golden opportunity he would not pass up. He might not have this chance again.

He and Lou did a line of coke and went to the bedroom. Thirty minutes later they came back out. He told her to keep her mouth shut if she wanted more. It would be their little secret.

The telephone was ringing when they came back into the office. "Yeah?"

"Hey, baby. It's me. When'd you get back?"

"Oh, just a few minutes ago."

"How'd it go?"

"Fine. We just went and straight back. No lollygaggin', just business. We'll cut it and bag it up tomorrow."

"I miss you. Did you miss me today?"

"Sure, baby. Sure, I miss you." Ray slipped his hand underneath Lou's tank top and gave her a wink.

"Well, is everything okay? You sound strange."

"Nope. All's just dandy here. Well, listen, I gotta scat. People are startin' to line up here." Ray hung up and kissed Lou. Then he went to let Zip know it was okay to come back into the office.

***

She had finally done it. She had slept with Ray. It was over a lot quicker than she wanted, but he had to get back to business and people would be coming in soon. Didn't matter; she got what she wanted.

Fuck you, Darlene! I had your man, and I will have him all weekend.

Lou had dropped her kids off at her mother's and planned to spend the night right here with Ray. Good thing Doug had decided to go fishing this weekend. She couldn't wait for him to leave. He got on her nerves more every day.

Ray wanted to keep their little thing a secret. She could do that. She would just need to be careful and not say anything. She decided not to drink too much, for fear that she would spill the beans. She had a tendency to talk too much when she was drunk.

CHAPTER TWELVE
Tell Me Something Good

"…it won't be long before she's gravel in your mouth, a pain in your gut, a wound in your heart." — Proverbs 5:4

"Darlene?"

"Yeah? Who wants to know?" Darlene looked at the unfamiliar man leaning against a black SUV. Another man was gassing up the vehicle.

It was not often that strangers in Matewan knew Darlene, and she was on guard immediately. Ray had instructed her to be careful when she was out and not to be out talking about his business in public, because people listened.

She reasoned the guys could simply be out-of-towners here to ride the trails. Someone inside the Gas 'n' Go may have told them she could hook them up with drugs. She continued to watch the gas pump as the numbers spun around like the numbers on a slot machine.

"Darlene, my name's Dan, and this is John." He pointed to the man holding the pump. "I understand you're a good friend of Ray's."

"Ray? Ray who?" Darlene looked at him. "Who are you and what d'ya want?"

"Come on, don't play dumb. We know who you are." Dan removed his sunglasses and hooked them on his shirt collar. "Darlene, Ray's in way over his head. He's potentially looking at some big trouble. We want to help you not be a part of that trouble."

"What kinda trouble? I don't know what you're talkin' about. Ray's just a guy I know. I eat at The Place sometimes and hang out with my friends there. That's all. We ain't friends."

"Now, Darlene, we know he pays your bills. He takes you on trips to Columbus and Detroit about once a month. We know what those trips are for, and you are an accessory to a crime. To several crimes, actually."

"You're crazy, mister. Ray has a wife and a couple of kids. He don't pay nothin' for me, and I've never been to Columbus or Detroit." Darlene absentmindedly started chewing the nail on her left thumb.

"Darlene, we have pictures and video of all this," Dan said as John tossed an envelope on the top of her car. Darlene froze and just looked at the envelope without taking it. She returned the gas nozzle back to the pump and replaced her gas cap. She turned back to Dan and took the envelope from the top of the car and sat down in her passenger seat.

Dan hadn't lied. He did have pictures of Darlene and Ray kissing; Ray leaving Darlene's trailer at North Matewan; Darlene and Ray in Columbus and Detroit; Darlene and Ray with Sammy, in Sammy's Jaguar; and Darlene, Ray, Mickey, Zip, Sammy and some other guys at the strip club in Columbus. Darlene felt sick to her stomach and was afraid she would get sick right there in the passenger seat of her car. So the Feds had been watching them. Ray had told her they had approached him about ratting on Sammy and a few other dealers. It never entered her mind they would come after her.

"What you want with me? So what, I date a married man. Is that such a crime?"

"No, that is not such a crime. Immoral, yes, but we're not here to judge you on that or your poor taste in men. Being a conspirator to buy, transport and sell illegal narcotics is such a crime. You could be looking at five to ten years in prison, Darlene, for trafficking drugs. This is pretty serious stuff. I guess you need to ask yourself if you love Ray enough to do time for him. Maybe never see your little girls again? We tried to talk to Ray and get his cooperation to provide info on his connections, but he isn't being very cooperative."

As she sat frozen in her car looking at the pictures, she was getting sicker, and her stomach started churning. She *could not* go to prison. She would never see her girls again. She *could not* rat on Ray either. Maybe they wanted her to rat on Sammy. Sammy was a scary character who would kill her and her entire family if he thought she was working with the FBI.

"Now Darlene, this is pretty simple. We just want some info on Ray and his connections. We play this right, and no one will know you were the one providing info. We might even be able to help you with that nasty custody issue with your ex-husband."

Dan gave her directions and told her to follow them and park her car so they could talk where people weren't watching everything.

Knowing she was going to be sick, Darlene ran into the ladies' room of the Gas 'n' Go as Dan and John drove away to the designated meeting spot. She still felt queasy as she drove to meet them. She kept wondering what kind of videos they must have since they had those pictures. How could she get out of this mess? How could she tell her mother? Her father would completely disown her with no chance of reconciliation. What about her children? She had a hard enough time getting to see them once every two weeks. If she went to prison or even got in trouble with the law, Dave would never let her see her babies again.

She arrived at the designated spot, parked her car and got into the Tahoe. As John drove them around to Williamson and back up the Kentucky side, Dan explained to her what would be involved. She listened. As they threatened her with prison, she listened. They wanted her to wear a wire and go into Ray's and act as though all was normal. Get Ray to talk about Sammy and the other dealers from Detroit, get him to name names.

She couldn't do this.

"Well, first of all I can't wear no wire. He'll know immediately. He's always touchin' me and huggin' me and feelin' me all over. He would know in two seconds. What other bright ideas you got?" Darlene's hands shook as she lit another cigarette.

"Well, then, you'll just need to feed us information daily. We can meet or you can call or both. We'll be watching you and him, so we won't be far away," Dan said.

"He doesn't tell me details. I swear. He just shows up and tells me to get ready 'cause we're goin' on a field trip. That's what he calls it, a 'field trip.' He never tells me ahead of time. He just shows up, and we go. I never ask about this stuff. If I start askin' now, he'll know somethin's up. He's real smart *and* real paranoid. He doesn't trust anybody. Not even me."

Darlene figured she could tell them what she knew, and they would leave her alone. Sammy was the only one she knew well. From what she knew, he was the main cocaine dealer, and he lived in Columbus. He had lots of money and big goons with big guns who served as his bodyguards. She knew he was Puerto Rican. He was the one they met frequently. He even came to Matewan a few times to drop off the drugs. Not often. He said he hated that hellhole, and he complained about how dirty his Jag got every time he came there, and the potholes messed up his rims. Not to mention his fear of meeting a coal truck around every curve. Sammy was not a mountain boy, and it showed. Ray called him a little pansy-ass. Never to his face, though. Sammy hated the mountains, but Ray was his largest distributor of cocaine, and now they had started moving pain pills—OxyContin and Lortab.

The deals with the gang from Detroit that started earlier in the year were still mostly pills, and Ray continued to think the trips were too risky. Too far, too many unknowns, and he didn't trust them. The Detroit deals were rare, and, by this time, the Detroit gang had started bringing the merchandise to Matewan. Sammy had also started moving pills a few months earlier, and he and Ray were thick as thieves.

Ray and Sammy had mentioned Chicago a few times, but no names, and Ray never went to Chicago. Sammy guarded his Chicago connection and insisted on being the middle-man and not letting Ray have direct contact with them.

Sammy was scary with his skinny little body and his cheekbones sticking out on his face. His nose was all boney and crooked and looked as though it had been broken a few times. He had an accent, and when he was angry he would burst out in Spanish. He also had lots of money, a nice car, expensive clothes, and he always had a big-boobed blonde with him—never the same one twice. Darlene often thought he was making them in his basement—his own private collection of fembots. Sammy scared the hell out of Darlene, and she didn't like being alone with him.

Maybe Dan was right and Ray was way in over his head with Sammy. Maybe Ray didn't realize how much trouble he could be in. He had spent five years in prison for dealing drugs and the attempted murder of his drug provider. Another bust and he could spend ten or even twenty years in prison.

"Why not just tell Ray and let him give you the info? Let him be the one. He ain't scared of Sammy. I am. I'm scared of Ray, too. Ya'll don't understand these people. They'll kill me."

"Darlene, that won't work. Ray hates the Feds and won't work with us. If you want to save yourself and save Ray, you need to do this. Just get us the information we need, and you won't be looking at prison time. We can help you get custody of your girls again. And we might even be able to save Ray from going back to prison."

John drove them back to Darlene's car. As she got out of the Tahoe, Dan handed her his business card and told her to call him when she was ready. He reminded her not to wait too long, or they would get someone else to help them and the deal would be off the table.

She was shaking so badly she could barely get her key in the car door. When she finally made it home, she was sick and had a miserable headache. She dug in her purse for something to take and came out with an OxyContin. *Like one would do the trick.* She needed more, but she couldn't go to Ray's until she calmed down, and Ray had all the drugs. She crushed the Oxy and snorted it. As insane as what Dan had suggested, she knew what she had to do if she wanted to get her girls back.

***

"Dan, you sure are making that girl a lot of promises you might not be able to keep," John said.

Dan sat in the passenger seat rubbing his chin, thinking about what he was asking Darlene to do, wondering if Ray and Sammy were really as crazy as she thought and whether he could protect her if they were.

"Yeah, I know, but that's part of the job. We need to get the information on Ray, and we'll figure out the rest of it on the back end. Let's go meet our other informant and see if there's any new information on that front."

***

It had been a long day, and Dan was glad to be back at his rented house in Williamson. He was not thrilled with his latest assignment, but he had been promised that a successful bust would lead to a promotion and a move back to D.C., where he had started. Southern West Virginia was at the bottom of his list of desirable assignments, but it was currently the hottest drug area in the agency. The amount of drugs moving out of Mingo County was astonishing, and some of the big dealers in Columbus, Detroit and Chicago were involved. Busting any avenue leading in or out would lead—could lead—to the big guys, and that was Dan's ultimate goal.

165

He had been with the FBI for five years, a rising star on the fast track to success. On the surface, this particular assignment seemed to be a step in the wrong direction, but if he could make this work, he could get the big fish—the Chicago Cartel. The plan was to start with the low man on the totem pole—Ray—and work their way up to Sammy and the Detroit gang and then to the cartel. The Chicago Cartel could be the bust of the century. He just hoped he could make it work. Something he hadn't counted on was the level of people involved with Ray. State politicians in West Virginia and Kentucky were either bought off or drug customers or both. This included senators, judges, prosecutors, attorneys, state officials—the list was long. Any bust could net a slew of people they hadn't originally considered. It could also open a can of worms they didn't want opened.

He hated this place. The mountains loomed over him. They were so close together, it was like living in a crack. It hadn't been so bad at first, but after a few weeks it became claustrophobic. It had been four months, and he had about another six to go if everything went as scheduled. He was here to work, and that was all he did. There was little time for recreation, which was a damned good thing, since there was no recreation here other than riding four-wheelers, which he did often.

It had been a long week, and he was tired, but he still had some work to do. He poured himself a Scotch, sat on the couch and opened the folder he had on Darlene. He couldn't figure out how she had ended up with Ray. She had been a straight-A student in high school and college; she came from a good family; she was a sweet girl, a mother. His strategy was to play to this side of her, to appeal to her good qualities and convince her that this was her chance to get her life back on track. Funny thing is he really did want her to get her life back on track. He had seen this scenario too many times. His own sister had gone down this same path. She hadn't been so fortunate and had died of a heroin overdose her first year of college.

Darlene could turn out to be a great informant. He needed to keep the pressure on her and keep her calm. She had all the info on Ray and was the closest to him. She just needed to be convinced of all the reasons she should cooperate with them. He would save the info he discovered the previous day on Ray and his latest squeeze, Lou. Giving Darlene this information too soon might cause her to break up with Ray, and then she would be of no use to the FBI. The plan was to string her along and drop the Lou bomb on her when she started feeling sorry for Ray and wanted to change her mind.

He closed the file on Darlene and opened the file he had on Gabe. Gabe was a bit of a wild card. He was scared of both the FBI and Ray. Gabe would probably run at the first opportunity, so they promised him a change of scenery to Texas as soon as they had what they needed from him. Dan held the trump card here, though; Gabe had been implicated in the murder of a girl in Williamson, and they had enough evidence on him to arrest him for accessory to murder. If Gabe wanted out of that mess, he would have to cooperate with the FBI.

Gabe and Darlene were just scared little kids. Both in their late twenties, involved in something way out of their realm of understanding. "Time to grow up, boys and girls. Keep your hands and feet inside the ride at all times," Dan said to himself as he poured another Scotch.

***

Darlene hadn't slept all night. After her meeting with the FBI, she was scared and needed to see her mom. Her car rattled down the back alley and over the tracks. First, she went to the Gas 'n' Go for cigarettes and a Mountain Dew. She needed the caffeine to wake up. Normally she would have had a line of coke by now, but she didn't want to be high when she went to see her mother.

She wanted to show she was trying to do better. She also needed a clear head to think about things. She flicked her cigarette out the window just before she pulled into her parents' driveway. Her mother hated when she smoked.

She had called her mother earlier to make sure it was okay to stop by. Her father still didn't want her in the house unless it was to see the girls every other weekend. She had been desperate when they spoke by phone.

"I've gotten into somethin' that I need to talk to you about, Mommy. It's real important, and I think you should know."

"Darlene, you in trouble? You need bailed out of somethin' again? Your daddy won't—"

"This ain't about that, Mommy. Honest, I need you. I need to talk to you."

"All right, come by at noon, and we'll have lunch. Darlene, you gotta be out of here by 2:30, 'cause Daddy gets home at three."

"Lunch. Mmmm…" Darlene loved her mommy's cooking, and that was probably the one thing she missed the most since her daddy had kicked her out. She hoped Millie had made dessert. Her apple pie was the best.

As Darlene entered the back door to the kitchen, she could smell the most wonderful things. Her mother had made not only an apple pie, but a baked chicken with potatoes, onions, carrots and cornbread. Her favorite things. She missed home. She missed her mother. She missed this love and comfort.

She dropped her purse and keys on the counter. "Mommy? Where are you? I'm here." She finished her Mountain Dew and went to the fridge. She got the pitcher of sweet tea, poured herself a glass and leaned against the counter.

Millie walked into the kitchen and they hugged. She kissed Darlene's forehead.

Noticing that Millie looked exhausted, Darlene asked, "Mommy, you okay? You look tired."

"I'm fine, just gettin' old. Sit down. I need to take the cornbread out of the oven. I'll fix you a plate."

Darlene began telling her about her current situation. "Mommy, I think I've got into somethin' I might not be able to get out of."

Millie got the cornbread out of the oven, turned it onto a dinner plate and left it to cool for a few minutes while she fixed the plates. She cut a chicken leg and some breast meat, scooped out a few baby carrots and onions and spooned the broth over it all.

The chicken fell off the bone. Darlene put butter on one piece of hot cornbread and crumbled another piece into the broth from the chicken. Heaven in a bowl. Between bites of baked chicken and buttered cornbread, she told Millie everything she had told Dan.

They finished lunch and cleaned the dishes, and then it was time for apple pie. Darlene cut two pieces of pie and sat at the table.

Millie started to tear up. "Darlene, Darlene. What kinda mess are you in? I told you Ray was no good. He's an evil man. Now you're lookin' at prison? Or runnin' the chance these people'll hurt you?"

"Mommy, the FBI said they would protect me. They said they would be there to watch after me and jump in when it gets to be too much or I get too close."

"Darlene, unless they're with you twenty-four hours a day, they ain't gonna protect you from nothin', especially that crazy man. Don't be so naïve."

"Mommy, I just want you to know who I'm dealin' with. Just in case. This is who I talked to." She handed her mother the business card Dan had given her. His name and phone number were embossed on the card: *Dan Abrams, Special Agent.*

"Just in case what? You know this is a bad idea."

"I don't have much of a choice, Mommy. I could go to jail if I don't help them. I could die if I do. What am I supposed to do?"

"When is all this supposed to take place? This week, next week, next month?"

"I don't know, Mommy. There ain't a schedule. It'll happen when it happens, but sooner rather than later, I suppose."

"Well, you need to call me every day, or I will worry myself sick about you. I love you, Darlene." She grabbed her and hugged her tightly.

Darlene gave her mother a kiss on the cheek and assured her she would call every day with an update. It was two and time to leave. Her mother made her a doggy bag to take with her.

Millie stood in the back door and waved as Darlene pulled away. She felt guilty for dumping this on her mother, but she needed someone to know just in case something did happen to her, and her mother was the only person she trusted 100 percent. That sick feeling had moved from her stomach to the pit of her soul.

She rattled back to her trailer in her Civic and called Dan.

"Dan, it's Darlene. I'm ready. I'm scared, but I'm ready."

"Darlene, I'm glad you decided to help us."

"I will help you, but you have to help me. I want custody of my kids. Full custody. You said you could help me with that. Can you?"

"We can certainly influence the judge's decision, Darlene. It would all be behind the scenes, of course. We can't go to court and testify for you, but we can make sure the judge sees things our way."

"Okay. I want my kids, and I want to leave Mingo County. You have to help me leave here. You have to give me enough money to move and get started someplace else."

"Absolutely, Darlene. We will protect you. That's part of the deal here. Pick your place."

"Tennessee. I want to go to Tennessee. My cousins live there, and that's where I want to go." Darlene was determined to get the sweet end of the deal for her and her girls. "Okay, what do you want me to do?" Darlene settled into the realization that she needed to do this or go to jail.

She hung up with Dan, and her doubts began to settle down—not completely dissolve, but at least they were not jumping around in her head. She had a half-finished joint in her ashtray and decided to smoke it. Once it was done, she stretched out on her back porch to enjoy one of the last days of fall and the warm sunshine on her face. Jelly Bean curled up in a little ball on her chest. The trees moved gently in the breeze. The leaves were starting to turn slightly. Looking straight up, the mountains were amazing. "Always look up, Jelly Bean. Always look up," she whispered, and Jelly Bean purred and curled his tail around himself more tightly.

She kept repeating a line from a song she had heard in church years ago, something about *the hungry soul always reaching for a higher high*. The high was never high enough. There was always a great expectation, but she never reached the place she aimed for—not more drugs, not different drugs—nothing could fill the empty pit in her soul. Nothing could provide the high she reached for. Seemed nothing could satisfy the thirst in her soul. How did she end up in this mess? It was just so easy to keep using. So easy to go along with the flow. With Ray's flow. With Mickey's flow. With whatever came along. Before drugs, it was Dave's flow— whatever he wanted. After she got married, she never really had made much of an effort to create her own path.

After the divorce, Ray came along, and the drugs had just been too easy to get and too easy to take. They had opened a door to slip through, an opportunity to be someone else. They promised her control of her life and had soothed her restless mind. And they lived up to their promises—for a while. Then she woke up one day and realized she was being controlled by a lover far worse than Dave or Ray could ever hope to be. She had tried to stop using so many times. Really wanted to stop using, just not yet...*always reaching.*

***

Gabe was scared and tired. He wanted to get away from Ray and Zip and the whole crazy mess. It had been almost three years now, and he was done. Sure, he liked the drugs, and the money was good. He didn't have to work too hard, but when they asked things of him, they were big things—things that went against everything he knew was right and good. He didn't know how much more he could take. They had him beating up little kids and roughing up women. That was some messed up shit.

The tipping point for Gabe had been the night Ray's cousin Bobby needed a ride home. Bobby was hopped up on pills and had been drinking Jack Daniel's. He could barely walk, let alone drive. Gabe was ordered to drive him home to Delbarton, but halfway there, Bobby insisted Gabe take him to his girlfriend's house in Williamson. Gabe cut across Buffalo Mountain.

Susie lived on the other side of the mountain in a small house that sat off the road. When they arrived, Bobby told Gabe to wait in the car. Bobby went inside, and Gabe could hear them fighting. It sounded like a war, with things being thrown and Susie screaming. Then silence. Bobby came running out and was walking around in circles in front of the car, mumbling.

Gabe got out of the car. "What the hell is wrong with you, man?"

"I think I killed her, man. Fuck! I think she's dead." Bobby sat down on the ground with his head in his hands between his knees.

Bobby's shirt, hands and face were covered in blood. Gabe took one look at him and ran into the house. It looked like someone had hosed the kitchen in blood. It was everywhere, and Susie was curled up under the kitchen table in a puddle as it spread out around her. Her baby was sitting beside her, crying. Gabe figured the kid to be about three years old—old enough to identify Bobby, old enough to know something bad had just happened to his mommy.

Susie's face was bashed in, and she was unrecognizable. Blood was filling the kitchen floor. Gabe had tears in his eyes, and when he turned to ask Bobby what on earth he had done to her to cause this much damage, he saw the bloody baseball bat on the floor.

"She pulled the bat out to hit me. Told me to leave. Said she had no use for a loser like me. Said she had a job now and wanted a decent life for her kid. She said all I had to offer her was a life of drugs and Jack Daniel's. When she said I…was no good, I…I couldn't take it, man. I just…I lost it, and I took the baseball bat away from her, and I hit her, and then I hit her again. Fuck, man, I couldn't stop! Then she just stopped movin'. I shoved her under the table, 'cause I couldn't look at her no more."

Susie's little boy crawled from under the kitchen table, whimpering. He had blood on his pajamas and hands. The baby tried to wipe away his tears and smeared blood all over his face and in his hair.

Gabe didn't know what to do. He wanted to take the baseball bat to Bobby's head and do to him what he had done to Susie. He knew he needed to call Ray and let him decide what to do. He just wanted to run, but he couldn't leave the kid alone.

Bobby was now sitting in the doorway with his head on his knees, crying. The baby was crying. Gabe heard something moving under the table. He looked and Susie was moving her arm and moaning.

"Holy shit! She's still alive, Bobby. She ain't dead." Gabe went to Susie and knelt in the puddle of blood that was now spreading across the tile floor. "Susie, hang on. Just hang on. We're gonna get you help."

Susie mumbled something that sounded like "Baby," to Gabe.

"He's okay, Susie. He's right here. He ain't hurt. We're gonna get you help. Just hold on. Hold on."

Gabe yelled at Bobby to call the ambulance, but when he turned around Bobby was gone. "Fuck! Where'd he go?"

Gabe looked around for the phone, and then he heard the fast beep beep beep of the phone. It was under Susie. She had managed to call someone. That meant it was a matter of time before the cops showed up, he hoped with an ambulance.

Gabe made sure the baby was safe in his crib. He put Bobby in the car and destroyed what evidence he could think of that they had been there, which included taking the baseball bat, wiping their fingerprints off of the floor and the doorway and anything else they might have touched. He apologized to Susie and tore out of there as fast as he could and took Bobby straight to Ray's with one stop on top of Buffalo Mountain to throw the baseball bat over the side. And one more stop at the bottom to throw up.

By the time they got to Ray's, Bobby was passed out. There was blood all over both of them and the car. Ray came out and helped drag Bobby inside. Once inside, he threw cold water on Bobby to wake him up and then beat him nearly to death.

"What the fuck were you thinkin'? You're an idiot. Now the cops are gonna be lookin' for you. You gotta get the hell out of Mingo County. Everybody knows you have a temper and that you'd been fightin' with her. You're the number one suspect, you fuckin' idiot. Damn! You know better than to bring this shit to my door. Gabe's gonna take you to Hazard. You're gonna stay with your brother for a few weeks, until this dies down some. I can't afford to have this kinda heat on me. You need to keep your sorry ass there until I say you can leave. Do you understand?"

Bobby shook his head yes and sat on the floor, crying. Gabe went home and changed clothes. He cleaned the blood out of his car as best he could, and then he drove Bobby to his brother's in Hazard.

On the way back to Matewan, Gabe had a sick feeling in the pit of his soul. Seeing what Bobby had done to Susie for no reason was more than he could handle. But it was just another day in the life of Ray and his lair of lunatics. Gabe knew he needed to get away from Ray and this craziness or he would end up in jail or dead. These people were crazy. No, they were more than crazy, they were evil. He couldn't do this anymore. This was more than he had bargained for. Ray was mean and nasty and not beyond killing anyone. He needed to find a way out of this mess.

A week after he made it back to Matewan, the FBI gave him the perfect opportunity to make his exit.

The FBI made Gabe an offer he couldn't refuse, but one he knew could get him killed. His choices were go to jail for being an accomplice in the attempted murder of Susie or work with them to arrest Ray. He knew if Ray found out he was even talking to the FBI, he would kill him. Or have Zip kill him. Zip didn't like Gabe anyway and never had. Gabe knew Zip would take great pleasure in slowly torturing him to death.

Gabe also knew he couldn't stay in this situation. He wanted to leave Mingo County. He wanted to go to San Antonio, Texas. So he made a deal with the FBI. They agreed to move him to Texas and give him cash to get started. There was nothing for him in southern West Virginia anyway. His family didn't really care what happened to him. He welcomed the fresh start and had always wanted to go to Texas. He agreed to provide them with information—dates, times, names, places. Whatever he knew.

Two days later, Susie was taken off life support and died from trauma to the brain.

CHAPTER THIRTEEN
The Darkest Hour

"…the road of wrongdoing gets darker and darker…"
— Proverbs 4:19

It was 2 a.m. and freezing. Had she forgotten to turn the heat on before she went to bed? Went to bed? What a joke. Passed out is more to the point. She got out of bed and made her way in the dark through the trailer; her old friends, guilt and shame, came crawling alongside her. The shame ate away at her nearly every day, especially on the days she got high, which was most days. She would get high, feel shame, then get high again to not feel the shame, then come down and do it all over again.

She tried to quit so many times—actually made it a few times for a pretty damned long time. It just never seemed to stick, and she always fell back into the miry clay of addiction. Without a job, there wasn't much to occupy her mind and time. Getting high seemed to be the only option most days. Being Ray's girl made it too easy to get drugs and too hard to stop doing them. It was their lifestyle. What they did. Just thinking about making any kind of change for a better life drained her energy. She was tired. Tired of the constant partying, the lack of direction, the paranoia that oozed out of Ray. Tired mostly of the crazy shit that floated around Ray— junkies, whores, beatings, and God only knew what else she wasn't even aware was happening.

She wanted to just erase all the mistakes, but there was always someone there to remind her of them—Dave, her daddy, Ray. Trying to forget her mistakes was like using the worn down eraser of a No. 2 pencil. The more she tried to make them disappear, the more obvious they became—black smudges on white paper. Dan and the FBI had offered her a way out, a path to freedom from all of it for her and her girls. Maybe she couldn't undo what she'd done, but she could start over.

The heat was on, but nothing was happening. Probably broken. Again. *Why can't anything ever work around here?* She would call Gabe to come look at it tomorrow morning. She lit a cigarette, picked up Jelly Bean and stumbled back to bed. The anxiety was mounting again, and she lay in bed and thought about the FBI and what she had told them about Ray. If Ray found out about Dan and the FBI, she knew he would kill her or tear her up so badly she would wish she were dead. She didn't have any pills left, so she smoked the last joint she had. She was supposed to go with Ray to Columbus on Saturday. That gave her only two days to pull herself together. If Dan would just stop hounding her for more info—he always wanted more info. He made her nervous. She knew it was a matter of time before Ray or Zip saw them together, and then it would be all over. Matewan was a small town; everybody knew everybody, and all the druggies knew she was Ray's girl.

How did her life get this out of control? She started crying and thinking of her babies and what a terrible mother she had been. Dave called her a junky when she tried to talk him out of the custody battle. Well, she wasn't a junkie, and he could kiss her ass. Junkies use needles. She'd never used a needle. Ever.

She felt so alone. So miserably alone. It was as though everyone in the world had suddenly disappeared and she was the only one left. Perhaps the rapture had come, and she was really left here, the only human being on planet earth—maybe her and some poor schmuck in Japan. And they would never find each other because Japan was a long freaking way away.

She had no one to turn to. No one to run home to. Her mommy was always there, but she had dumped so much on her mother already; Darlene didn't think Millie could take much more. Darlene just wanted to find some kind of peace of mind. Why couldn't she find that peace? Maybe it was hiding under the bed or had crawled into the furnace and caused a malfunction. She took the last hit of her joint and eventually slipped into a fitful sleep, dreaming of the schmuck in Japan.

Darlene woke up again at ten on Thursday. She called Gabe to come fix the furnace. "Gabe, please hurry. I'm freezing. Don't take your sweet ass time. It's cold."

Gabe pretended he was Ray's bodyguard or something. Always sponging off Ray, waiting around for drugs. Like a dog expecting crumbs to fall from the table. Well, that was how most of the losers who hung around Ray played it. At least she had sex with him and helped him as much as she could. And she really did love Ray, even if it was a twisted relationship.

She didn't bother with the shower, since it was freezing anyway. She put on her baseball cap to cover her hair and to partially hide the acne on her face. Her nerves were really getting to her in more ways than one. She got dressed in the same jeans she had worn the previous day, put on a flannel shirt over the T-shirt she had slept in and clean socks. At least her socks and underwear were clean. She lit a cigarette and waited for Gabe.

"Where are you, Gabe? The heat won't fix itself. It's colder inside than it is outside. Please hurry up." Why was he not answering the phone? If he didn't get here to fix the heat soon, she was afraid she would surely freeze to death.

She sat alone in the cold and let her mind walk around over the events that had landed her here. She couldn't believe three years had melted away so quickly. She had gotten a divorce, lost custody of her baby girls, and become a drug addict. Oh, and a whore, if you believed her father and Dave. She had had such high expectations of life. Of her life and what she could do. What she was capable of doing. She didn't regret divorcing Dave; she regretted marrying him in the first place. Regretted that she was not the person she needed to be. Dave was controlling and angry. Now she was mistress to something much more controlling and angry—Ray and drugs. She should have left Matewan as soon as she had divorced Dave. She was on a train headed nowhere.

When Ray came along, the ride downhill picked up speed. At first the drugs were fun; they provided a certain comfort and relief from her anxiety. Then when the honeymoon phase was over, Darlene woke up and realized she was bound to a monster from whom she might never shake free. The drugs ruled everything and controlled all of them with the high they gave, the money they brought in. The drugs fed Ray's ego while they robbed his soul. Ray took delight in getting young kids hooked on coke and pills. It was just another dollar for him. He always joked, "One more addict is one more customer, baby." His goal was to create as many addicts as he could. He called himself "The King of Coke." And he was; he was making tens of thousands of dollars a week selling coke and pills to pretty much everyone in the county.

Age didn't matter to Ray. There were some kids Darlene knew were only in eighth grade, stopping by for drugs. They had probably robbed their grandma for the money. Darlene once told Ray it was horrible to sell drugs to those little kids. He just laughed at her and said, "Wait until your little girls are old enough to stroll up to the coke window, baby."

She knew then she must get away from this person. What was she doing? But she had continued on the crazy train with Ray. She kept telling herself she would leave, she would get away from him, but she just kept kicking that can down the road. Now she had no choice but to leave—leave on her own and have a life, or leave at the hands of Ray and die.

Here she was alone, terrified, cold and confused. She had taken the last Xanax yesterday and really needed something to calm her nerves. She hoped Gabe had something on him, a joint, a pill, anything.

A gentle knock at the back door startled Darlene. Jelly Bean bolted from her lap and scurried into the bedroom.

"Darlene? You in there? It's me, Gabe. Open up."

That fool, what on earth was he doing coming to the back door? No one ever used the back door. She stood and wrapped her blanket tighter around her tiny frame and walked to the back door of the trailer. As soon as she had the door unlocked, Gabe pulled the door open and hurried inside.

"Gabe, what on earth is wrong with you? Why don't you use the front door like most civilized people?"

He looked like hell. "What the hell happened to you? You look like shit." Gabe was barely twenty-seven years old. He was six feet, two inches tall and a lean two hundred pounds. He was a tough-looking young man, but today he looked like a scared little kid.

"Darlene, we're in some trouble. Big trouble." Gabe sat on the couch next to Darlene and held his face in his hands. "I know about the FBI. I know about Dan. I know what they're wantin' you to do."

Darlene thought Ray had probably put Gabe up to this to trap her. "What're you talkin' about, Gabe? You take some LSD or somethin'? I don't know who Dan is or anything about the FBI."

"Darlene, I know. Stop bullshittin' me. I know. Dan and that other guy picked me up the other day and drilled me and told me I would go to jail right along with Ray and you if I didn't tell them everything I know. Darlene, what we gonna do? We are fucked."

As Darlene listened to Gabe and watched him shake and look out the window every ten seconds, she realized he was telling the truth and he really was afraid. He had a lot of details about Dan, and it was the same stuff Dan had said to her.

She looked at Gabe and started crying. She couldn't stop.

CHAPTER FOURTEEN
Mother and Child Reunion

"…to the hungry soul, every bitter thing is sweet."
— Proverbs 27:7

Dave agreed to let the girls spend the entire Christmas weekend with Darlene while he visited his wife's family in North Carolina. They would have four whole days and nights together. Of course, he had a list of conditions he was more than eager to lay out for her: her parents had to be there, and she had to be there the entire weekend, no smoking in front them, no drinking, no profanity, and she had to have them back Sunday morning so they could go to church with his parents. He even provided a list of things they were not allowed to watch on TV, all written in his new bride's handwriting, which Darlene was certain was done just to piss her off even more. Darlene thought Dave's list of conditions was excessive, but she agreed to everything and bit her tongue when she really wanted to tell him to kiss her ass. She didn't want an argument; she just wanted a weekend with the girls. He spoke to her as if she were a complete idiot who had never been near children.

The alarm went off at six, and she bolted out of bed. Normally it was ten or eleven before she crawled out of bed, usually hung over or still groggy from the pills she had taken to go to sleep. She packed her bag for the weekend and gathered Jelly Bean's essentials—cat litter, food and toys. The girls loved Jelly Bean and couldn't wait to see him. He was the official baby of the family. Of course, he considered himself supreme ruler of the family. Cats!

She wanted to get to her parents early and give Jelly Bean a chance to settle in before the girls arrived. Her mother wanted to do some last minute grocery shopping, and they planned to leave for Piggly Wiggly no later than eight.

After an hour at the Piggly Wiggly playing bumper cars with every shopping cart in the store, they had made it home around 11:30. Millie shooed Darlene away from helping unload the groceries and told her to shower and get ready.

The girls got out of school at one—early for the holiday. The plan was for Dave to pick them up at school and Darlene would meet them at his parents'. Her hands were shaking when she put on her eyeliner. She was a tangled mess of nerves and excitement. She was nervous about seeing Dave and excited to see Amy and Renee. If she were honest with herself, she was also nervous about spending the entire weekend with the girls and her parents. No drugs, no booze, no cussing, no Ray. Could she do it? She prayed she would not do something crazy and mess up the entire weekend. How many times had she messed up? Too many to count. She had let everyone down, including herself, repeatedly. It was hard for her to believe in herself or even trust herself anymore.

She pulled on her blue panties and snapped the matching bra Ray had bought her the previous month on a shopping spree in Columbus. The trip to Victoria's Secret had resulted in $350 worth of panties, bras and pajamas. No, she would not think about Ray. Thinking about him would only make her miss him and then miss getting high. Then she would wonder what the gang was doing. Then she would want to go there and join in the party. No, she would not think about Ray. This was her weekend. The girls' weekend. She wanted to be right here with her family. The people who truly loved her. No room for Ray, Mickey or any of the noise that had polluted her life.

She zipped her jeans and wondered if Dave would think she looked good. He had been so holier-than-thou when he rattled off his list of conditions. He had always thought more highly of himself than he ought. Being good enough for Dave was something she knew she could never do, and meeting his expectations was impossible. God knows, she had tried for years to be the perfect wife and mother, but she always derailed, and her vision of herself became more distorted with each failure. She looked in the mirror and promised herself and God that she would not derail this weekend.

The previous three weeks had been rough. Backing off the pills, the coke and the booze had been torture for the first week. It was much harder than she imagined it would be or could be. Going cold turkey would have been impossible. Getting clean, or at least clean enough for the weekend, was too important to fail, so she stuck with it and backed off a little more each day. She wanted to be, needed to be, clear-headed. Ray and Mickey had laughed at her attempts to get clean.

A hardness and sharp edges.

Sleeping had been the hardest part, and the first few nights she tried to sleep without a pill, she was up all night.

Mountain Dew and coffee would be substituted for coke to get her through the days and to keep up with the girls. She considered bringing a couple of Xanax or something to help her sleep but was afraid her parents or the girls would find the pills or she would black out as before. She desperately wanted to get clean and regain custody of her kids, and she didn't want anything to mess up the weekend. If she couldn't sleep, she couldn't sleep; it was only four days. She wanted a normal life, a home, no drugs. Some days, like today, it seemed possible, but most days it seemed like a far away dream. She just wanted a chance and knew that she had to give herself one before anyone else would.

Dave had agreed that she could come alone and get the girls, but they had to go straight to her parents. It was only one mile down the road; she assured him she could handle it.

Dave's truck was not there when she pulled into the driveway. She could catch her breath and calm down. *Stop shaking.* She checked herself in the rear view mirror. *Not bad.* She had spent the last few days getting everything ready for this weekend—cleaned the car, bought new clothes for the girls (*thank you, Ray, for the shopping spree*), and rented the latest Disney movies. She bought new clothes for herself and made sure the smell of cigarette smoke wasn't lingering on her clothes or in the car. She wanted this weekend to be perfect.

As much as she was glad to be away from Dave and his everyday control, she sometimes missed him and the life they had or the chance they had had at a normal life. Well, as normal as it could be. She was nervous about seeing him. She also wanted him to notice how good she looked and that she was straight. Some tiny part of her still wanted and needed his approval.

She was sitting in her car waiting for Dave when his mother stepped out on the front porch and motioned for Darlene to roll down her window. Determined not to let the old biddy get to her, Darlene smiled and got out of the car. "Hi, Betty. How ya doing?"

"It's a darn shame you're takin' the girls for Christmas. A darn shame. I told Dave he ought not let you have 'em. You ain't fit to spend a holiday with 'em. You'll probably go and leave 'em with your mommy while you go out honky-tonkin'."

"Betty, I ain't goin' nowhere this weekend. I don't want to fight with you about this. We're gonna stay at Mommy and Daddy's and watch movies, bake cookies and just be together. I just want to spend some time with my babies."

"Just ain't right. Ain't nothin' but…well, there's Dave with the girls now. You listen to me, Darlene. You better take good care of those girls and have 'em back here on time for Sunday school." She waved at Dave and went back inside. Darlene could feel her watching from the kitchen window.

Dave's new truck pulled into the driveway and parked behind Darlene's beat up Civic. She walked out to the truck, and her heart started beating faster as Dave got out and looked at her with a bit of surprise on his face. "Your car's awful clean. What happened? You pay somebody to clean it?"

"I cleaned it. Why is that so surprisin'?" She was trying hard not to be defensive, but to keep it playful. She knew he could turn nasty in a heartbeat.

"You ain't known for a havin' a clean car, that's all."

"Well, this is a special day, and I want my princesses to ride in style."

The girls came running around the truck with shrieks and giggles, hugging Darlene as Dave loaded their Beauty and the Beast and Dora the Explorer suitcases in the back seat.

"Remember, Darlene, they gotta be back here by 9:30 sharp Sunday morning. If anything happens and you need me, call. No matter what time it is."

"Dave, ain't nothin' gonna happen unless they giggle themselves sick. We'll be back at 9:30 Sunday. Sharp."

This was the happiest she had been in a long time. Her babies were so glad to see her and were talking a mile a minute about what they had done in school. Amy was rambling non-stop about the girl who sat behind her in class. Savannah had kissed yucky Cody Hill while they were on the playground, and it was super gross. Renee agreed; it truly was the grossest thing ever. They provided a download of the day's events on the short ride to Darlene's parents' house.

All three were giggling when they entered the kitchen, and Millie was thrilled to see them. They ran to hug and kiss her while Darlene took Dora and Beauty and the Beast to the bedroom.

Jelly Bean had more attention than he could handle and eventually fell asleep in front of the fireplace. Darlene and the girls baked cookies, cakes and pies with Millie, and the children were thrilled to get to lick the cake batter bowl. While they were baking, Darlene's dad came home from work. He half-hugged Darlene and said hello. Or at least she thought it was, "hello." It could have been, "go to hell." He had made it clear he was not happy about having Darlene in the house all weekend, but he was thrilled to have the girls.

She felt good and was happy to be home. It felt solid. Real. And most of all, it was home. The smells of her mother's kitchen were pure comfort. Her mother's singing as she cooked and cleaned was the sweetest sound this side of heaven. Seeing her mother smile and laugh with the girls and her father telling them stories was the best part, and Darlene videotaped most of the weekend. Her father and the girls fell asleep in his giant recliner, and she snapped a picture of them—one she knew she would cherish for the rest of her life.

The weekend was full of food, games, stories, giggles and more food. Early Sunday morning Darlene got up and got the girls ready for church as her mother made breakfast. As promised, Darlene dropped them at Dave's mother's on time. She said good-bye to the girls with lots of hugs and kisses. They waved frantically to each other as Darlene pulled out of the driveway. As she drove back to her parents, joy and sadness jumbled together in her mind. The weekend had been wonderful, and she wanted more. She wanted normal.

For what little time she had left in Matewan, Darlene wanted to move home with her parents. Knowing her father wasn't ready for that, she didn't want to push her luck with him. When she entered the kitchen, he was sitting at the table drinking coffee.

She sat down across from him in the same seat she had occupied that horrible morning he laid his .38 on the table. "Daddy, I wanna come home." He started to shift nervously in his chair. She put her hand up to stop him from saying anything. "I know you ain't ready for that. I hope this weekend is a good start at least. The girls were thrilled to be here, and I want more of that. Daddy, I need more of that, and so do you and Mommy. I know I've made really big mistakes and done some stupid stuff, but I'm truly ready to turn it around and make a better life for me and my girls. So, just think about it."

As she got up to leave, her father said, "We'll see."

Darlene packed her and Jelly Bean's bags and left. *We'll see?* What does that mean? She kept playing his words over in her mind as she drove back to her place. She could still not call her place home. Home was her parents' home. Home was where the only real life she knew existed. She wanted to show her father she had changed. She wanted his acceptance and love, but it seemed to be encased in armor. Maybe she had gone too far and messed up too much.

"We'll see, Jelly Bean. We'll see."

CHAPTER FIFTEEN
Somebody's Watching You

"Betrayal is the only truth that sticks." — Arthur Miller

Ray could tell something was wrong with Darlene. She was more nervous than usual. She always had anxiety, which he brushed off because she was young and inexperienced. This was different, though; she had taken to biting her nails again, especially her left thumb. She would chew on it when she was nervous or anxious. It drove him nuts. It had taken him a year to get her to stop biting them. He hated nasty looking nubby nails, and Darlene would bite and chew until she bled. He had bitched at her and berated her and embarrassed her enough that she finally stopped, and her nails had grown. He insisted she get a manicure once a week, and finally her nails looked good. He was pissed when he saw her nails all chewed into the quick. What he couldn't figure out was why. Why was she so nervous all of a sudden?

At first he thought maybe she was cheating on him. Gabe was the logical choice. They were about the same age. They grew up together, and they were always joking around and talking about stuff they did as kids in North Matewan. But Gabe was a scared little punk who knew better than to mess with his bitch. So, who? Zip? Never. Zip didn't even like Darlene, and he was loyal to the death to Ray.

His friend Senator Steves had sent a message that he wanted to meet at his office in Charleston; as instructed, Ray went alone. On his drive to Charleston, Ray thought about Darlene's recent anxiety and wondered if she were cheating on him.

"Ray, I got word this week the FBI has launched a full-blown investigation into your business." The good senator never used the word drugs or cocaine or any code names, even though he had purchased enough of it. It was always, "the business."

"The FBI has been snooping around into everyone in the county who has any dealings with you. They have several people in the business in their cross-hairs. You need to watch your back. Maybe lay low for a while, calm things down a little. You're running wide open, Ray, and everyone in the county knows what you're up to. You're a sitting duck for the FBI."

"Nothin' you can do to stop it? You stopped it in the past. You stopped the West Virginia State Police from raidin' my place several times. You stopped that one FBI idiot from startin' his investigation. Hell, you even got me out of prison and had my probation reduced. You can't do nothin' about this?" Ray sat back on the leather sofa in the senator's office and took a sip of his eighteen-year-old Scotch.

"Not this time, Ray. There's some new asshole there trying to make a name for himself. Says he wants to clean up Mingo County of all the drugs and corruption." Senator Steves sat down on the other end of the sofa and swirled the ice in his drink.

"Well, fuck, Jack. I doubt they have the balls to get me. Besides, I'm careful. We don't take kindly to strangers at The Place. No pizza sold to out-of-towners." Ray chuckled. He was overconfident and feeling cocky. He couldn't imagine anyone having the balls to come into his place to set him up.

"Ray, I'm not sure how to tell you this, other than to just tell you. From what I understand, they have someone on the inside. Someone in your inner circle is feeding them information. They know when you leave and where you go and what you do. Probably have your phones tapped, cameras, the works. This is serious."

Ray sat up on the edge of the sofa and demanded to know who was feeding the FBI information.

"Now, don't get all riled up. It could be one of those characters you do business with in Columbus or Detroit setting you up. The FBI may have come down on them, and they're turning you in to keep their own asses out of jail. It isn't necessarily one of your crew. Just be careful who you trust."

After the meeting, Ray climbed into his Suburban, madder than damn. He sat there mentally going through everyone in his camp. It was suddenly all clear to him. He beat his fists on the steering wheel. "That fuckin' little bitch! Darlene. Who do you think you are, rattin' on me?" This explained her change in mood and anxiety level. Those nasty fingernails were a dead giveaway. If she wasn't the one, she knew who was.

He drove back to Red Jacket from Charleston in record time. He had calmed down by the time he arrived. He didn't want to give it away that he knew anything about the FBI being in town. He wanted to be sure. If Darlene, then who else? She couldn't and wouldn't do this alone. Maybe she was in it with others. Mickey? Gabe? God only knows who else. Maybe her daddy convinced her to do it. Promised her something if she would get rid of the vermin. Maybe someone else had threatened her. He would kill whoever it was. He didn't think Darlene had the nerve to do this alone. He'd just have to keep an eye on her.

Ray was a patient man; he would wait them out. He would just watch and see who acted strange. He would figure out who was the traitor or traitors.

The days wore on, and Ray's paranoia grew. He didn't trust anyone, not even his wife. When he confronted her about it, she denied knowing anything about the FBI.

"You think I want you to go back to prison? I have two kids to raise. How will I do that if you're in prison? How would we eat and pay the bills? I'm not that stupid."

To make sure she understood he was serious, he grabbed her throat and shoved her against the refrigerator. He pushed his finger into her face. "You fuck me over, and I'll slice your face to pieces. I won't kill you. I'll just make you look like a freak. Even your own kids won't be able to look at you without screamin'. Do you understand me? If you know anything about this or hear anything about this, you better tell me."

Zip was the only person Ray trusted. "Zip, I want you to follow Darlene. I think she's fuckin' around on me. Not sure who with. Just keep an eye on her and drive by her trailer at night. Look for strange, out-of-town cars. I want to know everywhere she goes and who she talks to." Ray didn't tell Zip the truth about the FBI, just in case he was the one feeding them information.

***

Zip did as he was told. He didn't like Darlene anyway, and this was just the assignment he had been waiting for. Zip thought Darlene was a little tease who always thought she was better than everybody else. Smarter than everybody else. She was just a stupid, washed up whore. She had a scholarship to go to Marshall and decided to just drop it all and stay here for her moron ex-husband. She just wanted to get married and have babies. Well, that worked out real well for her, didn't it? Unlike Darlene, he had wanted to go to school. Wanted to play professional football and was well on his way, until the accident. He didn't like people like Darlene. Just another whore looking for an easy ride. *No wonder Dave got rid of her sorry ass. Lazy bitch.*

Sure, he would tail her, and if he caught her doing anything, he would beat the shit out of her. Ray said he could. He followed her, but she didn't go anywhere but to her parents' with that stupid cat. He thought about breaking in and taking the cat when she wasn't there. He hated cats.

After a week he reported back to Ray. "Ray, she ain't doin' nothin'. Boring as hell. Not sure what you see in her. She goes to her mother's, her Aunt Penny's, the grocery store and here. That's it. She aint' doin' nothin'."

"Is anyone else at her parents' house when she's there?"

"Nope, just her parents. Usually just her mom, but sometimes her dad. Then the kids every other Saturday. Pretty borin', actually."

Ray was surprised Darlene was there when her dad was home. That must mean they had made up or at least were trying to. Maybe that was why Darlene was so nervous. She had been fighting with her old man.

"Does she go there every day?"

"Pretty much, either there or her Aunt Penny's. Same thing, though. Just her and that damned cat."

"Keep an eye on her for a couple more days, Zip."

***

Darlene knew Zip was watching her every move. He was not very good at this game and didn't really try to hide the fact that he was following her. He wanted her to see him. He wanted her to feel threatened and scared. She made sure to never leave Jelly Bean alone at home. She knew Zip would take him just to be mean. She went to her parents and called Dan to report in every day. She had even spent the night a few times with her parents and once with Aunt Penny.

She tried to act as normal as ever, but she was a nervous wreck. She really needed a Xanax, but most days she was scared to take anything…or at least too much of anything. She didn't want to be wasted if something bad went down. She never knew when she would need to get out of town in a hurry.

After a couple of weeks, Zip backed off.

CHAPTER SIXTEEN
A Rat in the Stew

"I'd rather die like a man than live my life like a bitch,
I'd rather be in the pen than walk the streets as a snitch."
— Mac Dre

Paranoia coiled around Ray's mind like a python, squeezing tighter and tighter every day. He felt himself losing control, and that made him even more angry and scared. Going back to prison was not an option. The nightmares had never stopped, but now they were worse. He woke up in a cold sweat more often than he wanted to admit. No, going back to prison was not an option. He would find out who the snitch was, and when he did...

Was it Darlene? Gabe? Mickey? Someone else? Every customer was a suspect. All the hangers-on were suspects. Hell, even his wife was a suspect. Zip had been watching Darlene and his wife for a few weeks now. According to Zip, they hadn't been doing anything out of the ordinary. Zip was the only one he could trust. No, Zip was no snitch. He was loyal to the bone.

Ray had implemented a new rule: no selling to strangers. Only the die-hard regulars. At least for the next few weeks, maybe even a month or more. He wanted to let the heat die down and smoke out his snitch. This would cost him a lot of money, maybe even ten grand a week.

His worst fear was that Sammy was the snitch. What if the Feds had gotten to Sammy and threatened *him* with prison and so he rolled and offered Ray as the sacrifice? Yeah, Sammy was at the top of the snitch list, but he was scared of Sammy. Sammy was the only one crazier than Ray. He knew Sammy would put a bullet in his head without even thinking about it. No, he couldn't and wouldn't confront Sammy. But he would keep an eye on him.

Darlene had been acting really nervous. Jumpy and still biting those damned fingernails of hers. She and Gabe were both chicken shit little punks and would turn on their own mother if they thought it would keep them out of trouble. Darlene was a sweet piece of ass. Too bad if it was her. He hated to mess up that pretty little face and those perfect tits, but this was war, and no one gets a pass in war. Not even Darlene.

Gabe was at the top of the list, as well. He was an idiot. He proved what a pussy he was with that girl of Bobby's in Williamson. Gabe wanted all the fun but none of the ugly stuff. He was scared of his own shadow. He would turn for no reason. The Feds just had to say boo, and he would spill his guts. Ray never did trust him. Darlene sure seemed to like him, though.

Ray just needed to keep it together long enough to find out who the snitch was. He really wanted to punch someone in the face. He needed to keep his cool just a little bit longer. This bunch wasn't smart enough to pull this off. None of them could keep their big mouths shut long enough to be a good snitch. No, they would talk soon enough. Spill the beans and then all hell would rain down on them.

***

A few weeks had passed since Ray met with Senator Steves. Everyone was on edge because Ray was on edge. Wanting to keep them on edge, he decided it was time to start turning the screws. He wanted everyone around him to feel the pain; the snitch would crack under the pressure.

It was a typical Saturday night, and The Place was hopping. The kitchen staff couldn't make pizzas and subs fast enough. There were also a lot of orders for cocaine. If they hadn't bought anything in the past month, they were turned down and told to come back in a few weeks. Ray hated to turn down business, but he had to. For just a little while. Losing money and possibly customers made his anger spill over.

He walked into the back office, and there they were, like river rats, waiting to be fed. Darlene, Mickey, Gabe, Zip, two girls he didn't know (he assumed they were with Zip), Lou (without her husband) and Sally. The regular guys. The regular leaches. They all wanted something—drugs, money, sex, street cred from hanging out there. They all had an angle. They all wanted something for nothing.

He was in a foul mood, and seeing them sitting there waiting for him didn't improve it any. Normally it did. He liked it when they all waited for him; he liked being the center of his universe. The king of coke. Yes, he was king, and he would stomp any piss ant that tried to bring him down.

"What are ya'll lookin' at?" He slammed the door behind him. "What do you want?"

He walked over to his desk and got a cigarette and lit it. He spun his chair around but didn't sit. He just stood there with his cigarette. No one moved; no one said anything.

Finally, Darlene spoke up. "Hey, baby, is everything okay?" She got up and came over to him. He brushed her off, and she stumbled back and half fell, half sat down in the desk chair.

"No. Everything is not okay, darlin'. Apparently, we have a snitch in the soup. A little smarmy, slimy, no good, son of a bitch, snitch." His words were measured as he looked at each of them. "So, who is it? Gabe? Is it you?" He turned to Darlene. "Darlene? Mickey? Lou? Sally? Zip? Who?"

Ray enjoyed the look of fear on their faces. Yeah, this is exactly the response he wanted. He searched each face for telltale signs. They all looked like they had just pissed their pants. He felt the control returning as he tightened the noose. This could be fun after all…if he weren't so concerned.

"Mickey, you know anything about a snitch?"

"Hell no! Ray, I ain't heard nothin' on the street, man. Nothin'. When did this come up? Who told you there was a snitch?"

"That don't matter, but I got it on good authority. Mark my words, I will find out who it is and when I do…" He put his cigarette in his mouth and used his right hand to grab Darlene's hair and pull her head up and back against his stomach; he ran the thumb of his left hand across her throat. Then he pushed her away from him; the chair rolled and banged into the desk.

He set his sights on Gabe. "You, Gabe? What do you know about the Feds havin' their nose all up in my shit? You been talkin' to them? You been contacted by those assholes?"

"Ray, man, you know I ain't talkin' to those sons-a-bitches. Like Mick said, man, I ain't heard nothin' on the street, either. Nothin'."

Ray crossed the room to where Gabe was sitting on the love seat. He grabbed his shirt with both hands and pulled his face into his. "You little punk ass son of a bitch, I didn't ask you what Mickey knew. I want to know what *you* know. Who *you* been talkin' to and what *you* been sayin'. Do you understand?" Zip was up and ready to finish the job for Ray if needed.

"Ray, I don't know nothin'. I swear." Gabe didn't fight back. He knew better. He knew Zip would kill him.

Ray let go of Gabe's shirt and gently slapped him on the cheek. He fell back into the love seat, next to one of Zip's girls.

"Keep it that way, little boy. Don't fuck with me or I *will* kill you." Ray pointed his cigarette at Gabe. "And you know I mean it."

Ray backed up until he was at the desk. With his right arm outstretched and his finger pointed, he moved his arm back and forth to include everyone. "Any of you snitch on me, *any of you*, and I will fuck you up. Forever. I ain't playin'. This is war. This includes all of you. If there's a snitch in this room, you *will* regret it for the rest of your sorry little lives.

***

Darlene had never been so scared. She was afraid she was going to be sick, but was more afraid to show it. Any little thing could set Ray off and cause him to suspect her. When he grabbed her and mimicked slitting her throat, she had been certain he knew she was the one. Then he let her go and went after Gabe. Maybe he knew it was both of them. He went after Mick, too, so maybe he was just fishing. She had to calm her mind and fight the urge to run to the bathroom. He *didn't* know it was her. There was no way. He might suspect Gabe or just want to make an example of him. He never liked Gabe anyway. As for her—she was just a convenient prop for his throat-slitting demonstration.

Just stay calm. Breathe.

She had never seen him so angry and crazy. She wanted to run home but knew she couldn't. The party mood had certainly disappeared in a hurry. Maybe he would make everyone leave.

She couldn't fight the sickness any longer. She got up to go to the bathroom, and Ray barked at her. She assured him she just needed to pee and would be right back. Once in the bathroom, she had diarrhea. She fought the urge to cry; that would be a dead giveaway. She needed to calm down. She tried a trick she read in a magazine a few months earlier. It was supposed to bring your heart rate down and stop the anxiety. She sat on the commode, placed her hands on her lap, relaxed (as much as she could) and focused on her breathing.

Deep, slow, steady, through the nose. In, one…two…three…four…five. Out through the mouth, one…two…three…four…five…six. Calm.

When she thought her stomach was going to be okay she fluffed her hair and smiled into the mirror.

Just act normal.

She returned to the back office. Lou, Sally and Gabe had left. Zip was outside with his two girls. Only Mickey and Ray were in the office.

"Ray, man, I can't think of anyone who would rat on you," Mickey said. "Who? Who could be that stupid? What could the Feds promise them that would be worth your wrath?"

"Mick, I was told it's someone here. Someone I trust." Ray sat on the couch smoking a cigarette. He had a glass of Jack Daniel's on the table. He patted the spot beside him for Darlene to sit. She sat and rubbed his thigh, something she always did.

Normal, just act normal.

Ray took her chin in his hand and turned her face toward him. "Darlene, you'd tell me if you knew anything, wouldn't you? You wouldn't try to protect Gabe, would you? I know he's your friend, but if you know somethin' and don't tell me, I'll be very angry."

Breathe.

"You can't mean that! Really? Baby, I love you. You're my priority. You're my man. I would never take Gabe's or anybody's side over you. You're the one I love. Gabe's a friend, but I'd never let him get away with somethin' like that. Ever." She hoped she was convincing. He let go of her chin and took a drink of his JD.

Deep…slow…steady…in…one…two…three…four…five…out …one…two…three…four…five…six.

She was focusing on breathing when Zip came in alone. He must have sent his girls home or Ray had told him to get rid of them.

Darlene wanted to ask Ray who tipped him off but knew he would never tell her. She listened and hoped he would slip up and give a clue. If whoever it was told him there was a snitch, how long before that same person told him who it was?

Breathe.

Ray told Zip and Mickey to leave. He was not in the mood for a party. He wanted to be alone. Darlene prayed he would send her home, too. She was not so fortunate. He told her to stay the night. He had two more drinks, and they went to bed. No sex, no discussion, nothing. She had a sleepless night and prayed for the daylight so she could go home and pull herself together. She needed to call Dan and tell him Ray was on to them. Morning couldn't come fast enough.

***

Ray woke up and was not nearly as angry as the night before. They had sex, and he sent her home. It was Sunday, the day he typically spent with his wife and kids.

As soon as Darlene got home, she was sick again. She fed Jelly Bean, took a shower and called Dan.

"He knows! He knows there's a snitch. It's just a matter of time before he knows it's me. You gotta get me outta this mess...*now*. I mean it, Dan." Darlene lit another cigarette. "I thought he was gonna kill someone last night. Either me or Gabe or both of us. He's determined to find out who it is."

"Darlene, calm down. Listen to me. Nothing is going to happen to you. We have this under control. We were right outside last night and ready to jump."

"You tryin' to convince me or yourself? He could have slit my throat, and that would have been the end of it. You mighta been able to grab my dead body and take it to my mother, but I would be dead. This man is really over the edge and ready to kill. I'm out. You need to make your move soon. I'm out." Darlene put her cigarette out in the ashtray and started to cry.

"Darlene, don't cry. We're almost at the finish line. We're almost there. Just a little longer. We just need to know when Sammy is coming to town. We need to catch the two of them together. We bust Sammy, and Ray runs. We bust Ray, and Sammy runs. We need them both in the middle of the deal."

Darlene agreed to try to find out who was feeding Ray information about their operation. She agreed to find out when Sammy was coming back to town. The same conversation she had with Dan every day. She had already provided him with a lot of information, and she longed to be done. She was more scared than ever and just wanted out.

"Jelly Bean, after last night, I think we need to be ready to run at a moment's notice. We need to pack a bag that we can just grab and go. You in?" Jelly Bean purred and gave her a head butt. He was ready.

She called her mother, and they made plans for that afternoon to go to Walmart to shop for a few essentials she would need—an overnight bag she would pack and leave at her parents', toiletries, stuff for Jelly Bean (food, cat litter, toys). She couldn't risk taking her overnight bag out of the house with Zip watching, so she decided to just buy a new one. Everything else, she would take to her parents', one thing at a time.

It was early March. She hoped to be out of Matewan by the end of the month.

***

Dan had placed the intel guys in an apartment across the road from The Place. The apartments were low income housing, and it had been a bitch to get the apartment they wanted, but he had pulled some strings and made it happen. They had the phones wiretapped and had placed listening devices all around and inside the restaurant. They couldn't get into the back office to place a listening device, however, and had to rely on Darlene and Gabe for information on that front.

To video traffic going in and out of the back office, they had installed a camera on the utility pole adjacent to the building, but it was having technical difficulties. From the apartment, they had a good angle for photographs and video on the front and side of the restaurant, but not on the entrance to the back door to the office. They had cameras and 24/7 surveillance on the building and customers. They could see who went around the side of the building, but not what happened at the door.

Jason, who was in charge of surveillance, was not happy with the camera on the pole. "Dan, we have an issue with that camera. It keeps shutting itself off. I think it's getting hot. The only way to fix it is to go back up on the pole. We've been up there a few times now, and I think it might draw too much attention if we go back right away. Stan and I recommend waiting about another week or so. We can keep taking photographs, and we have the camera here in the apartment." Jason had been assigned to this project at Dan's request. He was the best surveillance guy, and Dan trusted him.

"Jason, do what you need to do. The cameras in the apartment can't get a good shot of the back office, but you're right. We don't want to draw attention to it. See what other options you can come up with. Word is Sammy is coming to town soon, and we need to document as much activity as we can."

Jason agreed to explore other options and get back to Dan with an update by the end of the week.

The team had been working around the clock on this one. Dan hoped they could wrap it up in the next couple of weeks. Their intel indicated Sammy would be in town the following week with a huge delivery for Ray. Now he just needed to get Darlene and Gabe ready.

CHAPTER SEVENTEEN
Twisted Souls

"Do not envy a violent man or choose any of his ways…
God can't stand twisted souls." — Proverbs 3:31-32

Mickey supposed it was true that time does change things. It changes people. Changes their motives, their reasons, desires. Mickey didn't know when the change in her actually happened; maybe it was just a gradual transition, a slow burn. She had turned that corner, though, and she was now going full speed on the roller coaster. She needed more pills to go to sleep and more cocaine to stay awake. She also realized she now relied on Ray for everything—money, drugs, self-worth, purpose. She hated needing him as much as she loved needing him. She loved Ray. She had always loved Ray, and she would do anything for him. She knew he would never love her, or at least not be in love with her. Especially with Darlene in the picture.

Before she introduced him to Darlene, she had thought, had hoped, she could be his girl. It had never even come close to that. But, it *had* become something more. Something more special and deeper than anything Darlene could ever have with him. Darlene was just a convenient blowjob. He *trusted* Mickey. She was his confidante and he, hers. In the past year he had started trusting her more and sharing vital information about his business. He had even sent her to meet

Sammy for a few pickups. He gave her a lot of responsibility to keep the others in line and the snitches out.

She would do anything he asked. Sure, he supplied her with drugs and money, but it had grown to be more than that. They shared a mutual respect and had each other's back. They were a team. That had to matter to him as much as it did to her.

Didn't it?

As if Darlene weren't enough, he was now sleeping around with Lou whenever he had the chance. Mickey had never cried over a guy, but this hurt to the core and really pissed her off. The night Lou got drunk and started bragging about sleeping with Ray, she had wanted to slap the stupid right off her face. Lou was a liar and would lie about anything and everything to get what she wanted. Lou had been crazy about Ray from day one and hated Darlene because she was cute and tiny and Ray's. Mickey refused to believe Lou's lies, then Ray started asking Mickey to cover for him and keep Darlene occupied while he and Lou hooked up in the back room. Not often, but enough to be a thing. She felt used and foolish, like a little school girl. How could she have let herself get emotionally wrapped up in this man? She knew what he was. She also knew what *she* wasn't; she wasn't physically the kind of woman Ray would want. She was tall, big and rough. Darlene was dainty, cute and bubbly. Lou had big tits and would do anything that involved sex. One was a naïve child, and the other was a whore.

No, Mickey wouldn't let this get to her. Couldn't let this get to her. It was just sex and meant nothing to Ray. Ray's devotion to her was greater than any sex he could have with anyone. He needed Mickey, and that was enough for her.

Besides, Lou was a passing fancy. Darlene was his main squeeze, but he had lost trust in her, and Mickey didn't know why. Why would he suspect Darlene of ratting to the FBI? He had no proof it was Darlene, and quite frankly, Mickey couldn't imagine Darlene having the balls to even talk to the FBI, let alone set up Ray. She was as scared as a little church mouse most of the time. It had taken her five years to leave Dave—actually it was Dave who called it quits. She would have stayed married to him forever. No, Darlene didn't have the balls to cross Ray. She couldn't be that stupid.

Or could she?

Mickey was keeping an eye on Darlene, just as Ray had asked. She had tried every trick she knew to get her to talk. Darlene wouldn't cough up the truth. She would probably spill her guts if she knew about Lou, though. But Mickey knew she couldn't tell her about Lou, or Ray would be pissed.

Darlene wasn't talking, but she sure seemed more nervous than usual. All she would tell Mickey was that Dave was trying to keep her from seeing the girls ever again. He wanted his new wife to adopt the girls and be their legal mother. That made sense; Dave was such an asshole.

Mickey even stopped by unannounced a few times, and Darlene was the same as she ever was. Mickey tried to bait her with talk about Gabe. She talked about his hot body and how she would like to get hold of him. Darlene always rolled her eyes and said Gabe was too young and dumb to fuck. Mickey reported all this back to Ray, but he wasn't convinced. Mickey wasn't convinced either, not completely. The custody issue made sense, but there was something else; Darlene was quieter than usual and on edge. She seemed distant and cautious, even with Mickey.

Mickey had tried for weeks to get anything out of Darlene that was proof she was the snitch or proof she wasn't. Nothing. Now she had been summoned to The Place. Ray wanted to talk. Probably wanted to know if she had come up with anything on Darlene. She would just tell him they were beating a dead horse on this one and should look elsewhere.

Mickey entered the office at The Place. Ray was the only one there. He was sitting on the couch smoking a cigarette. A bottle of Jack Daniel's and a half-empty glass were on the coffee table. He refilled his glass. Mickey closed the door behind her.

"Pour yourself a drink and have a seat. We need to talk." Ray took a long drag off his cigarette and swirled the ice in his JD.

"What's up? You look like death." Mickey got a glass, poured herself a Jack and Coke and sat on the couch with Ray.

"It's her." He tipped his head back and exhaled the cigarette smoke. "It's Darlene."

"Man, I don't think Darlene has the balls to do somethin' like this. What would be her motive, Ray? I just don't think it's her."

"I *know* it's her. She's the one." He took a drink and stared straight ahead.

"How?"

"Stanger. Sgt. Stanger of the West Virginia State Police. He told me. Actually, he showed me. He had copies of the FBI file. It's her. No doubt. For seven months, seven *fuckin'* months, that little cunt has been tellin' those assholes my business. Everything. She has told them every damned thing she knows. And she knows a lot."

"Shit, Ray. Can you trust Stanger to be tellin' you the truth? Maybe he's settin' her up to take the heat off the real snitch? Can you trust a cop?" Mickey took a drink of her Jack and Coke and lit a cigarette.

Ray finally turned and looked at Mickey. His eyes were dark, and his face was like a stone. "It's her."

"So, what are we gonna do?"

He looked Mickey straight in the eyes. "Kill her." He looked away and took another drag off his cigarette.

"What? *Kill* her? Man, you can't be serious? Darlene? You want *me* to kill *Darlene?*"

"Yes, *kill* the fuckin' little bitch."

"Ray, she's…she's my best friend. I…I don't know if I can do that. You know I'd do anything you want. I'd go to hell and back for you, but…they's gotta be another way, man. What if we just fuck her up real good? Break her legs, cut her face up. Somethin', anything besides kill her. I just don't know if I can do this."

Feeling sick, Mickey set her drink on the table and put out her cigarette. She wanted desperately to change his mind.

Before she could say another word, Ray jumped up and threw his glass against the wall, "I said kill the fuckin' bitch!" He pounded his fist in the air as every muscle in his body became rigid. His face contorted and turned red. The veins on his neck bulged and looked as though they might explode. "Am I clear? Do you fuckin' understand what you need to do?" He was yelling at the top of his voice and leaning in toward her.

"Yes. Yes, I…I do." Mickey could hear her voice coming from far away and from someone else.

Ray paced back and forth for a few minutes, running his hands through his hair. Mickey sat motionless on the couch, her mind racing. Ray calmed down a bit. "I want it done quick. Don't waste any time. Do it this week. We need to shut her up."

"Okay. This week. Okay."

"It's Gabe, too. Both of them. He doesn't have too much to tell them, but he spilled what he does know. So, he's gotta go, too. But Darlene goes first, before she tells somethin' we can't recover from."

Darlene, her best friend since second grade? Little Darlene?

She couldn't imagine actually killing her. Maybe Ray was just angry and would change his mind. Mickey wanted him to change his mind. She needed to leave and think about this, but leaving was not part of the plan. Zip was on his way, and they needed to figure out how to do this and not have murder added to any drug charges the FBI was concocting.

Ray's voice was calm now, and quiet. "Mick, you do this and you get the keys to the kingdom, baby. Anything you want—all the cocaine you can do, money, a house, a car. You name it." He was pacing again. "I'm relyin' on you, Mickey." He stopped in front of the coffee table and looked at her. "You're the only one I can completely trust these days. I *need* you to do this for me, and do it right. I'll take care of you, Mick. We're in this together. I *need* you, Mick."

She had been waiting to hear those words for a long time. Needing her was so much better than loving her. Needing her meant he couldn't be without her. Needing her for this meant they would be joined forever. A shared secret. A deed that would bond them for life.

Zip showed up, and they devised a plan. Mickey spent the next few days in turmoil. She knew what she had to do, but she wouldn't do it alone. She told him she wanted Zip to help. However, when it came time to do the deed, Zip was out looking for Gabe, so Ray sent her with Lou and Sally. Two little pansy ass idiots. Sally was scared of her own shadow, and Lou would throw Mickey under the bus without hesitation if this got out.

Ray told her exactly what to do and when to do it. Ever obedient to Ray, Mickey loaded the gun and put it in her jacket pocket.

CHAPTER EIGHTEEN
The Bed You Lie In

"It's the way you've lived that's brought all this on you.
The bitter taste is from your evil life." — Jeremiah 4:17-19

"Okay, Gabe, where are you?" Darlene muttered to herself as she peered through her car's windshield into the dark, abandoned parking lot of Montgomery's Super Market. The store had been closed for nearly a decade. The current occupants were wayward dogs, cats, rats and God only knew what else. Weeds were sprouting up through the asphalt parking lot, which was the unofficial meeting place for drug swaps, hookups and other cover-of-dark activities.

When Darlene was a child, coming to Montgomery's was a Saturday morning ritual for her and her mother. The owner's name was Charlie, and he was always being paged over the intercom.

"Charlie, pick up the PA."

"Charlie, red line."

"Charlie, green line."

Darlene had thought they were saying "lime" instead of "line," and she always wanted to see the red limes.

Her cousin Rachel made up a song about the store to the tune of an old David Allen Coe song. Darlene stared into the darkness of the parking lot and laughed as she thought of Rachel singing, "I was thumbin' from Montgomery's. I had my groceries on my back…" They were at Aunt Penny's the day Rachel first sang the song and acted out a little skit—her version of an MTV video. They were so young and innocent. Entertainment didn't include drugs or alcohol then.

Darlene had been waiting for Gabe for almost twenty minutes, when a couple of cars came and parked at the far end of the parking lot. They made their exchange and pulled out. Gabe had said to be here at eight, and she was a few minutes early. He had information from Dan and didn't want to talk about it on the phone. Darlene looked around the lot and out the passenger window. She heard something thumping on the back of the car. She froze. She suspected Ray was onto her and was terrified it was Zip, sent to kill her. The thumps grew louder. Darlene looked around and was ready to put the car in gear and get the hell out of there. She looked around again and was suddenly looking into two eyes through the passenger window. She screamed.

"Open the fuckin' door, Darlene."

Her eyes adjusted. It was Gabe. "Shit, Gabe. You nearly scared the life out of me," she said as she leaned over and unlocked the passenger door. "You gotta stop doin' that shit."

"Well, who else were you expectin'?" He shook his head, sliding into the passenger seat.

"Well, I don't know, Gabe. I'm a little bit paranoid. For all I know Ray had crazy Zip follow me. This whole mess has me checkin' closets and lookin' over my shoulder all the time."

"Well, you should be careful. This thing is way out of control. Ray's paranoid as hell and suspects everybody. If anybody refuses to do what he says, he right off thinks they're workin' with the Feds." Gabe looked around the parking lot and then at Darlene.

He lit a cigarette. "Darlene, you really need to be careful. Ray asked me if you was workin' with the Feds and if I had any reason he shouldn't trust you."

"What did you tell him?"

"I told him no. That you were too much in love with him to do that."

"Crazy thing is I *am* too much in love with him to do this. But I love my kids more, and this may be my only chance at gettin' 'em back."

"Well, I think he suspects me now, too. Zip's been runnin' his mouth. He thinks if he tells Ray what he wants to hear, he'll get more drugs and be the only one in the inner circle. Between him and Mickey, I don't know who's more power hungry. This whole thing has gotten crazy, Darlene."

"You think Mick's part of it? You think she would turn on me?"

A hardness and sharp edges.

"In a fuckin' heartbeat. Don't be so naïve, Darlene. That bitch is as crazy as Zip. She would do anything Ray told her to."

Darlene didn't want to believe Mickey would turn on her. She wanted to get to the point of their meeting. "Well, what's up with Dan? Why did he want me to meet you?"

"This is where things get really crazy. Dan says Sammy's comin' to Matewan real soon…like next week. But he wants you to find out exactly when. They're gonna bust 'em both right in the middle of the deal. They're ready to move, but they want to catch 'em both in the act. They want to take down the entire operation in one giant bust. And they want you to be the one to set it up."

"Me? Is he crazy? I've told that man a million times I don't know what Ray is doin' until we are on our way out the door, and I don't know when Sammy's comin' until he shows up. This is not info Ray announces. To anybody."

"Well, Dan is determined that you find out exactly when and that you be there when it all happens. Darlene, I don't think you should be around when this goes down. It could get real ugly, real fast. Sammy is one crazy man, and his posse would just as soon kill you as look at you. If they have any idea you set this up or had anything to do with it, they'll kill you before the FBI can move. You ain't got a good poker face, Darlene. I'm afraid they'll make you as soon as the cops come bustin' in."

"Well, me not bein' there will look worse than if I am there. What am I supposed to do? Either way I'm screwed!"

"Well, I've been thinkin' about it. You could tell Ray that your mommy is sick or that Aunt Penny is sick or somethin'. You just can't be there when this goes down."

"What about you? What are you gonna do?" Darlene asked.

"I don't know just yet. Dan says they'll get me to Texas and give me money to get started, but that won't happen until they arrest Ray. I plan to lay low until this thing blows over, maybe have Dan hide me somewhere. Zip would kill me just to be killin' me. I won't be goin' back to The Place. It's too risky, especially after the other night when Ray was questionin' all of us."

Darlene felt sick to her stomach and wanted to throw up. She put her hands on the steering wheel and leaned her head against it. She didn't know what to do. She was too far in to back out now, but she couldn't go any further into this. She could be killed. She just wanted to take her kids and leave this God-forsaken place.

"Dan wants you to call him tomorrow and let him know what you find out," Gabe said.

"Tomorrow? I'm supposed to find this out by tomorrow? That man is crazy. I think he's tryin' to get us both killed." Darlene looked around the abandoned parking lot and started to cry. "Tell him I'll see what I can do."

"Darlene, we're in this together. We need to find a way out for both of us. Here's what I'm thinkin'. You go to Ray and tell him Aunt Penny is really sick in Myrtle Beach, and your mommy wants you to go with her to visit. Tell him your mommy is really upset and begged you to go with her, and you think you may leave Thursday or Friday. If Sammy *is* coming, he'll say somethin' to you about needin' you to be there to entertain that slimy fucker.

"This is the only way I can think of to get him to tell you when Sammy's coming. If he says somethin' about wantin' you to be there, you can ask when he's comin' and tell him you'll try your best to be back by then.

"Then you leave there and tell Dan. I think you should have your shit packed and ready to go. As soon as you hang up with Dan, you get the hell outta here. Do you hear me?" Gabe said. "You can't hang around for one minute after you tell Dan when Sammy will be here. Ray has ways of findin' out stuff, and he'll figure out it was you who told. If you're gone, he won't have any real reason to suspect you. Besides, if you stay, Dan will expect you to be there when this all goes down."

"I can't just leave, Gabe. What about my kids? I want to leave *with* my kids!"

"You can come back for 'em, Darlene. Dan said he would help you with the custody thing, but he can't do nothin' until this all goes down. It may be months before he can do anything. You need to leave. *Now.*"

"What will my girls think? They'll think I just abandoned them. They'll think I'm just gone and not comin' back." Darlene was crying hard now.

"You can call them every day, Darlene. They know you love 'em. Your mommy can tell them you're comin' back." Gabe tried to reason with her. "You can't stay here."

Darlene knew he was right. She would need to tell her mother first thing tomorrow morning, before she went to see Ray.

***

The next morning Darlene was up early and gathering her clothes. She would go visit her mother and do her laundry. That way she would have her clothes in her car and could just swing back by her place, grab Jelly Bean and be on her way.

She gathered up Jelly Bean's favorite toys, the five cans of tuna in the pantry, and his favorite fleece blanket her mother had given him, putting them in a small bag by the door. She sat on the couch, holding Jelly Bean close to her face. She kissed his silky head. "Sweetheart, you be ready around two. I'll be back for you and we'll head south." Purring, Jelly Bean placed a velvet paw on her cheek to show his approval.

Darlene left her house with her basketful of clothes, some dirty, some clean. When she got to her mother's she went straight to the washer and started loading her clothes. "Darlene honey, what's the rush? Sit down and let's have some coffee and talk about this," Millie said.

"Mommy, I'm leavin' this afternoon to go stay with Rachel for a while. This whole thing with Ray and the FBI is gettin' real ugly, and I need to leave. But only for a little while."

Millie teared up. "Darlene, what's happened? Did that man threaten you? I swear I will tear him apart if he tried to hurt you."

"Mommy, no. It ain't that. I just don't want it to be that either, so I'm leavin'. The FBI is movin' in, and I am not gonna stick around to be a part of it. I got just one more thing to do for them, and then I'm outta here."

"What? What is this one more thing?"

"I'm goin' to see Ray when I leave here. I need to get him to tell me when Sammy is plannin' to be here, date and time. Gabe and I concocted a story. I'm tellin' him I need to go with you to visit Aunt Penny in Myrtle Beach sometime this week. Hopefully he'll get all upset and want me to be here when Sammy arrives and will tell me when I need to be back. Once I give this info to Dan, I'm gone. Ray's gettin' too close to findin' out it's me and Gabe talkin' to the FBI. I don't trust any of them now. Not Ray, not Zip, and Gabe says I shouldn't trust Mickey, either."

"Oh, dear Jesus, Darlene. This is terrible."

"Well, I hope to be outta here by two. I'm gonna do my laundry so I have my clothes in the car. I'll stop and get Jelly Bean and go."

"What about the girls? What will you tell them?"

"I wrote this letter for them and want you to give it to them after Ray is arrested and in jail, not a minute before." Darlene took the envelope addressed to Amy and Renee out of her purse and handed it to her mother.

"Okay, okay. I'll give it to them." Millie got up from the table. She walked over to the sink and started crying.

Darlene got up and went over to her mother. "Mommy, I love you so much, and I'm so sorry for every mean, hurtful thing I've done to you and Daddy. I never, ever meant to hurt you. I never meant for any of this to happen. Things just got out of hand."

"I love you too, baby." Millie wrapped her arms around Darlene.

"Mommy, it's like you always said about the little choices we make in life and how they can lead to a really bad end. I made some terrible choices and had no clue it would get this crazy. I thought I was just havin' a good time. I wasn't, though. I was havin' a really horrible time and ruinin' my life and my kids' lives. I'm so sorry, Mommy." Darlene started crying again. She got up and started putting the first wash load into the dryer.

"What time does Daddy get home?" Darlene asked. "I'd like to say goodbye to him."

"He's workin' second shift today and won't be home until around ten tonight. But he's goin' to Tennessee to the lake to fish next weekend with your uncle Johnny. So you can see him then. He'll be real pleased you made the decision to leave here."

"Tell him I love him, Mommy, and I'm truly sorry for everything." Darlene turned back to the laundry so her mother wouldn't see the tears she couldn't hold in any longer.

"Darlene, why don't you go on? Do whatever it is you gotta do with Ray and get outta here as soon as you can. I'll finish up your laundry. After you stop and get Jelly Bean, you can swing by here and grab your clothes and go."

"Are you sure, Mommy?"

"Yes. I'm sure. Do you want somethin' to eat?" Millie asked.

"Lord, no. I'm afraid I might throw up."

"Okay, I'll have a little somethin' ready for you to take with you. You'll need to eat somethin'. I'll have all your stuff packed and ready."

Darlene hugged her mother and told her she would be back as soon as she could. They agreed that if she were going to be later than two, she would call.

"I love you, Mommy."

Darlene closed the back door and left.

CHAPTER NINETEEN
The Road to Hell

"There's a way of life that looks harmless enough; look
again—it leads straight to hell." — Proverbs 14:12

She pulled out of her parents' driveway, going over again
what she would say to Ray. She didn't want to slip up. She
just needed to keep it together for another hour or so.

She couldn't quite wrap her mind around the mess her
life had become. She had made so many bad choices, it was
hard to pinpoint the one that had sent her over the edge.

They were small, simple choices.

Seemingly insignificant yes-or-no decisions. Each one had
led her one small step further from where she was supposed
to be, from where she truly wanted to be. Step by simple step.
Piled together the choices were one huge mountain of chaos
and noise. But one at a time, who could tell any difference
from the moment just before she made the choice, to the
quiet moment just after?

Simple choices.

Her mama always told her, "Think before you leap,
Darlene." She always thought that meant big leaps, big
choices. Stuff like getting married, having babies, moving
across the country, joining the army. Real life-changing
choices. Big ones that you could reach out and touch
immediately.

Not little ones.

Spending time with Mickey seemed to be an easy choice. When Darlene had been having a difficult time after the miscarriage, Mickey came to visit. To check on her. That's what friends do.

They hadn't spent too much time together after Darlene got married and she had missed her friend. But that one visit turned into more visits, and that turned into more drugs and more bad decisions on Darlene's part.

Visiting with Mickey didn't seem like a bad thing to her at the time. Sure, she brought drugs, but so what? It was just a little pot and a few Lortab; sure seemed like it was no big deal at the time.

Just one small choice.

She knew she couldn't blame it all on Mickey, though. Mickey just wanted her to lighten up and have some fun. Truth is, she had been bored, lonely, and had been carrying around a mountain of disappointment and shame and anxiety for years. She just wanted to escape for a little while. She was tired of the way her life was. Tired of who she had become. Some days the anxiety of living her life just gnawed at her from the inside like a parasite. She just needed some relief from being her.

Yeah, having her friend come visit sure seemed like the right thing to do at the time.

If it were only that simple.

She approached the turn to the back alley and her trailer and thought about just running in and grabbing Jelly Bean and leaving. To hell with Dan and the FBI, and to hell with Ray. If Dan wanted Ray so much, he was going to need to do it another way.

She pulled off the highway and stopped before crossing the tracks that would take her down the back alley to the first left turn, to her trailer, seventh on the left, and to Jelly Bean. She played it out in her mind. *Grab Jelly Bean and his traveling bag. Stop at Mommy's and pick up the clothes whether wet, dry, dirty or clean. Grab the other items we've been stashing away. Grab my money.* Jelly Bean would curl up in her lap asleep as she drove. Three or four hours later, she would cross the bridge on Tennessee Highway 33, across Norris Lake. Just a few more miles and she would be at Rachel's. Tomorrow she would wake up and be free.

She wasn't sure how long she had been sitting there, crying, on the side of the road in North Matewan. It felt like hours. Her body felt like lead. Everything in her was pulling her to put the car in drive, cross the tracks, get Jelly Bean, and go. But leaving like this and not helping Dan would pretty much guarantee she would never see her kids again, and she couldn't take that chance. With a sick dread, she pulled back onto the highway and headed toward Ray's.

CHAPTER TWENTY
Mountains to Climb

"I am not a little sparrow
I am just the broken dream
Of a cold false-hearted lover
And his evil cunning scheme."
—Dolly Parton, "Little Sparrow"

It was a beautiful day for a drive. As the mountains passed by, she noted the early bloomers—red buds, golden rods. Not many, but enough to dot the mountainside. Darlene loved springtime. She couldn't wait for the dogwoods to bloom. She would be in Tennessee by then, in time for the Dogwood Festival in Knoxville. Her mother's crocuses had been up for a while, and the tulips were shooting out of the ground. Mingo County was beautiful in the right season. The mountains were tall and tight, with a straight-up mountain, the road, the railroad tracks, the Tug River and another straight-up mountain. And then after that mountain, another and another and another. The early spring rains and melting snow created waterfalls and streams flowing out of the hollers and crevices—pure mountain beauty. The sun came up at ten and was gone by five. She would miss these mountains. She hoped, in time, she could return. At least to visit. She would be glad to get away from here, though, and to get her girls out, too. This place was home, but there were no opportunities for a young, single mother. There were also too many demons pulling her down a no-good path. Leaving was the right decision, and today was the day.

The truth was that she just wanted to run away from everything that was her life, not necessarily the place. A change of geography was only part of her reasons for wanting to run. She needed to get away from Ray, from the drugs, from the FBI, from Dave, from her father. She needed a new life for herself and the girls. She didn't want her girls growing up here. The drug scene was taking over. Everyone she knew was on pills, pot or cocaine. The frightening part was that it was not just the typical druggy using these days. It was professional people, moms, dads, politicians, businessmen, hard working coal miners needing a little something to take the edge off from crawling around underground all day. No one was untouched by it. For Darlene, it all had become too much to absorb.

Matewan would always be home. She had grown up here and spent her entire life here—playing in the creek that ran behind the house, climbing up in the mountains to Devil's Tea Table, and riding four-wheelers up on the Hatfield & McCoy trails. She remembered the first time she saw the wild horses—what a sight to see. Beautiful, gentle beasts. She loved going up to Grapevine and just sitting and watching them. A bag of carrots was always a welcomed treat. She watched the mountains pass by as she rode along, wishing she had spent her last day here with her girls and the horses instead of with Mickey, Lou and Sally. But she still had one last thing to do before she could leave.

She just wanted to get home now, grab Jelly Bean, and go. Everything was packed and ready. When she arrived at The Place, Mickey came out to greet her and insisted they go for a drive. She told Mickey she needed to get home soon, but Mick was all jacked up on coke and seemed like her mind was a million miles away.

They had been driving around forever. Darlene didn't think she could do one more line of coke. Mickey, Lou and Sally were working themselves into a frenzy. The car was full of coked-up women, music and cigarette smoke. Darlene decided just to go with it. It would be her last night of partying and probably the last time she would see Mickey. Darlene looked at her watch. It was five. She really needed to call her mother. She had told Millie she would swing by to get her clothes at two. Her mother knew Darlene and knew she was almost always late. But this time was different, she was leaving town, and her mother would be worried. Mickey was hell-bent on not stopping or listening to her.

***

"Millie knows how you are. She knows you're never on time for anything anymore. We'll stop and call her later." Mickey didn't want Darlene talking to Millie. She didn't want Millie to know Darlene was with her.

Mickey kept driving, working up the courage to do what she had been ordered to do. She loved Darlene and hated her at the same time. No, hate was taking it too far. Mickey resented Darlene's being so cute and girly and that Ray had chosen Darlene and not her. She wished she had never introduced them. But Ray trusted Mickey. He *needed* her. He counted Mickey as one of his best foot soldiers. A true confidante. Now that he knew the truth about Darlene, maybe Mickey would have a chance to be Ray's girl.

She had tried to convince Ray to let her just beat up Darlene, but he was hell bent on killing her. Make an example of her, he said. An example that no one, not even a good piece of ass, crossed him and got away with it. Mickey was having a hard time doing this because she and Darlene had been friends for so long. Darlene had been a huge part of her life. They were like sisters. Yeah, she loved Darlene, but she loved Ray more. She worshipped Ray and would do anything for him. Ray had been good to all of them. Especially Darlene.

How could Darlene turn on him? How could she be such a snake? The FBI? What was she thinking? Why would she do this? What had they offered her or threatened her with?

Oh, well. It didn't matter now. They were stepping through a door they couldn't close.

Mickey stopped on top of Mary Taylor Mountain and cut out four more lines of coke.

CHAPTER TWENTY-ONE
Sin and Bones

"You don't want to end your life full of regrets, nothing but sin and bones." — Proverbs 5:11

Thursday, April 16

At two, Millie was waiting by the telephone for Darlene's call. Then came three…four…five…no call. Millie waited all night for Darlene to return for her clothes and get on the road to Tennessee. She had gone to the Dollar Store and bought a case of cat food and a large bag of cat litter for Jelly Bean. Rachel's mother, Emma, had called earlier to let her know she was more than happy to have Darlene stay with her as long as she needed. Her daughters had been in a tight spot before, and she understood how distraught Millie must be. Family had to stick together. Millie knew Emma would take care of Darlene as if she were her own. If Darlene would just hurry up and come on, Millie could relax.

She hadn't wanted Darlene to go back to Ray's for any reason. Millie didn't trust the FBI to make sure Darlene didn't get hurt. Darlene trusted Dan and had called him before she left to let him know she was making her last trip to Ray's before she left town. She had done all she could for them and would make one last effort to find out when Ray would see Sammy again.

Millie called Gabe to find out if he had heard from Darlene. Gabe didn't answer his phone. Perhaps they were together.

***

Ray had been pacing for hours. No news was not necessarily good news in this case. What if the FBI had followed them and arrested the girls? Mickey had his .38 on her and about two grams of cocaine—enough to send her to jail for a while. What if the FBI had come busting in when they were killing Darlene and they had turned on him. Rats! All of them were rats.

Zip came in about ten. He had no news on Gabe. Zip had staked out Gabe's mother's place and even followed her to work. Nothing. Not a sign of Gabe anywhere. Zip suggested that maybe the FBI had him in protective custody. That made sense except for one thing—why Gabe and not Darlene? She was more vulnerable than Gabe.

Ray had been surprised when Darlene showed up that afternoon. He expected her to leave town as fast as she could. She had to know he was on to her. If the Feds sent her back to get more info, then they were probably following the girls.

He had doubts that Mickey could go through with it because he knew she loved Darlene. On the other hand, Ray knew Mickey would do anything for him; he had complete control over her. He was only slightly concerned that she wouldn't finish what she started, but he had sent Lou with her just to hedge his bet.

Lou hated Darlene. She was so damned jealous she couldn't see straight and would do anything to get her out of the picture, even murder. That, coupled with the amount of cocaine he promised her, guaranteed she would make sure the deed was done.

Sally was the one he wasn't sure of. She was addicted to Oxies, and he had promised her a life-time supply. Hell, he promised all three of them all the drugs they could do for as long as they could do them.

***

The four women returned to Red Jacket and approached The Place. Darlene was relieved; she just wanted out of the car, but Mickey didn't stop. She was headed toward Newtown. Darlene was pretty wired up on cocaine and just wanted to go home and straighten up. She couldn't go back to her parents like this, but she was afraid to go home alone. Staying with Ray was out of the question. She didn't want to be anywhere near The Place when Sammy arrived. She decided as soon as she got back to Ray's, she wouldn't even go in; she would just get in her car and go.

Mickey wasn't about to stop, though. Darlene had asked three dozen times to stop so she could call her mother. Mickey ignored her. Now Mickey was turning off Mate Creek Road going up Double Camp.

"Where we goin', Mick?"

"Oh, never you mind that, Darlene." Mickey just kept driving.

About two miles up Double Camp, they turned onto a dirt driveway. On a small hill on the right sat an old, rusty trailer. The front porch was no more than a few cinderblock steps and four pieces of rotting wood.

Darlene peered through the car window. "Does somebody actually live here? It looks abandoned."

Mickey just laughed.

A hardness and sharp edges.

Lou and Sally hadn't said anything for the past several miles.

Darlene was getting worried. What was Mickey up to?

Mickey stopped the car and Lou and Sally got out of the back seat. "What are we doin' here, Mickey? I don't understand."

Lou opened Darlene's door. "You will."

Mickey got out and came around and pulled Darlene from the front seat. Darlene tried to break free, but Mickey was twice her size and determined. She held Darlene firmly by the arm.

"Mick, what on earth's wrong with you? Why you actin' like this?"

They know. They know it's me.

Darlene tried to play this out in her mind and prepare for the worst. What was the worst they would do? Beat the shit out of her? Probably break her legs and leave her here. Or Mickey would let Lou and Sally do the beating. Ray must have threatened Mickey. Her best friend would never treat her like this.

A hardness and sharp edges.

Maybe her mommy had been right. Maybe Mickey wasn't her friend. Maybe Mickey didn't love her like a sister. Or maybe Ray had made her choose.

Mickey dragged Darlene up the cinderblock steps. She kicked open the door and tossed Darlene inside, where she fell to the floor. The only light was from a street lamp on the road directly in front of the trailer. Mickey, Lou and Sally came in and circled her. Darlene tried to stand up, and Lou kicked her back down.

"Why you doin' this?" Darlene didn't understand why Mickey was part of this. She knew Lou hated her, but Mickey was her best friend. She crawled backwards on her hands and knees until she hit the wall. They moved in closer.

"You're a rat, Darlene. Ray knows all about your little chats with Dan, the FBI guy. It ain't a secret no more." Mickey towered over Darlene. "I told you before you even met Ray he was wired all the way to the top. Did you think he wouldn't find out about you workin' with the Feds?"

"Mickey, I don't know what you're talkin' about. I swear. I would never do that."

Mickey picked up Darlene and dropped her onto a rusty metal chair that was pushed up against the window. She leaned over and put her finger in Darlene's face. "Well, little

Darlene, all cute and sweet, stop playin' the innocent victim. We know all about you and the FBI. What I don't understand is how you could turn on Ray after he's been nothin' but good to your sorry ass. Don't you know that turnin' on Ray, is turnin' on all of us?"

"Mickey, I swear…I ain't talked to the FBI. Do I look that stupid? I love Ray and would never turn on him." Darlene saw Mickey's hand coming up and she put both hands in front of her face to ward of the blows. Mickey ordered Lou and Sally to hold down her hands. Mickey slapped her two, three, four times. She knew Mickey was going to beat the shit out of her, and she was scared. How far would Mickey go? Would she leave her there to crawl home? It could be days before anyone found her.

Lou was yelling for Mickey to hit her again. Sally just stood there holding Darlene's left arm, looking as though she might faint.

"Let me at her, Mickey," Lou screamed.

Mickey stood back. Lou kicked Darlene in the shin.

Darlene was sure it was broken. She doubled over in pain and threw up on the floor at Lou's feet. Lou was pissed that she threw up on her shoes and kicked her again and then gave her an upper cut to the chin.

Mickey told them to back off for a minute. When they were far enough away, Darlene got up and ran down the hall, dragging her leg behind her. She was going for the back door to get out. Her leg was throbbing, and she only made it as far as the first bedroom. Mickey caught up with her and pushed her inside.

Darlene tried to stand up but only made it as far as her knees. She was kneeling in front of Mickey when she pulled the .38 out of her pocket. Mickey told Sally to watch the front door and make sure nobody came up the driveway.

Darlene thought this must be a dream. Mickey would never shoot her. Ever. They loved each other like sisters. Maybe Mickey just wanted to scare her.

"Why, Mick? Why in God's name are you doin' this? This is me, Darlene. Your best friend. Your *sister. Why?*" Tears flowed down Darlene's face.

"Cause you're a traitor, and Ray wants you dead. His orders." Mickey aimed the gun at Darlene's head.

"Please, Mick, I have two little girls who need me. Please don't do this."

"Well, you ain't exactly been mommy of the year, Darlene. You should have thought about them long before now." Mickey pulled back the hammer.

"Please, Mickey, at least let me pray before you kill me."

"Pray? Are you serious? God don't hear the prayers of whores like you, Darlene."

Mickey pulled the trigger.

Darlene ducked. The bullet grazed the right side of her head. Darlene put her hand to her head. There was blood, but she was still alive. She tried to stand up, and Mickey fired another shot into her chest. Darlene felt the bullet go in, hot and stinging. She held the spot on her chest as blood oozed through her fingers, soaking her sweater.

"Why?" Darlene asked, crying. She couldn't believe Mickey had just shot her. She loved Mickey.

A hardness and sharp edges.

Her girls. What about her girls? What would they think had happened to her? Would they know how much she loved them? Would they ever know she had done this for them? The letter. Her mother had the letter. What about her mother? Her mother would die from this. This is the last cruel thing she would do to her mother.

Oh, sweet Jesus, save my soul. Please don't let me die here. Forgive me, dear Lord. Forgive me.

"This bitch ain't gonna die. Let me beat her fuckin' brains in." Lou grabbed a broken cinderblock from the living room and started beating Darlene in the head.

Darlene saw Lou coming at her with the cinderblock, but she couldn't move. She was dying. She felt the first hit on the left side of her head, then the second hit on the back of her head as Lou moved around. She was anticipating the next hit when everything went black. Their voices sounded so far away. It was dark and quiet for a few minutes. Calm even. Then it started getting brighter and brighter still. There was no sound. Then peace. Sweet peace.

***

Darlene fell over. Her face was a mangled mess of blood and hair and exposed bone. Blood was everywhere—on the walls, the carpet, Lou, Mickey.

Still holding the gun, Mickey just stood over Darlene, watching her best friend since second grade bleed to death. Darlene lay there with her eyes still open, looking into space.

Fuck, what have I done?

Mickey knew she couldn't get all emotional now. Not now. The deed was done. It was what Ray wanted, and Ray always got what he wanted. Even if it meant killing Darlene. She did it for Ray. He *needed* for her to do this.

Okay, now what?

Mickey's panic rose to her throat and choked her.

Dear God, what have I done?

She couldn't show her weakness to Tweedle-dee and Tweedle-dum. Couldn't let them see she was upset or even worried about the consequences of what had just happened. Did she really just kill her best friend? They really hadn't been best friends for a while. Actually, she had grown to hate Darlene and her whining about everything all the time. Darlene had it made with Ray and just took it for granted. She was sleeping with the man who controlled all their lives. It was Darlene who got to go on the trips. It was Darlene who got all the drugs she wanted without having to work for it. It was Darlene who got a free place to live and money.

Whiney-ass bitch. Traitor. She deserved it.

"What are you two standin' around snivelin' about? Help me put her body in the car."

"The car? What are we gonna do with it?" Sally cried. "I thought we were leavin' her here, and Zip was gonna burn the place down?"

"Well, there's been a change of plans. I ain't sure yet what we'll do with the body. We'll put it in the trunk for now and figure it out after we talk to Ray."

"Oh, God. I'm gonna throw up." Sally ran into what used to be a kitchen and vomited violently.

"Great! They send me with the two most simple-minded, pansy asses of the bunch," Mickey said with a moan. Inside, she wanted to throw up herself. She would miss Darlene; she had loved Darlene, even when she hated her.

I'll think about that later.

She needed to focus on cleaning up the mess and getting the body out of there.

She looked at Darlene's dead body. She was wearing the diamond stud earrings Ray gave her for Christmas. She was also wearing a diamond necklace and a watch Ray had given her. Mickey decided there was no reason to bury those. She took all the jewelry off Darlene's dead body. She stood up and noticed the new boots Darlene was so proud of and decided her niece would like those. She jerked the boots from Darlene's tiny feet and one of her socks came with the boot. Darlene lay on the floor, bloody, with one bare foot.

As Mickey was putting the jewelry in her pocket, she screamed, "Lou, take the keys and bring the Budweiser banner from the trunk of the car. And close the trunk when you're done. Here, put these boots in the back seat. Hurry. *Now!*"

Lou fumbled the keys from Mickey and dropped them twice before she could get to the door. All the while, Mickey was growing more agitated. Lou tripped down the three steps to the cinderblock landing. She tossed the boots in the back seat and closed the door. She was shaking so badly she couldn't get the keys in the trunk lock. With the trunk finally open, she grabbed the banner and ran back inside. Mickey grabbed the banner from Lou and spread it out on the floor.

"Sally, grab her feet and I'll get her arms. On three, pick her up and put her on the plastic." As Sally picked up Darlene's feet, she grabbed Darlene's bare foot. Feeling her flesh, still warm, she dropped both legs and screamed.

"What now? Good grief, it's just a foot."

"A dead foot! Dead. She's dead, Mickey! What if her soul's still floatin' around here and she, she—"

"She what? Kicks you? Her soul went straight to hell. It ain't floatin' around anywhere. Now pick her up or your soul will be floatin' with hers."

As they dropped her body onto the banner and folded the ends over her, Lou started crying uncontrollably. "For the love of God, what is it now?"

"I just can't stand to see her like this. I can't believe you killed her."

"*I* killed her?" Mickey turned, grabbed Lou's throat and slammed her into the wall. She backhanded Lou across the face, busting her lip and nose. "You mean *we* killed her don't you, sweet cakes? *We* killed her. You were the one who took the cinderblock and smashed her brains in. Do you remember that part? We don't know *what* killed her—the bullet or the head bashin' *you* gave her. Either way, both of you snivelin' little bitches were as big a part of this as me. So don't say *Mickey* killed her. We *all* did this. Not just me. Besides, you hated her fuckin' guts, and now you're gonna get all sentimental about killin' her? Shut the fuck up with your baby cryin' and help us before you find yourself wrapped up in plastic. Do you understand? Now, Ms. Cry Baby, go open the trunk if you think you can handle that."

Lou nodded and wiped the snot and blood with the back of her sleeve and ran outside to open the trunk again. Mickey and Sally finished wrapping the body in the plastic sheet. Sally took the time to put the sock back on Darlene's bare foot, and they carried her outside.

"I don't understand how someone so small could be so damned heavy. She feels like a ton of rock," Mickey said as they maneuvered their burden down the steps to the trunk. A cold, drizzling rain had started.

"I'll put my end in first, since it's the heaviest," Mickey said as she carelessly tossed the top half of Darlene's lifeless body into the trunk, causing the banner to fall away from Darlene's head and neck. Sally gently placed the feet in the trunk and tried to smooth Darlene's hair out of her face. It was matted in blood.

"What the fuck are you doin'? It don't matter what she looks like. Move so I can close the trunk. We need to get out of here. Get in the car." Lou and Sally quietly got in. Mickey closed the trunk and they drove away.

"She hated to be cold," Sally said. "She hated this weather."

"Well, she won't have to worry about that anymore, will she? Where she's gone to is nice and hot," Mickey snickered.

They finished the drive with the only sound coming from the windshield wipers screeching on the upward motion.

CHAPTER TWENTY-TWO
The Aftermath

"We are each our own devil, and we make this world our
hell." — Oscar Wilde

Friday, April 17

A little after midnight they arrived back at The Place and
parked at the very rear of the restaurant, entering the office
through the back door. Ray was there waiting with Zip.

"Where the fuck you been? I been sittin' here waitin' for
fuckin' ever! Where is she? Did you do it?"

"Yeah, we did it." Mickey sat on the couch and put her
head in her shaking hands. "It's done."

"Well, where is she? Where's her body?"

"In the trunk of Sally's car, wrapped in a Budweiser
banner."

"What?" Ray screamed. "In the trunk? What are you
plannin' to do with it? You can't just drive around with a
dead girl in the trunk of the car, you idiots."

"Well, I didn't think leavin' a dead body there was such a
good idea with the FBI watchin' every move we make. We
thought you would tell us what to do with it, since it was your
idea to kill her. What did you want us to do with her, just
leave her there?"

"You were supposed to leave her there, and Zip was
gonna burn the place with her in it. Damn. This fucks up the

entire plan, Mickey." Ray paced back and forth for a few minutes. Lou and Sally sat on the couch next to Mickey and said nothing. Sally was still crying.

"So she's wrapped in the Bud banner?"

"Yeah."

"Good, we'll bring her in here and put her in the freezer in the storeroom. It's pretty much empty and no one ever looks in there. We'll leave her in there until we can think of what to do next. I'm sure the Feds will be lookin' for her soon enough." Ray was still pacing and running his hands through his hair. "Well, what are you waitin' on? Go! Zip, help her. Bring her in here. Lou, you and Sally clean out the freezer."

Mickey and Zip went to the car and carried the body in through the back door, careful that no one was watching. They entered the storeroom as Lou was pulling the last few steaks out of the freezer. They dumped Darlene's body wrapped in the banner in the freezer and placed the freezer contents on top of her. Ray looked around the storeroom, turned the light off, and closed the door.

***

By 2 a.m. they had been sitting in the office for about thirty minutes, no one speaking. Darlene was in the freezer, dead, but she was bigger than any life they had ever known, and she hung in the air between them. Accusing them. Taunting them. Ray had been pacing the entire time. "How much evidence did you leave just layin' around in that damned trailer? All of it? I assume you left fingerprints, footprints, bullet casings, her purse? What else did you leave? Or do you even remember?" Ray was worked up into a frenzy now. He couldn't believe they had brought her body back to his place. He needed to figure out what to do. They couldn't very well load her in the car now and take her back to the trailer. The FBI would be watching their every move. Getting her out of the car was risky enough.

"Zip, you need to go tonight and burn the trailer. Do it just before dawn so no one will see you. Don't park your car there. Park somewhere in Newtown or above Double Camp and walk. Don't leave any evidence. You gotta do it tonight, before they get wind of the place."

***

Millie woke up at 3 a.m. Bill was already up and pacing. "Darlene ain't back yet, Millie. I'm worried somethin's happened to her. I've called her house ten times, and she don't answer." He walked into the kitchen and started a pot of coffee.

Millie got dressed and joined her husband in the kitchen. "I'm gonna drive to her house. Maybe she's there and just not answerin' the phone. Or she could be there and be hurt." She wrapped her hair into a ponytail.

"No, you stay here in case she comes back. I'll go and check her house. You don't need to be runnin' into that crazy bunch and get hurt." He took his .38 and left. Millie told him to feed the cat while he was there.

Millie's anxiety grew as she sipped her coffee and waited for Bill to return. After an hour she heard Bill's truck in the driveway. She met him at the door and knew from the hollow look on his face that he hadn't found Darlene.

"She wasn't home, and it looked like she hadn't been there all night. The bed was made, her stuff was sittin' by the door. The cat hadn't been fed. I gave him a can of food and some fresh water. I scooped the litter, too. No sign of Darlene. I drove on up to Ray's. Her car wasn't there, either. Let's try to get some rest and call that FBI guy first thing. This just feels wrong all over."

Millie fought back the tears as Bill sat at the kitchen table and took off his shoes and emptied his pockets, a ritual he had performed since they had gotten married. As familiar as it was, Millie felt as though she were in someone else's body. Someone else's life. She knew in her gut Darlene was hurt.

Resting was the last thing she could think about. She stood at the counter next to the coffee pot and started to cry. Bill moved slowly across the kitchen to hold her for a long time.

***

Zip had left The Place around 2:45 a.m. to burn the trailer as Ray had instructed, even though he wasn't sure if trying to start a fire in this rain was a good idea. He stopped at his house to get the small amount of gasoline he had there for his lawnmower, a can of lighter fluid, and a box of road-side flares. He sat in his living room in the dark and waited for the rain to die down. He wanted to get the fire started before daybreak. He didn't have any concerns about the fire starting, just that it would keep burning long enough to destroy any evidence. The rain tapered off to a drizzle and then stopped.

At 4:15, he left his house with his supplies. He parked about a mile from the trailer and walked. He wore gloves and was careful not to leave any further evidence. After kicking the door open, he poured gasoline and lighter fluid on the walls and floor all through the trailer—in the bedrooms, the hallway, living room and kitchen. He put extra on the blood in the bedroom. He lit six flares, one for each room of the trailer. Needing to stay long enough to make sure the fire was going to keep burning, he stood at the door to the trailer, ready to dash out when the fire got roaring.

After fifteen minutes the fire was blazing, but he continued to stand ready with his gas can and the lighter fluid can and with the remaining three flares in his back pocket. It would be sun-up in about an hour, and he needed to be out of there and home before daybreak to make sure no one saw him. The fire was starting to roar, and the smoke was getting thicker. He stepped back, just beyond the heat of the fire, remaining until the back end of the trailer went up in flames and collapsed. He ran back to his car and drove home. He didn't turn on the headlights until he was a couple of miles down the highway. He was home and in bed before the sun came up.

***

Jason, the FBI's surveillance expert, woke up to the blare from the fire trucks' sirens. He rolled over and tried to go back to sleep; it was barely six. He tossed and turned for five minutes and then decided to turn on the scanner they had been using to monitor the local police channel. Fire at Double Camp. It was an abandoned trailer and probably nothing, but around here everything was suspect. He made a note of it in his log book, just in case it turned out to be something, and then turned off the scanner and went back to sleep.

***

Dan fumbled to find the phone. God, what time was it? 6:24? Who on God's green earth is calling this early? He got out, "Hello?" and then Millie launched into a whole lot of stuff about Darlene that he couldn't understand. She was talking very fast, bordering on hysteria.

"Dan, this is Millie. Darlene's mother. I know it's early, but we have a huge problem. Darlene left here after she called you yesterday. She went to Ray's and she ain't come back. She ain't home. And her car ain't at Ray's. Have you heard from her?"

"Millie, Millie! Slow down and breathe for a minute. Darlene called me yesterday and said she was making one last effort to find out when Ray was meeting with Sammy. She said she would call when she got back to your house, before she got on the road to Tennessee. Millie, let me tell you…I had two of my men staking out Ray's place all day. Darlene showed up there and then left with Mickey and some other girls around one yesterday afternoon. My guys left their post a little before midnight. According to their report, Darlene and Mickey hadn't returned, and Darlene's car was still there."

"Why didn't your guys follow 'em? Why would you send her into this mess knowin' what Ray's capable of?"

"Mickey was never a perceived threat, Millie. Ever. Even Darlene said she was not to be a concern. They've been friends forever. We're after Ray, not Mickey."

"Don't you see? They're all a threat. They're all alike! Mickey's as evil as Ray. I can't believe you just let her go off with that crazy woman." Millie was getting angry and tried to calm herself. "Well, your men left at midnight. My husband drove by Ray's Place at 3:30 this mornin' and Darlene's car wasn't there. So sometime between midnight and 3:30, somebody moved her car. I thought you had cameras on the place. Is there nothin' on the cameras?"

"I'll have my guys review the video right away. Have you checked with your relatives in Tennessee? Maybe Darlene got spooked and just left."

"She would have called me. She would not have left without her cat and her clothes. Oh, dear God, maybe she did. Maybe she was afraid to stop. I'll call Rachel again and see if she's there. In the meantime, you need to check around Ray's and see if they did somethin' to her. By the way, where's Gabe? He don't answer his phone."

Dan tried to calm Millie, but he was concerned now. He knew Darlene well enough to know she would have stopped on her way to Tennessee to call him. She had been out of sight for almost 18 hours now. She checked in every day— twice, most days. She was scared and nervous. What really concerned him was Gabe. Where could he be? He had checked in around 2 a.m. with some critical information about the next drop from Sammy. Dan told him to lay low, but check in. He decided to send his guys to check on him.

Millie called back in less than thirty minutes. No one in Tennessee had heard from Darlene. He would send someone to check on her place. They had Ray's phones wired for sound; they needed to determine if anything had come across. It was now eight on Friday morning.

***

Dan showed up at Millie and Bill's around noon. He instructed Millie to call Mickey, whose phone was wired. The phones of all Ray's mules were wired. Dan gave Millie some key things to ask Mickey.

"Mickey, this is Millie… I'm doin' fine. How's your mother? I heard she was sick. Oh, that's good. Mickey, have you seen Darlene? She was supposed to stop by here yesterday, and I've not heard from her, and she don't answer her phone. Yeah, I figured she might be off somewhere with that no-good Ray. Probably on a binge and not wantin' to come around. When did you see her last? That long ago? That's not like you girls to go two or three days without seein' each other. Ya'll ain't fightin' again are you? Oh, okay. Well, if you hear from her, please tell her to call me right away. Bye."

Dan knew Mickey was lying. His men had photographs and video of them getting in Sally's car and driving off the previous afternoon at one. Why would Mickey lie, unless she was hiding something? He called his men immediately and told them to put a tail on Mickey, Lou, Zip and Sally. And somebody needed to find Gabe.

CHAPTER TWENTY-THREE
Paranoia

"…just because you're paranoid doesn't mean there isn't an invisible demon about to eat your face."
— Jim Butcher, *Storm Front*

Tuesday, April 21

Darlene had been missing for five days, and Dan knew in his gut she was dead. She would have called by now. It was possible Ray had her tied up somewhere to keep her quiet or had beaten her nearly to death and left her somewhere. But Dan knew that was just hoping against hope. Darlene's parents were not about to give up and had called Ray and Mickey several times a day for the past two days. Her father had even gone to Ray's looking for Darlene and demanded that Ray talk to him. Dan had his guys stay close by, and they waited in the parking lot ready to move in if things turned ugly.

Jason and Stan had provided the video of the parking lot at The Place for the day Darlene went missing and the day after. Jason had provided a report along with the video to inform Dan what he was seeing. He read the entries for each video time stamp for the fifth time.

<u>SURVEILLANCE – THURSDAY (16 APRIL)</u>
10:30 a.m. – The staff arrives

11:07 a.m. – Ray arrives.

12:16 p.m. – Mickey arrives.

1:06 p.m. – Darlene pulls into the parking lot and sits in car for a few minutes.

1:10 p.m. – Sally's car pulls in behind Darlene Occupants are Sally and Lou.

1:11 p.m. – Mickey comes out of back office and approaches Darlene as she gets out of her car. They talk for a few minutes with Sally and Lou (they are still in Sally's car).

1:15 p.m. – Mickey and Darlene get in car with Sally and Lou. Mickey drives; Darlene is in front passenger seat; Sally and Lou are in back seat.

1:18 p.m. – They pull out of parking lot heading south towards Matewan.

11:35 p.m. – Zip pulls into parking lot; enters back office.

<u>SURVEILLANCE – FRIDAY (17 APRIL)</u>

12:05 a.m. – Rain becomes heavy at this point and obscures passengers in vehicles entering and leaving parking lot until around 3:30 a.m. (working on video to clear and identify occupants of all vehicles).

12:14 a.m. – Sally's car returns to The Place and pulls around to the back of parking lot. Appears to have three passengers. Car is out of view of cameras at this point. Only shadows visible as occupants emerge from car and enter back office.

12:46 am – Shadows appear around car and at door to back office. Unclear what is happening. Audio picks up muffled voices, nothing clear. Rain is heavy at this point (working on audio to clear).

2:32 am – Darlene's car leaves parking lot heading south towards Matewan. Appears to have one occupant.

2:45 am – Sally's car leaves parking lot heading north towards Newtown. Appears to have two occupants.

2:46 am – Zip's car leaves parking lot heading north towards Newtown. Appears to have one occupant.

3:37 am – Darlene's father pulls into parking lot and sits in car for a few minutes. He departs heading south towards Matewan.

NO ACTIVITY UNTIL 10:00 A.M. NEXT MORNING – STAFF ARRIVES AND ENTERS RESTAURANT.

Note: Ray's car and Mickey's car do not leave parking lot. It is assumed Ray was there all night. If occupants of vehicles are assumed to be Darlene, Mickey, Lou, Sally and Zip—someone is missing. It could be assumed Darlene stayed with Ray. If so, who left in her car?

Dan had reviewed the video four times already and hadn't spotted anything other than what Jason had provided in his report. What had they done with Darlene? Had she been in the trunk of Sally's car? Had they dumped her body someplace else? He needed to get a search warrant before they had a chance to destroy any evidence.

Dan and Jason were going over the videos, phone conversations and logs for the past week. Dan noticed the entry Jason had logged for the trailer fire. "What's this? This fire?"

"Oh, that was a trailer burning at Double Camp last Friday morning. The fire trucks woke me up, and I turned on the scanner. Thought I would log it just in case it turned out to be something. Why? What are you thinking?"

"I'm thinking this could be where they killed Darlene or at least where they took her. The timing is just too close to be coincidental. I think it might be worth checking into."

Dan called his contacts with the state police and the Mingo County Sheriff's Department. He informed them that the burned trailer at Double Camp was officially a federal crime scene and the FBI would be taking over the investigation. He got some push back and a lot of questions he wasn't going to answer. Officer Stanger with the state police had a whole lot of questions—too many questions, in Dan's opinion. Maybe just being territorial, but there was something else in his tone that Dan couldn't quite put his finger on. He had too many other things to think about than officer Stanger's line of questioning.

***

Thursday, April 23

The FBI had been looking for Darlene for the past week. Her mother had called two or three times a day, every day. Her father even showed up a couple of times. Each time, Ray told him he didn't know where she had gone. She just up and left—he assumed with Gabe, since they were both missing.

Ray knew it was a matter of time before they got a warrant and came to The Place to look for her or at least evidence of her being killed there. They had to move her.

"Zip, we gotta get that damned body out of here. It's been a week. The FBI will be comin'. Get her out of here."

"What you want me to do with her? Bury her? Drop her down a mine shaft? What?"

"Bury her. Take her back to the trailer and bury her. Put her behind where the trailer was—out of the way, off the road."

"This rain ain't supposed to stop for a few days. Gonna turn to a freezin' rain tonight and tomorrow mornin'. I'll do it as soon as the rain stops." Zip wondered why he was the one who had to dig the grave. He hadn't killed anybody.

***

Darlene's body had been in the freezer for a week, and Ray hadn't left The Place. He had trouble sleeping but wouldn't leave as long as her body was in the freezer, in case somebody got nosey. The first night he drank half a fifth of Jack Daniel's before going to bed. He wanted—no, needed—to be numb. He was pissed those stupid bitches brought the body back to him. That is not what he had told them to do. Couldn't any of them get anything right? But, there she was in his freezer in the back storage room wrapped in a Budweiser banner.

He finished his last drink and crawled into bed. He drifted into a restless sleep, tossing and turning, somewhere between asleep and awake. The light from the parking lot slipped through the curtains and cast a blue shadow in the room. He rearranged his pillow. He rolled over to face away from the window. That was when he saw her. Darlene was standing at the edge of the bed. No, he was dreaming; it wasn't her, it couldn't be. She was *not* there. He closed his eyes tight and went back to sleep. An hour later, he woke up again. He could smell her perfume—probably just on the pillow.

What was that?

There was something beside him in the bed. He inched his hand out to the right and felt around.

There. That's it.

It was cold and wet. Sticky. He had a hard time adjusting his eyes in the darkness. It *was* Darlene. He couldn't breathe. He tried to say something, but all he could manage was a grunt. His chest was tightening. She was just lying there in his bed, looking at him with those green eyes. She was naked and covered in blood. She had a hole in the center of her forehead, her hair bloody and matted to her face.

Ray could hear someone screaming. Who was screaming? He woke up enough to realize the screams were coming from his own throat. He jumped out of the bed and turned on the light.

He was fully awake now. There was no one there.

It's just me. Darlene isn't here.

He pulled the blanket and sheets off the bed.

She could be hiding.

His heart was racing and felt as though it might explode out of his chest.

He looked under the bed, in the closet and in the bathroom. No Darlene. Was she really dead? Had anyone thought to check her pulse? She could have crawled out of the freezer and left.

No, it was a dream.

His heart was pounding as though he had just sprinted up a hill. He sat on the edge of the bed. That couldn't have been a dream. It was too real. He *touched* her. He could *smell* her perfume. He could still smell it.

He ran to the freezer to make sure she was still there. He threw the boxes off the top and opened the lid. It was cold. He pulled the frozen steaks and chicken and boxes of fish and threw them aside. There was the Budweiser banner. There was her body. When they dropped her in the freezer, the banner had fallen away from her head. She was face up, staring at him. The fucking dead, frozen bitch was staring at him. Her bright green eyes were lifeless and hollow.

"Fuckin' bitch, stop lookin' at me!" He screamed at her lifeless body.

He went to the kitchen and found a garbage bag. He returned to the freezer, grabbed her tiny body and wrapped the garbage bag around her head. He tied it off at the ends, dropped her body back into the freezer, put the banner over her and covered her with the steaks, chicken, and fish, then slammed the lid shut. Now, maybe he could get some sleep.

He took two Xanax and tried to go back to bed, but each time the dream returned. He wanted to go home, even though he didn't want to deal with his wife, but maybe he could get some sleep. Leaving with the body there was not an option, though. The last thing he needed was for someone to open the freezer and find the body. Ray got very little sleep.

***

Saturday, April 25

Millie couldn't eat or sleep. Bill paced the floor and drank what seemed like five gallons of coffee every day. Aunt Penny had cut her trip to Myrtle Beach short, coming home as soon as Millie called her. The three of them had set up camp in the kitchen. Rachel had come from Tennessee to help find Darlene.

Dan enlisted Rachel's help in going to Ray's to see if she could gather information about Darlene. Rachel wanted to help but had never had a good feeling about Ray and refused to go alone. She agreed on two conditions: she would wear a wire and her friend Jeff would go with her. Ray knew Jeff, and it would be a good cover. She agreed not to tell Jeff the whole story behind Darlene's disappearance and the connection with the FBI. She'd just say Millie had asked her to see if she could find out where Darlene was.

Rachel and Jeff went to The Place Saturday night. Ray looked haggard and old. He escorted them to the back office where the usual crew was gathered, all but Darlene and Gabe. Rachel and Jeff were there under the pretense of buying a bag of pot, which Ray gave them. He offered coke, but they turned it down.

Rachel waited until Ray was comfortable with them being there, just as Dan had instructed her. Then she asked, "Where's Darlene these days?"

"That little whore took off a week or so ago. Who knows? Good riddance. She was a lyin' little bitch. Her and Gabe were messin' around, as best I can figure. Ain't seen either one of them in over a week, I guess." Ray lit the pipe and never made eye contact. As he exhaled, he looked at Rachel. "What do *you* know about it?"

Rachel was glad to have a couple of joints under her belt. Ray made her very nervous. "*Me?* Nothin'. I just got into town. I can't believe she would take off with Gabe. He ain't her type. Too young." Rachel was starting to get nervous, despite the amount of pot they had smoked. She never left Jeff's side.

Around eleven, Mickey and Zip came in. Mickey was surprised to see Rachel there. Rachel was surprised to see Mickey looking so rough. She looked as though she had aged fifteen years since they had spent time together during the holidays.

"Hey, Mick! How're you? I heard your mom had been sick. Is she any better?"

"How'd *you* hear about *my* mom?" Mickey's paranoia had her on edge.

"Don't forget, pretty much every cousin I have is a nurse. They keep me posted on who's sick, who died, who's in jail. All the good stuff."

"Oh, right. She's fine. She's out of ICU, but still in the hospital. Hopefully, she'll come home sometime this week. I doubt she'll make it much longer. She has a bad heart, colon cancer, diabetes and is fifty pounds overweight. But she keeps pullin' through."

"Well, I sure hope she gets better." Rachel was feeling braver and calmer. It was much easier to talk to Mickey than it was to Ray. Ray gave Rachel the creeps and always had. She waited until Ray was in a discussion with Jeff to ask Mickey about Darlene. "Where's Darlene? Ray said they split up? I can't believe she would leave him. She's crazy about him, and she sure likes the money and free drugs."

Mickey looked at Rachel as though she had seen a ghost and looked away. "You know Darlene. She just took off. She ain't too reliable, Rachel."

Mickey began bouncing her left knee.

"What the hell you two talkin' about over there?" Ray demanded. "Mickey, I told you don't be talkin' about that little bitch." Ray gave Mickey a cold stare, and she got up and went into the restaurant.

When Jeff dropped Rachel off at Millie's around midnight, the older woman was nearly frantic.

"Dear Lord, girl, where've you been?" Millie asked Rachel. "I was worried they'd hurt you, too. What'd you find out?"

Rachel reported what she had learned and how everyone reacted when she asked about Darlene.

Rachel drove around with Millie and Aunt Penny to all the possible places Darlene might have gone. She called her mother twice a day to see if anyone had heard from Darlene in Tennessee. Sunday she had to leave and promised to look for Darlene's car along the road on the way home. With a tearful hug, Millie said goodbye, and Rachel pulled out onto the highway.

***

Ray knew they were watching. He didn't know from where, but he knew they were watching. He could feel them. He had searched the back office ten times a day for cameras and listening devices. He wasn't sure what exactly he was looking for—anything looking like something that didn't belong. Darlene could have planted anything in there. He hadn't found anything strange, but that hadn't stopped him from looking. He was afraid to leave the office as long as the little bitch was still in the freezer. He needed to go home and sleep in his bed.

Maybe tonight. Maybe tonight.

He needed to get rid of the body, and he had the perfect plan. He needed to talk to Zip and get it arranged.

***

Sunday, April 26

Sunday morning Millie went to Darlene's for the fifteenth time in the past week and a half. She couldn't stand the thought of Jelly Bean being there alone for one more night. She wanted him to be there when Darlene got home, but now it looked as though Darlene would not come home. She gathered up Jelly Bean and all the stuff Darlene had packed for her trip and took them to her house. She left a note for Darlene, explaining that she had Jelly Bean and to come straight to her house. She tore up the other fourteen notes she had previously left.

***

Monday, April 27

Ray was getting more paranoid about the freezer and its contents. Darlene. Cute little Darlene was dead and in his freezer wrapped in a Budweiser banner with a garbage bag over her head.

Darlene. Dead.

He had a hard time saying it and never out loud. Only to himself, when he was alone. Damned shame she turned out to be a narc. He really liked her. She was cute and fun and a fine piece of ass. Being a snitch was not an acceptable quality in his line of business. So she had to go. He had to do it. Had to make an example of her or the others would think they could get away with that shit. No, she got what she deserved, and now the rest of the leaches would know better than to double cross him. Stanger had sent word that the Feds were investigating the trailer, so they couldn't bury her yet. Just a matter of time before they showed up with a warrant.

***

Wednesday, April 29

"What the hell's going on over there? Anything?" Dan was at the apartment with Jason, watching The Place. Dan was waiting for them to slip up. Ray wasn't smart enough or clever enough to not slip up eventually—either that or his minions would turn on him; they were the ones who wouldn't be able to keep their mouths shut. If Sally and Lou had helped kill Darlene or knew anything about it, they would talk. Just a matter of time. Dan wanted to give Ray and his crew a little breathing room. Let them wonder what was going on and let the paranoia and fear build. Wear them down. Let them turn on each other.

Dan had been doing this long enough to know people like Lou and Sally wouldn't be able to stand the pressure. They would be ready to spill their guts in another week or so. They were all under tight surveillance. His men had been following Ray, Mickey, Zip, Sally and Lou for the past three days.

"No. It's been quiet. Ray hasn't left for the past week. He hasn't even come out."

"Good. Paranoia is a paralyzing monster that just gets bigger and bigger. Darlene said Ray was getting more paranoid by the day. I'm sure killing Darlene has sent him into a complete tail spin. We'll just let this thing cook a little longer."

***

Thursday, April 30

The fire marshal had concluded the onsite investigation of the fire. They had all the evidence back at their lab and would have the final results in a couple of weeks. The preliminary results indicated the fire had been set with gasoline and possibly lighter fluid. There were several sets of foot prints on the grounds and tire tracks up to the front door.

Dan's men had used cadaver dogs to search around the trailer with no results. They had sent their evidence back to the FBI lab. They would wait to see if any of it pointed to Ray. The police tape remained around the perimeter and would stay there until all evidence had been examined and the results finalized.

It had been two weeks since anyone had heard from Darlene.

***

Ray got word that the FBI had finished their investigation of the fire. Word spread fast in Matewan. Rumor had it they had even used cadaver dogs to sniff around for her body. Dumbasses; he had her body. They were bigger idiots than he first thought. Now Zip could bury the body. They would do it right under the Feds' noses at the trailer. They had already searched the area and wouldn't go back. They would never find her. Idiots. Ray instructed Zip to dig the grave behind the trailer where no one would see it.

"Dig two," Ray said.

"Two? What we need with two graves?"

"One for Darlene and one for Gabe."

"Gabe? Where the hell is he? You know where he is?"

"Not yet. He can't stay out of sight for too long. He'll show up. And when he does, he'll end up right beside Darlene. In the ground on his way to hell."

CHAPTER TWENTY-FOUR
Hell's Coming for You

"She's dancing down the primrose path to Death;
she's headed straight for hell and taking you with her."
— Proverbs 5:5

Monday, May 4

April became May, and Mickey's life had become hell. It had been three weeks since Darlene died. No…was murdered. A murder she had committed. Sure, she had help, but she did it. She pulled the trigger with Darlene there on her knees begging her not to kill her. Asking her why. Why was she, her best friend in the world, her sister, killing her? Mickey didn't have any answers other than for drugs, money. But mostly for Ray. For some sick need she had for Ray to love her and want her and need her—the way he had Darlene. Darlene was a snitch, a rat, but was that reason to kill her? Reason to kill the mother of two little girls? Two little girls she loved. At the time, that seemed to be reason enough. But now, in the quiet, when Mickey was alone, there was no answer. Truth is, she was never alone; Darlene was always there with her. Begging her not to kill her.

The day Millie and Aunt Penny had showed up at Mickey's asking what she had done to Darlene had been one of the hardest of her life. Millie was a wreck. She had lost a lot of weight, and she looked empty; she was crying and screaming at Mickey. These people were her family. They had been part of her life for as long as she could remember. Aunt Penny had to pull Millie out of Mickey's house and back to the car. Yeah, that had been a hard day. She had done this and could never make it right. Ever.

Mickey had been drinking more and using more pills as the weeks passed. The booze helped her not to think and allowed her to pass out every night. For a while at least. Sleeping had been impossible. The dreams of Darlene were vivid and frightening. One night she dreamed she went to hell and Satan was there with all his demons and Ray—all laughing at her.

Now that the deed was done, Ray didn't seem to need her so much, other than to keep her mouth shut. He kept her close for the first few days, then he started pushing everyone away, saying they needed to avoid drawing any attention to him. He complained and whined about how he had to deal with this and how *he* felt, how *he* was trying to cope with it. It was all about *him*. She could see that now.

*****

Thursday, May 7

Gabe was restless. He had been in the safe house, which was actually a cabin, for the past three weeks. Dan's men had found him hiding out in his grandmother's garage the night after Darlene went missing. The garage was detached from the house and sat about twenty-five yards behind the house. It hadn't been used for a garage in years, and his grandmother had filled it with stuff she would never use again. Gabe had parked his car under some bushes behind the garage and made himself as comfortable as he could inside. He had food and water and a flash light. His grandmother didn't even know he was there.

Now, here he was in a safe house, and he had no clue where he was. It looked like West Virginia, but it could have been Kentucky or Virginia. Hell, it could even be

Pennsylvania for all he knew. Two agents had been assigned to watch him around the clock. He was allowed outside for an hour each day. He couldn't call anyone. No email, no letters, no communication. He could watch TV and drink beer, but that was about it. He was getting restless. He was worried about Darlene; they still hadn't found her. That son of a bitch Ray had killed her; Gabe was sure of it. No, Ray was too much of a coward to do it himself; he had Zip do it. They had killed Darlene. She should have left when he told her to, and now she was dead. If the FBI hadn't found him, he would be dead with her. Ray was evil, and everyone who got close to him was destined for a sorry end.

***

Tuesday, May 19

The shovel chewed through the earth. With each load of dirt, Zip muttered to himself about the assignment of this particular task. There were others who could have done the deed as easily…or at least helped. Frustrated, he just picked a spot—the easiest spot for him, not where he had been instructed to dig. Perhaps not the best spot for a grave, but what the hell. It worked, so what if it was a little close to the road? Not like it was a major highway, just a stupid back road in Mingo County, West Virginia.

He continued digging, and he continued muttering. "Digging graves is not what I signed up for. Stupid bitches. They killed her. They should dig the grave." It was a moonless night, and he couldn't see his hand in front of his face, let alone what he was digging. "Whose idea was it to dig a grave in the pitch black of night in these God-forsaken mountains? And why two graves? They only have one body. Stupid bitches."

***

Ray, Mickey, Sally and Lou were waiting at Ray's mother's house. Ray's mother was eighty-nine years old and had gone to bed hours earlier. It was midnight, and Ray had turned off all the lights. Lou's aunt's car was backed into the garage, and Darlene's body was in the trunk. It had been in there since yesterday afternoon. The weather was still pretty cold, so the corpse was still partially frozen, still wrapped in the Budweiser banner, and the garbage bag was still tied around her head. They knew the FBI had been following them, and Ray's crew had had a hell of time getting away from Dan's people. Ray and the three women snuck into the backseats of cars they knew the FBI would not be tailing, and they all met at Ray's mother's house. It had taken them almost all day to ditch the FBI. Zip was digging the grave, and they would meet him at the gravesite at an hour past midnight to bury the body. They were all in this together, and they would all go down together if it came to that. They snorted another line of coke and decided it was time to go meet Zip.

They drove to Double Camp and found Zip sitting at the bottom of what used to be a driveway to the trailer. The police crime tape was gone, and the frame of the torched trailer was hollowed out and black.

Mickey parked the car at the top of the driveway so it wouldn't be seen. Ray got out of the car and walked over to Zip. "What the fuck you doin' sittin' here? Anybody could see you!" Ray whispered.

"Well, they ain't been not one car go by since I been out here. So I think we're pretty safe."

Ray started walking toward the trailer. "Where's the grave? Let's do this and get the hell outta here."

"Graves are down here." Zip pointed back toward the road away from the driveway.

Ray walked over to him and grabbed his shirt. "What the fuck you mean down here? I told you to dig the grave behind the damned trailer. Not on the side of the damned road!" Ray was furious that Zip would do something to disobey his direct orders.

"Well, you ain't the one that had to dig—not one, but two—graves in this pitch black dark shit out here. I couldn't find a spot up there that was soft enough. It's all rock. This is what we got, so let's just go with it."

"Did you at least dig *two* graves?"

"Yeah, even though we only got *one* body, we have *two* graves."

Ray just stared at Zip. He didn't want to argue with him here. "Let's just get the body out of the trunk and bury it."

Mickey, Sally and Lou got Darlene's body out of the trunk. She wasn't as cold now, not nearly as frozen. The plastic was wet from the thawing. Sally was crying. They carried Darlene's body down the dirt driveway to the grave. The spot was about fifteen feet from the pavement, between a cluster of trees. The weeds and grass were overgrown, and unless someone was looking for it, they would never see the grave from the road.

They placed Darlene's body on the ground while Zip got the shovel out of the grave. The five of them stood around the shallow grave like mourners waiting for the eulogy. The moon broke through the clouds just as Mickey and Zip picked up Darlene's partially frozen body.

Ray said, "Make sure she's face down. I want that little bitch to see hell comin' for her."

They did as instructed without uttering a word. Zip and Mickey hurried to cover the body with dirt, while Lou and Sally gathered leaves and weeds to cover the grave. Ray watched, never getting dirty, except for the mud on his shoes. Ray didn't ever get his hands dirty. The moon disappeared behind the clouds.

They drove back to The Place in silence. Now that they were done, they didn't care if the FBI saw them. It was late; they were all tired.

"Ray, what about Gabe? What we gonna do about him? Ain't nobody seen him in a month," Mickey said.

"I don't know. He's still out there. He'll turn up soon enough. He ain't too smart. We'll just wait him out, and when he shows his sorry face, we'll stick him in the hole next to Darlene.

CHAPTER TWENTY-FIVE
Your Sins Will Find You Out

"…for dust thou art, and unto dust shalt thou return."
— Genesis 3:19

Saturday, June 6

May had not been a good month for Dan and his team. They had been following every lead they received on Darlene. The cadaver dogs had been to the trailer two times with no results. Not even a hit. The Fire Marshal's results proved the fire at the trailer had been deliberately set, but no evidence pointed to a culprit, let alone Ray and his gang. They had hit a wall. Darlene's parents had lost hope. They just wanted a body and justice for what everyone knew Ray had done to Darlene.

It was June 6, and Dan knew if they didn't find Darlene soon, any evidence would be destroyed and Ray would walk away from this without a scratch.

There was a glimmer of light in this darkness. They had Ray on drug trafficking, and it was a slam dunk. They had sent in an undercover agent to buy five kilos of cocaine. Ray was getting either cocky or sloppy. They arranged the deal with Sammy and met at The Place; it was all on tape. Even better news was that in exchange for a plea deal, Sammy had turned and offered up Ray, the Detroit gang and the Chicago Cartel. None of this would have happened without Darlene's help and the information she had provided. She had given them enough details about Ray and how he dealt, how much he kept on hand, and with whom he dealt to know how to arrange the setup. Thanks to Darlene, they knew to ask for more than two kilos, thus causing him to have to bring Sammy into the deal. He couldn't move that much by himself for one customer. They were ready with the warrant so they could move in when Ray and his crew were all there for their typical Saturday night soiree. Dan wanted to close it down— all of it. They were prepared to arrest everyone in the place.

The FBI had spread out all around Matewan. Jason and three agents were in the apartment providing a minute-by-minute run of what was happening and would join the others when they arrived. A helicopter was coming in from Charleston, and 35 agents were on the ground on standby— some at the new high school, some in the old Montgomery's parking lot, and a few sitting about a mile above The Place— ready to move in. The chopper would follow them in. Mickey had been there for about an hour; Zip had arrived ten minutes earlier; Lou and Sally had just pulled in. Dan gave the signal, and they surrounded the place within minutes.

Ray, Zip, Mickey, Lou, Sally, two of Zip's cocaine babes, and three customers were sitting in the back office. Ray had just cut out a line of coke for everyone when the FBI came busting in. They were like a swarm of angry hornets surrounding the place.

"Well, boys what took you so long?" Ray sat back and took the warrant Dan offered to him.

Dan instructed his agents to handcuff all of them and the restaurant staff. They sat on the floor, while Dan's men ransacked the place.

"So, where's Darlene, Ray." Dan stood looking down at him.

"Don't know nothin' about that little bitch. She took off awhile ago with Gabe."

"Now, Ray, we all know better than that. Mickey? You have any idea where Darlene is?"

"Fuck you. I ain't tellin' you nothin'."

"Really? Well, you and Lou and Sally were the last ones to see her alive. Maybe Lou will talk. Or Sally. I'm sure your little secret won't stay secret for too much longer, Mickey." Dan stood looking down at her. "I suggest you start talking now and maybe we can cut you a deal."

"Fuck you, asshole." Mickey glared at him.

"Zip, what about you? You sure are quiet. You got any information to provide on Darlene?" Zip sat on the floor just staring straight ahead.

Zip's two cocaine babes were crying, and one was bordering on hysterics. Dan told one of his men to take them out and load them in the van.

"Well, here's how this is gonna go down, Ray. We have you on drug trafficking now. When we find Darlene's body— and we will—we will then charge you, Mickey, Lou, Sally and Zip with first-degree murder."

"Well, if you ain't got a body, you can't charge us with a damn thing." Ray was feeling cocky.

"Not sure if any of you are aware, but in the great state of West Virginia, murdering a federal informant counts as a federal crime and is punishable by death."

Sally shot Dan a scared look.

"Yep, that's right, little Ms. Sally. The death penalty, and you can bet your sweet ass we will pursue it for all of you. Load 'em in the vans, boys. I'm sick of looking at this scum."

Dan's men conducted a thorough search of The Place, every car, every person, every closet, every drawer, every nook and cranny. They bagged up their evidence and sent it off to the FBI lab.

All totaled, eighteen people were arrested. Most were sent to the county jail, but Ray and his crew were sent to the federal lockup in Charleston. Bail had been denied for them, but Dan was certain this would be overturned within a week or so. He wanted them held for as long as it took to get one of them to break and tell what they had done with Darlene.

***

Sunday, June 7

Sally woke up alone in a cell equipped with a bed, a commode and a sink. The door had a small window with bars and a little hatch door that could be opened only from the outside. The walls and door were padded.

Why a padded cell? Do they think I'm crazy? Maybe all jail cells are padded.

Last night had been rough. They were all cuffed and thrown in the back of a huge black FBI van. Lou screamed and cried all the way to Charleston. Ray was yelling at her to shut up. Mickey and Zip sat in stone silence. When they finally arrived at the jail, Lou really went over the edge during booking and started beating her head on the floor.

Sally had just been scared. Very scared. She had never been in trouble for anything, not even a speeding ticket. Now here she was arrested for distributing drugs and a long list of other stuff she couldn't remember. Once they found out for sure about Darlene, they would add murder to that list.

How long have I been locked up? I really need an Oxy.

Based on how she felt and how bad she needed a pill, she estimated it had been at least five hours.

What if I don't get out today? Will they give me a pill? Will they give me anything?

***

Monday, June 8

It had been two days if she were counting correctly, and that estimate was based on the number of breakfasts they had brought her—one yesterday and one today. Two days without an Oxy, and she really didn't feel too bad, just a headache and a bit of anxiety so far. She hoped she would be bailed out today.

She hadn't been allowed any contact with the rest of the gang. For all she knew, they were out and had pinned Darlene's murder on her. She wanted to see her sister and father but was told she couldn't have any visitors for a few more weeks. *Weeks?*

The only people she had been allowed to talk to were her state-appointed attorney and the FBI guy who had arrested them. The attorney didn't tell her anything and seemed very uninterested in getting her out. The FBI guy promised her a deal if she would rat on Ray. But she saw what Ray had done to Darlene and was certain he would do the same to her or worse. She didn't trust the FBI. Ray had told them not to trust anything they said or promised.

***

Tuesday, June 9

She was stuck somewhere between dreams and reality and woke up to her own screams, more of a guttural moaning, as she ascended from the abyss. A no man's land of nightmares and anxiety. Everything was wet. Her hair, her clothes, the sheets, the blanket. The withdrawals had begun. Just like last year when she tried to quit cold turkey—night sweats and nightmares at first, then leg cramps, nausea. After that, the really bad stuff started, throwing up and diarrhea and utter misery.

There were no dry clothes to change into, no towel, no dry sheets. The only thing she had was a hand towel, which she used to dry off as best she could. The pillow was wet, so she turned it over; at least she had one dry thing. The thin blanket was soaked but not all the way through, so she decided to lie on top of it and wrap it around her. The air conditioning was blasting, and she was freezing.

Her head hurt, and she really needed a pill. Maybe her family would bail her out soon. She drifted in and out of sleep for the rest of the night.

Dan brought her breakfast that morning. He was very nice and calm and promised her that Ray would not be able to hurt her. She wanted to remind him how well that worked out for Darlene, but that would be like a confession. She told him to fuck himself.

***

Friday, June 12

Sally was sick. Breakfast was delivered, and she threw up just smelling it. They took it away and sent the nurse. She had been throwing up for two days, and it was only getting worse. The nurse gave her a pill, which stopped the vomiting, but she still felt like hell. With each beat of her heart, her head throbbed like a wrecking ball was inside her skull, swinging back and forth, back and forth, slamming into the sides of her skull.

The FBI guy had visited every day, promising her freedom, if she would just talk. She told him to kiss her ass. She could ride out this storm. At least she hoped she could.

***

Sunday, June 14

A charley-horse in her left calf woke her up. The pain was unbearable. She screamed and cried and begged someone to come help her.

No one came.

She cried most of the night, unable to sleep due to the leg cramps. Early that morning, they brought breakfast. She didn't eat. She couldn't eat. The anxiety was building higher and higher every day. She wanted to rip the skin off her face.

Why won't they give me one freakin' pill? Just one is all I need. Just one. For the love of God, they need to give me a pill. They can't keep me like this.

She went to the door and called out for someone to help her. Again, no one came. She beat her head and fists against the padded door; it barely made a sound. She begged for someone to bring her a pill. She scratched at the padded door and slammed herself into it over and over. Still, no one came. She fell to the floor and cried.

Dan came to see her in the afternoon and found her on the floor. Same questions. Same threats. Same promises. She didn't tell him to kiss her ass this time. She just shook her head no and cried.

***

Tuesday, June 16

She was itching all over, and her skin felt as though it was going to crawl off her bones. It had been ten days, and the withdrawal seemed to be getting worse by the minute. With the need for an Oxy and under the constant questioning, threatening, and promising, Sally finally broke. When they brought her breakfast that morning, she told them to get Dan. She wanted to tell him where to find Darlene. She told them everything. In exchange, they offered her a reduced sentence. Since she had not actually pulled the trigger or bashed in Darlene's head with the cinderblock, she would not be tried for murder but as an accessory to murder. She would serve two years. Her story had to check out before the offer would be guaranteed.

***

Dan got warrants that afternoon to search The Place, Sally's car, Lou's aunt's car, Zip's place, and the burned out trailer and the surrounding grounds.

Based on the information Sally provided, the forensics team went to The Place and Zip's house late afternoon and searched for evidence of Darlene's murder. Sally told them the freezer had been scrubbed and bleached. She and Lou had done it themselves. She doubted they would find anything. The trunk of her car had also been scrubbed, and the carpet had been ripped out and replaced.

The forensics techs used Luminol and found traces of blood and hair wedged in the hinges of the freezer lid. The trunk of Sally's car had been thoroughly cleaned, but they had forgotten to clean the inside of the car. Mickey, Lou and Sally had blood spatters on their shoes and hands and carried them into the car. They found traces of Darlene's blood on the door handles and floor at the driver's seat, the front passenger's seat and the back passenger's seat.

Lou's aunt's car was a goldmine of DNA evidence. They hadn't bothered to clean it, assuming it would never be suspect. They hadn't counted on Sally's spilling her guts. The trunk had a significant amount of blood and hair samples, and the front of the car had trace amounts of blood on the door handles along with the same dirt found at the grave site.

Zip's house was also a goldmine. The shovel itself still had the dirt on it and would need to be matched to any dirt they found at the grave site. That might have been a stretch, but Zip transferred Darlene's blood from the banner to the shovel, along with his fingerprints—in her blood.

***

Wednesday, June 17

Darlene's parents had bought a police scanner a couple of weeks after she had gone missing. They wanted to be able to monitor what the police were doing in the hopes of maybe recognizing some activity the FBI might overlook that would lead them to Darlene.

It was a beautiful June morning. Millie had been out first thing to water her roses. As she watered and pruned, she said a prayer for Darlene's safe return, as she did a million times a day, every day. This morning was different. She felt a shift in the air. A leap in her spirit. She had a great expectation in her heart, and the blooming roses held forth a promise for her that Darlene was safe, wherever she was, dead or alive.

After watering the roses, Millie went in and made breakfast. As she and Bill were eating, the scanner lit up and they heard the West Virginia State Police: "Back-up required at Double Camp, just north of Newtown. Federal investigation for missing person needs road blocked and traffic control. Repeat, federal investigation for missing person needs road blocked and traffic control. Double Camp. Over." Darlene's parents dropped their forks and looked at each other, neither of them moving for a moment. Millie's eyes filled with tears.

"Let's go. We should go, Millie," Bill said, getting up from the table and going for his shoes.

Millie slowly got up. She felt as though she were in a dream. A really bad dream. She had been hoping against hope that Darlene was alive and tied up somewhere or had just been in hiding. But not now. She prayed this missing person was someone else or no one.

Please, dear Jesus, let it not be my baby.

Three state police cars with sirens blaring went barreling by their house as Millie and Bill backed out of the driveway. They pulled out onto the highway and Bill floored it to keep up with the police. Bill took Millie's hand and held it as they sped along without speaking. By the time they got to Double Camp, the state police had blocked the road about half a mile after the turnoff. Bill pulled the truck off to the side and was parked halfway in the highway, but he didn't care. To protect the crime scene, the FBI had placed saw horses and orange cones to block the road, and they stretched black and yellow crime scene tape across from one side of the road to the other. Behind this initial barricade, there were two state police cruisers turned sideways, so no other cars could get through. Behind these cars, there was a line of cars up Double Camp including state police cruisers, unmarked cars and SUVs; Mingo County sheriff's cars; FBI SUVs and an FBI forensics van. The activities had drawn quite a crowd, and people were standing behind the crime scene tape trying to see what was happening.

As Bill and Millie approached the perimeter of the crime scene, people parted to let them through. They reached the tape, and Bill held it up so Mille could go under. A state policeman stopped them. "Ma'am, I'm sorry, but no one is allowed to go beyond the tape."

Millie's voice was hoarse and low as she fought back tears. "That's my baby up there you'ns is diggin' up, and I need to go through here. Now you need to let me pass, young man."

The young officer continued to tell Mille and Bill they were not allowed. It was a federal crime scene, and no one was allowed to go any farther up Double Camp.

Bill tried to get Millie to wait until they could speak with Dan, but she was a broken mother wanting to get to her child, and the hounds of hell couldn't hold her back. She started screaming at the young officer in a voice that startled even Bill. "You will let me through here so I can get to my baby. Let me see my baby! Get out of my damned way and let me get to my child!" Millie lurched at the young officer to shove him out of her way.

The officer, afraid she was going for his gun, jumped back and put his hand on the butt of his revolver as he held his other hand out to stop Millie. "Ma'am, you need to stay back or I will need to restrain you and put you in the back of the cruiser."

Bill held Millie and tried to calm her down.

Dan heard Millie screaming and came running. "It's okay. Stand down, stand down. She's okay. Millie. Bill. I was going to wait and call you when we had something definitive. Please come with me." Dan led them through the maze of cars, officers and agents.

"You can sit here in the van." Millie and Bill sat in the floor of the open doorway of the van. Leaning into Bill, Millie was whimpering like a wounded bird. Bill wrapped his arm around Millie and tried to comfort her.

Dan tried to convince them to go home. "I know this is hard, and I can't imagine what you must be feeling. It would be best if you waited at home. I can have one of my men drive you there. I will come to your house as soon as we complete the investigation. I can't let you go any farther than this for fear of contaminating the crime scene. It is very important that we don't do anything to destroy evidence. We don't want Ray to walk. Please, Millie, even if it is her, you won't be able to look at her or touch her. Please. It would be best for everyone if you wait at home."

"I ain't goin' nowhere. I'm stayin' right here! I *can't* leave! This is my *child*. My *baby*. My only baby. She needs me to be here. Don't you understand? She *needs* me!" Millie clung to Bill.

"Okay, you can stay, but you must promise me that you will not move from this spot and not try to come any closer, or we will have to take you home. Please understand that anything done to disturb the crime scene would allow Ray to walk." Millie and Bill assured Dan they understood and would wait in the van.

Millie and Bill watched as the cadaver dog was led around the front of the van. The forensics team removed equipment from their van. The forensics photographer took pictures of the area.

Millie and Bill could partially see through the cars and people. The dog was now under the trees just on the side of the road. "Why are they lookin' there? On the side of the road? I don't understand," Millie said to Dan.

"This is where Sally told us to look, and there is a shallow grave closer to the rocks over there. Apparently, it was reserved for Gabe," Dan explained.

"They buried her on the side of the damned road? Like a dog? This is what those animals did with my beautiful Darlene?" Bill cried to Dan.

The cadaver dog started at the bottom of the driveway that led to the burned-out trailer and worked her way down. After about ten minutes, the dog started barking and digging at the ground.

Millie's heart shattered into a million little pieces when she heard the dog barking. Her world slipped away and everything went black and very quiet. She fell to the ground on her knees and screamed. "Noooooo…nooooo…not my baby! Not my sweet Darlene! Noooo…" Her mournful sobs caused the forensics team to stop and allow this woman a moment for her heart to break. Bill knelt beside Millie as she curled up in the fetal position on the warm asphalt on a beautiful June morning, thirty feet from where a cadaver dog had just found her only child buried.

The forensics team excavated the gravesite and found Darlene's decomposing body less than three feet down. Her body was wrapped in the Budweiser banner, and her head was wrapped in a black garbage bag. She was face down, just as Sally had described. Several feet behind Darlene's grave was the empty grave that had been reserved for Gabe.

CHAPTER TWENTY-SIX
Justice

"But her end is bitter as wormwood, sharp as a two-edged sword." —Proverbs 5:4

Sally

Sally got her deal, but her family was unable to raise her bail money, so she served her two years in the federal lockup in Charleston while she awaited trial. She was sentenced to time served and was released on five years' parole.

Lou

Lou turned as soon as she knew Sally had provided the information on where to find Darlene. She told them everything she knew on Ray and corroborated Sally's story of how Ray told them to kill Darlene, how much he paid them, and how he had helped bury her body. In exchange for her testimony against Ray, she also got a reduced sentence. However, since she played a bigger part in Darlene's murder, she got a twenty-year sentence with no chance of parole. She would have to serve her entire sentence.

Zip

Zip pleaded guilty to his part. Although he didn't participate in the murder, he was an accessory to cover it up. With the drug charges and the accessory charges, he served a five-year sentence. Since he had no one to post bail for him, two years of his sentence was served in the federal lockup in Charleston while he awaited trial. He served the rest of his sentence in federal prison. He was released on five years' parole after he served his time.

Mickey

Mickey refused to turn on Ray. At first. She was loyal and dedicated and was willing to go down with the ship. She clung to the belief that Ray would somehow get them out of this mess. She clung to the notion that she loved him. She clung to the hope that he needed her. She had no one to post her bail and served two years of her sentence in the federal lockup awaiting trial.

Ray

Ray was out on bail from the drug charges as soon as he could arrange it. He denied everything about Darlene's murder. However, after being out for one week, he was arrested again for the murder of a federal informant. His bail was set at $1,000,000; there was no one who could or would post his bail. He served two years of his sentence in the federal lockup while awaiting his trial.

Mickey and Ray were tried together. Even with all the evidence against them, Mickey denied everything and protected Ray through the trial. They were both found guilty of first-degree murder, and both received the death penalty. Mickey was one of two women in the U.S. sitting on federal death row and the first woman ever to be sentenced to death in the state of West Virginia.

Three years after their trial, the verdict was overturned due to juror misconduct. Mickey and Ray were tried again, but separately this time. Three years of sitting on death row had changed Mickey's mind or jogged her memory about the events of Darlene's murder. She pleaded guilty to her role in Darlene's murder and agreed to testify against Ray. In exchange, prosecutors did not seek the death penalty. Mickey is now serving a life sentence with no chance for parole.

Ray was found guilty again on all counts in a twelve-count indictment. He is now serving a life sentence with no chance for parole.

Gabe got the deal Dan had promised him, and he moved to San Antonio. The FBI bought him a small house, gave him some cash to get started, and even arranged for him to get a job.

Darlene's children were adopted by their stepmother and are thriving despite the loss of their mother. The resilience of children is a mysterious thing. They visit the site where her body was buried every year on June 17, the day her body was found.

Millie was never the same. The trial took a huge toll on her and Bill. There is no cure for a broken heart. The murder of their daughter destroyed a piece of them that cannot be replaced. They get the girls once a month and are an important part of their lives. Millie is determined they never forget their mother.

CHAPTER TWENTY-SEVEN
Tricky Business

"Oh, what a tangled web we weave,
When first we practice to deceive."
— Sir Walter Scott, *Marmion*

Ray's mother was appointed trustee over Ray's property after his conviction. He didn't trust his wife to do the right thing, but he knew his mother would take care of everything the way he wanted. He could trust her and her alone, it seemed. After Ray's last appeal was turned down, she lost hope he would ever be released. Three years after his conviction, her health issues were getting worse and more frequent, and her arthritis was getting so bad she had difficulty with the simplest of tasks. Well into her nineties, old and tired, she was unable to do as much as she could just a year earlier. Making sure Ray's property was maintained as it should be was a chore. Ray had instructed her not to get rid of anything until he told her to, but it looked as though he wouldn't be returning anytime soon, and The Place was becoming too much to maintain. The equipment hadn't been used in three years and was just sitting there rusting.

A junker had been by earlier in the week to see if she was interested in selling any of it or if she needed anything hauled away. She was meeting him Friday morning at The Place to determine what he could take. She figured she might as well get rid of most of it; it was just becoming a breeding ground for rats at this point.

The junker showed up as scheduled, and they walked through the restaurant and back to the storeroom. The junker identified a few items he would take: the beer box, the cash register, a glass display case, Ray's desk in his office, and an antique Coke machine in the storeroom. Well, Ray said it was antique. It was very old and didn't work. It had been in the corner of the storeroom for years with a table and boxes piled on it and around it. It sat across from the freezer where Darlene's body had been hidden.

Ray's mom sold it all to the junker for $300. Seemed fair to her, and she was glad to get it out of the building. She took his cash and put it in her purse as he pulled out of the parking lot onto the highway. She would tell Ray tomorrow when she visited him that she was starting to sell the stuff. Surely he would understand.

***

After two turned-down appeals, Ray had accepted that he would die right there in prison—all because he trusted the wrong bitch with the wrong information. He never would have guessed that Darlene would be the one to snitch on him. She was so damned innocent and did whatever he wanted, whenever he wanted. She was *his* bitch. He couldn't believe he had been so blind to her cunning lies.

His wife had come to visit with the kids after he had been in for six months. She informed him that he would never see her or his children again. If the children wanted to visit him when they turned eighteen, that was up to them. But he doubted he would live that long.

His mother visited once a month for the first year, then her visits became sporadic. Her health was deteriorating, and her visits depended on how she felt. No one else ever visited him in prison. A local pastor wrote to him regularly, trying to save his soul from hell fire. But, he didn't see much need for Jesus at this point.

It was a Saturday morning and his mother was scheduled to be there for the afternoon visitation. He was excited to see her. He had something important to tell her. He was in his cell waiting when the guard came to get him to take him to the visitors' area. The guard escorted him through the first doors. The buzzer sounded and the door clanked open and then echoed through the hall as it shut behind them. They did this three more times before entering the visitors' area.

The guard took him to a table in the corner and handcuffed him to a metal hook in the middle of the table. Ray sat waiting for his mother. Other inmates were brought in and either cuffed to the table or sat and told not to move. Ray shifted nervously, he had something important to tell his mother. He couldn't give her anything in writing, so he hoped she could remember. The dementia seemed to be getting worse with each visit.

Ray could barely suppress a chuckle. He had waited three years to tell his mother his little secret. He wanted to wait until he was sure he would not be getting out and that the FBI was not watching The Place any longer.

Those bastards. Joke's on them. Nobody pulls too much over on me. I'm way too clever. He tried to contain himself.

The doors opened and the visitors came single-file into the room. His mother shuffled in, and a guard helped her over to Ray's table. The guard reminded her that touching was not allowed, and then he stepped away so they could talk in private.

Ray hoped his mother could contain her surprise when he told her that inside that old antique Coke machine in the storeroom, he had been stashing cash for years. His best estimate was that it contained a little over a million dollars. She needed to have it moved to her house and emptied right away.

***

At the head of Barrenshea Creek, the junker went out to his garage to inspect his haul from The Place he had made the previous day. He was especially pleased with that old Coke machine. As soon as he ate his lunch, he was going to open that baby up and see if he could get it to run again.

The End

ACKNOWLEDGEMENTS

Simple Choices is my first novel, but certainly not my last. Writing is a very solitary endeavor. You spend hours alone—just you and the voices in your head. However, *Simple Choices* required the help, assistance, patience, and many answers from many people.

First, I need to thank my mother, Deanna Collins; my sisters, Susan, Kathy and Dionne; my brother, Vernon; and all my nieces and nephews for providing a lifetime of good stories and adventures. I love you all to the moon and back.

My sister Dionne Collins—how many thanks can I provide? In addition to her shear enthusiasm for the project, I want to thank her for providing valuable research assistance for several key aspects of the story. She also had ideas that helped shape a few pivotal scenes. Along with Dionne, I must also thank Thomas Copley for providing a wealth of information and tidbits I would never have thought to include.

My niece, Morgan Seymour, not only did she provide answers and her expertise on the forensic details, she also showed extreme patience and understanding or just left when I went full tilt and became slightly obsessed with finishing the first draft. Thank you for not letting me throw the entire thing in the fire pit.

Drollene Brown was a jewel of a find and a great editor. She got me through the first and most crucial edits, formatting and much insanity. Thank you for your encouragement, mentoring and solid advice. I couldn't have gotten to this final product without you.

I also need to thank Drollene's sister, Sharon Reynolds. Sharon provided assistance that helped get the manuscript ready for primetime.

I had several "first readers" at crucial times during writing. Their feedback, comments, and keen eyes were vital in keeping the creation of the story moving. First, Bill Pehlivanian. Thank you, Bill, for providing targeted feedback and perspective, for loving the story and for encouraging me to continue. My dear mother read the manuscript in record time. Thank you, Mother, for asking questions, discussing key scenes and catching a few things I had overlooked. My niece, Natalie Harmon, read the manuscript just before the final edit. Thank you, Natalie, for your honest feedback, recommendations for changes and tweaks, and a dialect check. My dear friend Lee Keating was my final read before publication. Lee jumped into the manuscript with great enthusiasm. I appreciate your excitement and excellent comments—get ready for the next one!

There are some people you meet and you just can't believe how blessed you are to have them in your life at just the right moment. But, there they are, freely answering questions, offering solid advice, helping guide you down the writer's path. There are three such people in particular I need to thank and oddly enough, I have never met any of them in person:

Karen Todd Scarpulla (author of *Walking Toward the Light*). Karen is one of the most talented, generous, kind, giving people I have had the pleasure of knowing in a long time. When I started on this path, she was more than happy to share her author's experiences and lessons learned with me. She also shared a gold mine with me in the form of Jennifer Chesak (see below). I am forever indebted to Karen, and she is now a forever friend.

Dean King (author of *The Feud: The Hatfields and McCoys: The True Story*). I met Dean through my sister, Dionne, while he was doing research for his book, *The Feud: The Hatfields and McCoys*. Dean was the first person to read a few of the original excerpts from *Simple Choices*. His feedback and critique were crucial in those early stages in guiding me to tighten up the writing and stick to my story. He introduced me to people in the publishing world. He provided great advice and guidance. He took the time to listen to and answer my many, many questions. I can't thank him enough!

Keith Davis (CEO of Woodland Press and author of *The Secret Life and Brutal Death of Mamie Thurman* and others, and editor/publisher of more than 40 Appalachian-based book titles) is a fellow West Virginian. Keith became an unsuspecting mentor through a Facebook friend request. He never hesitated to answer my questions about publishing, writing, selling and signing. A generous man. A talented man. Thank you for the fountain of generosity and patience with my questions and uncertainties about this whole crazy world of publishing.

Jennifer Chesak (Wandering in the Words Press). Oh my! How do I even begin to thank you? A chance conversation with Karen Scarpulla and here we are. Jennifer provided a final edit, book design, cover design, encouragement, and solid business advice for getting the final product to market. You are a talented young woman and I am so thankful to have met you. Thank you for talking me in off the ledge (several times)! We will definitely do this again—soon!

Last and certainly not least—D&D. Cousins. Friends. Sisters. Thank you for your constant encouragement, support, love and overall being. I love you and could not have and would not have gotten through this journey without you. I love you!

I must extend a very warm head butt to my fellow office mates—Moose and Deuce (aka Jelly Bean, the original). My sweet, adorable Cornish Rex cats who sat on my lap or my desk (or keyboard, or shoulders, or…) through every chapter of writing *Simple Choices*. I love you!